RELATIVE CHAOS

RELATIVE CHAOS

•

Kay Finch

To Ron & Sandra,
I appreciate the
support of fellow
PA Texans.
Kay Finch

AVALON BOOKS
NEW YORK

Published by Avalon Books, an imprint of
Thomas Bouregy & Co., Inc.
160 Madison Avenue, New York, NY 10016

Library of Congress Cataloging-in-Publication Data

Finch, Kay.
    Relative chaos / Kay Finch.
       p. cm.
    ISBN 978-0-8034-7788-9 (hardcover) 1.   Self-employed
women—Fiction. 2.   Mentally ill—Family relationships—Fiction.
3.   Domestic fiction. I.   Title.
    PS3606.I53R45 2010
    813'.6—dc22

                                                              2010016362

PRINTED IN THE UNITED STATES OF AMERICA
ON ACID-FREE PAPER
BY HADDON CRAFTSMEN, BLOOMSBURG, PENNSYLVANIA

For their invaluable help with this novel, I thank my fabulous writing group—Amy, Bob, Charlie, Dean, Heather, Joe, Laura, Leann, and Millie. Special thanks to Susie and Isabella for sharing their home with us every week, to Scotty Harris for police procedure advice, and to Sherri Saunders for her probate know-how. Any mistakes or misstatements made in the novel are mine. For their encouragement and advice, I also thank Chelsea Gilmore, Julia Weis, and my agent, Mike Farris. Special appreciation to my husband, Benton, for always being there.

Chapter One

I clomped over Aunt Millie's threshold in my black steel-toed sneakers, wedging myself into a crowded, mildewy foyer that looked like the Goodwill drop-off after closing. My seventy-year-old aunt took one look at my yellow hard hat and rolled her eyes.

"You know, Poppy, everyone does *not* love a comedian," she said.

"Wasn't trying to be funny."

Heaps of papers, boxes, stuffed garbage bags, and stacks of books surrounded us. Millie's black cat, Jett, picked his way through the mess like a soldier negotiating a minefield.

I rapped on my hat. "This is self-preservation."

Millie tossed her head, making her tight gray curls bounce. "I call for help, and you insult me?"

"Nothing personal, Aunt Millie. Professional-organizer training stresses brutal honesty."

Okay, I *had* added the hat for a touch of humor, hoping to start this project on a light note. Guess that tactic bombed.

Millie puffed out a breath. "Training? Huh. You came out of the womb speaking your mind."

"Part of my charm," I said. "Besides, wouldn't be much help to my clients if I didn't tell the truth."

"Doesn't mean I have to like it."

I inspected an unfamiliar box labeled *microwave oven*. Next to the box, a sixty-four-piece set of stainless steel flatware sat atop an unabridged dictionary. "Where'd all this stuff come from? You promised to lay off the garage sales."

"I have." Millie took a calculated step to her right, but even her wide girth couldn't hide the set of rusty wrought-iron nesting tables, the misshapen throw pillows, or the cartons of yellowed paperbacks I knew hadn't been there last week. Jett hopped up onto a stack of fresh cartons near the front door—recent UPS deliveries.

1

I eyed the boxes. "Home Shopping Network?"

"Those were back-ordered," Millie said. "I haven't watched HSN in weeks."

"You won't have time for TV now. We'll be too busy." I gave her a bear hug, then backed off to meet her eyes. I cherished my childhood memories of this house—what I thought of as the clutter-free era.

"Do you know how thrilled I am that you asked for my help?" I said.

"Figured you'd be ready to dig in," Millie said. "Been harping on me since you were seven."

I grinned. The same year I'd insisted on going by Poppy instead of Penelope or, heaven forbid, Penny, which in my mind was just as dumb as calling someone nickel, dime, or quarter. The nickname had stuck.

Aunt Millie had known me as a pushy little girl, and she had me pegged now. I was as eager to dig in as a kid in a sandbox. I opened my tote and pulled out a work apron with handy catch-all pockets and my *Klutter Killer* logo embroidered across the bib.

I looped the apron over my head and reached around to tie it in back. "You'll be thrilled when all these dust-catchers are gone," I promised. "Just wait and see."

Her words on the phone earlier—"I need you to come over here and help me clean this place out"—were the best words I'd heard since the judge pronounced, "Your divorce is hereby granted" last year.

For the first time all month I was glad my business wasn't booming. When I finished with Aunt Millie—maybe a couple of months from now—I'd advertise in *Fort Bend Lifestyles* magazine to drum up new clients.

I picked my way around Millie's recent acquisitions and peeked into the dining room. I couldn't remember when I'd last seen the maple table I knew was hidden under gobs of papers, books, photos, and clothes. I scanned the room, noting a 1987 Federal income tax form that stuck out from a basket of petrified and permanently wrinkled laundry. A five-foot column of *Houston Chronicle* newspapers in a corner threatened to avalanche.

The scent of cinnamon wafted in from the kitchen—Aunt Millie's yummy cinnamon buns, I'd bet. A special childhood memory, and, with the big five-oh approaching like a freight train, I relished those memories more than ever. I headed for the kitchen, already tasting the soft, yeasty—

Wait a second. Baking was Aunt Millie's antidote for stress. What did she have to be stressed about when she knew I was on my way here to help?

I backtracked to find her standing by the HSN boxes, stroking Jett's silky black fur. The cat rolled onto his side, loving the attention, but Aunt Millie's shoulders drooped. I knew she would love the house after I finished organizing things, but no matter how badly I itched to get started, I'd have to take this in baby steps.

I walked over to Millie and gently touched her shoulder. "Remember that time I caught my prom dress in the car door and nearly ripped the skirt off?"

Millie smiled and nodded. "You were traumatized. Convinced your life was ruined forever."

"What I remember is that you dropped what you were doing to fix the dress. You made everything all right. That's what I want to do for you now."

"I know," Millie said.

"Then how about we get started? We can take it nice and easy. Tour the house, then sit down and map out a game plan."

Millie ran her knuckles down Jett's back and took a deep breath, then turned to face me. "Oh, I already have a plan in motion. I just needed an extra set of hands. Come on into the living room, and you'll see."

"O-kay." I consider myself a darn good professional organizer, but I like doing things my own way, using my own logical sequence. I suppressed my instinct to point this out and followed her, sniffing as a new odor hit me. "Maybe we can open some windows. It's a little stale in here, don't you think? Or"—I inhaled deeply—"is that paint?"

"Part of my plan." Millie slid double pocket doors aside to reveal the living room.

Light streamed through the windows overlooking Riverside Estates Golf Course, accenting the freshly painted walls and a zillion floating dust motes. A man in a sage green T-shirt and worn jeans with a tool belt slung low on narrow hips stood on a ladder, an electric drill poised in one hand.

"Who's this?" I said, annoyed by the stranger's presence and the fact that everything in the room had been shoved away from the walls to form a humongous mound of clutter over and around the furniture.

"Wayne McCall," said Millie, "meet my niece, Poppy Cartwright."

Self-conscious, I pulled off the hard hat and shook out my shaggy blond hair.

McCall gave me a once-over with the intensity of someone who planned to work with a police sketch artist later. "Right. The clutter lady."

"I don't clutter." My forced smile felt more like a grimace. "I *un*-clutter. Organize. Purge and toss." I gave Millie a pointed look. "Which we usually do *before* we start remodeling."

"To each their own," McCall said.

Judging by his lined, tan face and the sprinkling of white through his dark hair, I guessed him to be near my age—old enough to know we'd stir up plenty of dirt clearing out this room. Dirt that would settle on his cream-colored paint job.

McCall turned back to his work—screwing a metal shelving strip to the wall. I cringed at the buzzing drill that reminded me of a childhood spent in the dentist's chair.

"Where'd you find this one?" I whispered.

Millie ignored my question. "Wayne's a godsend. He did the painting for me, and now he's putting up bookshelves."

I took hold of her arm and pulled her with me into the hallway. Even out here, a good ten yards from the drill, I felt as if the bit was boring into my brain. "I'm serious, Aunt Millie. Where did you get him? I hope this isn't like the time you picked up that electrician who turned out to be a registered sex offender."

"Don't be rude, Poppy."

I sometimes thought Aunt Millie needed a bodyguard 24/7. "Where—did—he—come—from?"

"Well, if you must know, Kroger's," she said.

"He approached you in the *grocery store*?"

"Not exactly. I was leaving with my groceries, just like any other day, but then a man jumped out from between cars and snatched my purse."

I had heard nothing of this. "Your purse was stolen?"

"Would have been," Millie said, "but Wayne saved the day."

"Really?" I couldn't keep the skepticism from leaking through.

"He was right there—he'd left the store right behind me. Saw the whole thing and ran the guy down."

Leaving the store or following her? I wondered. "I'm surprised you never mentioned this."

"I told the story so many times, I forget who knows and who doesn't," Millie said. "Anyway, Wayne got my purse back. He's a hero, even though the thief got away."

"And now he's painting your house," I said. "Makes perfect sense to me."

What did she know about this man she'd brought into her home? Next to nothing, I'd bet.

Aunt Millie inched back a step, wearing her familiar warning expression. I'd sure seen enough of that look growing up. I had to back off or risk being fired before we even started.

"Okay, then." I pasted on a smile and hooked elbows with Aunt Millie. Walking her back into the living room, I spoke the words she needed to hear if I wanted to get this show on the road. "I'm glad you found such good help, and those shelves will be perfect."

Though you ought to donate all these old books to the library and put the space to better use.

"I'm glad you think so," Millie said, gloating.

I took a calming breath and scanned the mess. "Let's set up a sorting area for these other, um, belongings."

Magazines, more newspapers, broken straw hats, skeins of yarn, silk flowers, junk mail, cat toys.

Internal heavy sigh.

"No time to sort," Millie said. "Wayne picked up twelve dozen boxes for me."

"You ready for those?" McCall started down the ladder. "I'll bring them in."

"No!" I lowered my voice and tried to sound pleasant. "We don't

need boxes, Aunt Millie. Not yet anyway." Not *twelve dozen*. What was she thinking?

My face was beginning to ache from forcing a smile. "First, we categorize your things—those you use frequently, those to throw away, donate, store. . . ."

"I'm storing the whole mess," she said, throwing her arms in a big circle. "Rented two of those extra-large units at the Simply Storage place over on Highway Six. Think that'll be enough?"

"Wait, wait, wait!" I rubbed my aching temples. "You can't store all of this junk as is." I struggle against the urge to order my clients around, but this was Aunt Millie, and I couldn't take any more nonsense.

McCall pinned me with deep brown eyes. "Look, Mrs. Klutter Killer, if she wants to store her stuff, she stores her stuff. You shouldn't force people to do what *you* think they ought to do."

"I wouldn't *force* anyone," I said coldly. Who did he think he was?

McCall raised his eyebrows in silent reply, then went out the back door, presumably to fetch boxes.

I looked for a place to sit, didn't find one, then crossed my arms over my chest and faced Aunt Millie. "I thought you wanted to be organized—with *my* help."

"I do," she said, "but right now there's not enough time."

"What do you mean, not enough time?"

Millie chewed her lip, avoided eye contact, then said, "Janice is coming to visit."

"Here?"

"This weekend."

My snooty cousin Janice, Millie's daughter, hadn't visited since Uncle Hal's funeral three years ago. Even then she refused to set foot in her mother's house and took a flight straight back to her husband and her Wall Street job as soon as the service ended. Far as I knew, she spoke to Millie only on birthdays and Christmas.

"Janice is coming *here*, to *your* house?"

Millie nodded, and her eyes began to tear.

Janice coming home after all this time? "What does she want?"

"I—I'm not sure," Millie said, her voice trembling. "Probably to check out my will, make sure she's still inheriting. But I'm so glad she's coming, whatever the reason. And that reminds me, we need to find the papers from my lawyer in here somewhere." She scanned the mass of clutter. "If we don't, I'll have to ask Dawn to send out another set."

No one should have to put up with an uncaring, uppity, daughter like Janice—especially Aunt Millie. My son, Kevin, had caused me plenty of concern over the years, but I never doubted that he loved his family. My cold, calculating cousin was a different story.

I put an arm around Millie's shoulders. "We'll find the papers, but I wouldn't let Janice's visit interfere with your organizing the house. She grew up here, and I'm sure she won't expect things to have changed."

"Oh, but she will," said Millie, crying now. "I told her."

"What did you tell her?"

"That I was totally organized, that the house was all cleaned up, and she wouldn't even recognize the place."

Uh-oh.

"I swore on your Uncle Hal's grave it was true."

Millie cried harder, and I drew her close. *Now what?* I wouldn't want the catty, holier-than-thou Janice to prove *me* wrong either. And if that meant boxing up and storing Millie's junk, then so be it.

"We can compromise." I released Millie to make eye contact. "I have plenty of time to help you between now and the weekend. We'll organize the most important things, then box up and store the rest. What do you say?"

Millie nodded and pulled a tissue from the breast pocket of her plaid shirt to dry her tears.

"But you have to promise we don't keep everything. I mean, there's no good reason to hang on to magazines back to the seventies."

"Okay," Millie said.

"So we'll trash the older ones."

"Right."

"Even if you haven't read them yet."

She nodded her agreement.

"We'll need a slew of garbage bags."

Millie managed a smile. "I have some of those heavy ones out in the garage. Left over from the kitchen remodeling."

"Perfect. I'll be right back."

"In that blue cabinet by the workbench," Millie called after me.

I moved fast, hoping to return before she had a complete emotional meltdown. She was usually such a strong lady, and I wanted to slap Janice for hurting her.

Plenty of time for that later.

Outside, the day was cool but pleasant, perfect Gulf Coast February weather any northerner would envy.

Maybe *that's* why Janice was coming to visit—to escape the frigid New York winter.

Nah. She wanted something.

Two women riding a golf cart down a nearby path waved to me, and I waved back, thankful that Millie lived in this friendly Sugar Land neighborhood. Small consolation for having such a nasty daughter, but some emotional support was better than none.

Anyone acquainted with Aunt Millie knew better than to open the overhead garage door. The inside was stacked floor-to-ceiling with a lifetime's worth of belongings that she, for some obsessive reason, couldn't part with—junk that would spill onto her car parked outside without the door's support.

I entered the garage through the side entrance and flicked on the overhead light, then wasted a few seconds staring. A tower of empty shrubbery containers leaned against a wall next to boxes full of clothes hangers, piles of discarded shoes, and moldy lawn-furniture cushions. *Ick.*

I scraped past straggly potted plants Millie had dragged inside during a brief freeze we had around New Year's and squeezed through the rat maze, regretting that I'd left my hard hat in the house and feeling claustrophobic with the stacks pressing in on all sides.

The rubble blocked daylight from the garage's lone window, and the ceiling fixture's dim bulb didn't help much. Might be easier to run down to Home Depot and pick up some bags, but I liked the idea of using what Millie already had, so I forged ahead toward the blue cabinet next to Uncle Hal's workbench on the back wall.

God, it smelled putrid in here. Jett must have used the potted plants as a litter box.

I held my nose as I pulled my key ring penlight from my pocket. Shining the beam ahead, I spotted a tower of boxes labeled *JANICE* with thick black marker. That brat ought to be paying to store her crap somewhere else, and I wouldn't mind being the one to tell her so.

The smell was making me woozy.

Get out of here before you asphyxiate, I told myself, rushing to get the bags.

My foot caught on something, and I tripped, flying forward and barely escaping a collision with Janice's boxes.

I turned around and aimed the light at the floor.

A man's shoe. Which wouldn't seem that odd, given my surroundings, except that this shoe was connected to a leg protruding from a space between a stack of plastic storage tubs and an old washing machine.

What on earth?

I moved closer, my hand shaking as the light traveled from the expensive-looking loafer up a man's leg. He wore khakis and a yellow golf shirt stained with dark splotches. I trained the light on his gray complexion. My vision swam. He was definitely dead.

I backed away, feeling faint, and the light played over the man's torso, illuminating his arms and—

Holy God, his hands were gone.

Chapter Two

I stumbled back, gagging.

A dead man. In Aunt Millie's garage. Couldn't be real.

I blinked. Pinched myself. He was real, all right. Sweat poured down my face. The odor intensified. Flies buzzed.

For two seconds, my feet felt like they were superglued to the floor. Then I turned and hightailed it out of there.

Outside, I bent over the grass, hands on knees, and dry heaved. Mc-Call came up the driveway carrying an armload of flattened cardboard boxes. He looked at me, then at the open garage door.

"Pretty scary," he said, grinning. "Went in there once myself."

I wanted to call him a smart aleck, but my trembling lips wouldn't form the words.

He came closer and looked me over.

"You're kinda green," he said. "You sick?"

I shook my head and pointed at the garage. "In there. A man. He's de-dead."

"You're kidding," he said.

I stared at him. "Do I look like I'm kidding?"

The answer must have been no, because McCall threw the boxes down and ran into the garage.

He was back in ten seconds. "You recognize him?"

"No. Do you?"

McCall shook his head. "Whoever it is, my guess is he's been in there a day or so." He pulled out his cell phone. "Maybe you should prepare Millie. Cops won't be long."

I straightened and looked at the house. Aunt Millie would freak out at this news, but he was right. Better she hear it from me before cops came down on this place like the flood on Noah.

"Yes," McCall said into the phone. "I need to report a homicide."

He was silent for a beat, then added, "Unidentified male. Gunshot wounds. His hands are severed."

The word *severed* sent my stomach into a spin, and I didn't want to hear more. I approached the house slowly, my mission clear. Prepare Millie for news of a dead body found in her garage.

Impossible, but I'd give it my best shot.

Two hours later, I paced the neighboring driveway, watching as police officers scurried around Aunt Millie's property. McCall leaned against his truck, parked on the street, unable to leave because cop cars, an ambulance, and a fire truck that had responded to the emergency call blocked him in. Yellow crime-scene tape surrounded the driveway, garage, and backyard. I'd given Aunt Millie a sedative and put her to bed. Neighbors stood on the sidewalk gawking. Out on the golf course, carts slowed to see what the commotion was about.

Millie, McCall, and I had been separated and questioned individually, first by the initial officers who'd arrived on the scene, then by Rae Troxell, the lead homicide detective. They'd gotten no useful information because we didn't have any. We couldn't identify the dead man. We hadn't seen anyone or anything suspicious.

Even though I'd given Aunt Millie enough medicine to drug a horse, I caught her peering out the upstairs window every few minutes.

I wouldn't be able to rest either, didn't know if I'd ever be able to close my eyes again without seeing the dead man. Who was he? And why had someone stuffed him into Aunt Millie's garage? Clearly, the murder had happened somewhere else. I hadn't noticed any blood. There must have been a *lot* of blood. I shuddered, not wanting to dwell on *how* this had happened.

But why dump the body here? Could there be some connection between Aunt Millie and this man? I didn't think so. Maybe he lived nearby. I wondered about his family, whether he had children. I scanned the street, half afraid I'd see his wife or mother running toward the scene and screaming his name. My stomach rolled.

I turned my attention back to the police, who had opened the overhead garage door and jumped back when a pile of Aunt Millie's "collectibles" tumbled onto the driveway.

I knew they had to search the scene thoroughly, especially because of the missing hands, but I didn't like the way they were dismantling the garage contents, making an even bigger mess—if that were possible. I watched the measuring, photographing, and note-taking as they conducted their search for evidence.

They had to clear a path so they'd be able to remove the body from the garage, but why did they have to pile everything up haphazardly along the driveway? This project could work to everyone's benefit if done right. The woman in charge emerged from the shadows of the garage. Without consulting my better judgment, I marched in her direction.

Detective Rae Troxell was fortyish with a stocky, athletic build. She wore her brown hair in a tight ponytail and sported black-framed glasses and a manly navy suit, probably an image calculated to counteract her soft, feminine voice. Troxell's back was to me as I edged along the crime-scene tape, but she spoke before I reached her.

"Don't contaminate my scene, Ms. Cartwright."

I hopped back from the tape, raising my hands. "I didn't touch anything."

"Okay, then." She faced me. "What is it?"

"You know, I'm in the business of organizing, and—"

She nodded and made a hurry-up-and-spit-it-out hand motion, so I did.

"I couldn't help but notice the mess out here on the drive, and I'm thinking that if you decide down the road in this investigation that you need to take another look at something in particular, you shouldn't have to go through the whole cotton-pickin' pile all over again."

Troxell frowned. "You trying to tell me how to run my investigation?"

"No."

"As I remind my husband every day, *nobody* tells me how to do my job." She leaned toward me conspiratorially. "He's in the department. Pain in the neck to work with your spouse—know what I mean?"

I knew, and thank God I wasn't in that boat anymore. I took a deep breath and tried again. "I'm just explaining that if you'll take a few extra seconds to categorize things now, it will save you time later."

"Categorize," Troxell said.

"You know, make one pile of garden tools, one for seasonal decorations—"

"I'm trying to find a dead man's missing hands," Troxell interrupted, "and you want me to categorize?"

"I'm just trying to help."

"Don't."

"Sorry I wasted your time." I started to walk away.

"Ms. Cartwright," Troxell said.

I turned around.

"A few more questions, if I may."

"Certainly." So now she wanted something.

Troxell glanced toward the street, then moved closer to me. "What do you know about this McCall guy?"

"Wayne McCall?"

"You see any other McCalls around here?" Troxell said. "Who else would I mean?"

"Why do you ask?"

Troxell raised her eyebrows. "Just answer the question."

I reminded myself that she *was* in charge, and that she could make my life miserable if she didn't finish her job here quickly. I still had hopes of straightening things up before Janice arrived.

"I met Wayne McCall today for the first time," I said. "He and Aunt Millie seem to get along well with each other. He's handling some remodeling for her. Personally, I find him annoying."

"Huh," Troxell said. "Any idea how long your aunt's known him?"

Aunt Millie hadn't mentioned when the chance Kroger's meeting had happened. "No, but I can find out if it's important." I stole a glance toward McCall's truck, but it was gone. Apparently he'd found a way to worm around the emergency vehicles without my noticing. I turned back to Troxell. "*Is* it important?"

"*Everything* is potentially important in a homicide investigation," she said. "Can't find much on McCall."

"You investigated him?" I said.

"Preliminary check. Standard procedure."

"Does that mean you checked on me too? And Aunt Millie?"

"Sure," Troxell said. "Know everything about you from the date of your divorce to how much your son weighed at birth."

I stared at her.

"Kidding about that last part," she said.

When I didn't respond, she added, "Lighten up, I was joking."

"I don't find that amusing, and I'm not in the greatest mood. It's not every day I come across a dead body."

Troxell looked wistful. "Wish I could say that."

"Do you think Wayne McCall is suspicious?" I asked.

"Haven't decided. He's new to the area. Lived here three months."

A noise that sounded like another pile toppling came from the garage.

"Better get back in there," she said.

"I have a hard hat in the house if you need it."

Troxell laughed. "No need—I've got a hard head." She sobered and said, "I trust you won't mention this little conversation to anyone, right?"

I made a zipping motion across my lips.

She looked down at my apron. "And if I were you, I wouldn't wear anything with the word *killer* embroidered on it around here."

"Good point."

She walked away, and I trudged toward the front of the house. Neighbors huddled in a group on the sidewalk, no doubt gossiping about what might have happened. Aunt Millie had given up on her nap and stood by the street, talking with a man standing next to a golf cart. Her mouth and her arms were going ninety-to-nothing, and I figured the drugs must have pumped her up rather than calmed her down.

Millie saw me and waved. "Poppy, over here."

As I approached, I couldn't help but notice that the man was a hunk. Tall, slim, and tan, with impeccably cut dark hair and a bright smile. Ten or more years too young for me, but it never hurt to look.

When I got closer, Millie said, "Poppy, this is my new neighbor, Steve Featherstone. I told him all about how you came over to help me get organized and now we can't do anything because you found that dead man."

She sounded matter-of-fact, as if she was discussing the weather. The drugs were working in that respect.

Featherstone shook my hand. "Nice to meet you, Poppy. Sorry to hear about the trouble. Not something you expect to find, even in your line of work."

"This is a first for me," I said.

"Steve inherited the house at the end of the block," Millie said, "and he's staying there until it's sold. Unless we can convince him otherwise, of course. Nice young men are always welcome in the neighborhood."

Featherstone chuckled uncomfortably.

I jumped in to rescue him from further embarrassment. "Where are you from?"

"Here, originally," he said. "Been living in Los Angeles."

"You know any movie stars?" Aunt Millie asked.

Featherstone laughed. "Not well."

"Poppy loves going to the movies," she said. "You like movies, Steve?"

Now I felt uncomfortable. "Aunt Millie, this isn't the time, not with the police here and all." I put a hand on her arm and said to Featherstone, "If there's anything you need while you're in town, let us know."

"Actually, there is something," he said.

"Oh?" I waited.

"I noticed the Klutter Killer sign on your SUV when I went to the grocery store earlier, and that got me thinking. If there's one thing I could use in that big old house where my grandmother lived forever, it's somebody to get rid of the clutter. I'm overwhelmed."

"I understand how you feel," I said.

"Are you available?" he said. "I mean, do you have time in your schedule to take the job?"

"She's available," said Millie, giggling.

I shot her a look, then smiled at him. "I can pencil you in, after I'm finished with Aunt Millie's house."

"Nonsense," Millie said. "She can start in the morning. Bright and early. My Poppy's an early bird."

I tightened my grip on her arm. "Mr. Featherstone, I'm afraid my aunt is—"

"Call me Steve," he said.

"Steve," I went on. "Aunt Millie seems to be reacting badly to some medication."

He grinned. "Don't worry about it."

"Why don't I come by in the morning to give you an estimate? Then we'll discuss timing."

"Works for me," Steve said. "But I have to warn you, I'm on a short fuse."

"How short?" I said.

"I need to get the place shipshape by Sunday."

"That's short, all right."

"Can't be helped," he said. "A potential buyer is coming to town—a *cash* buyer."

"I don't know. . . ."

"I'm willing to pay extra," Featherstone said. "Matter of fact, I'll throw in a bonus. How does two grand sound?"

Chapter Three

The bonus sounded great, and though I didn't commit to taking the job, I agreed to meet with Featherstone at eight the next morning. He had just left when the cops decided they'd cleared a big enough path to wheel a gurney into the garage. I didn't think Millie would want to see them rolling the body out, and I turned to distract her from the morbid scene.

But she was running toward an officer carrying two of the boxes marked with Janice's name toward a police van.

"Stop," she yelled. "You can't take those."

I caught up with Millie and grabbed her arm. "Calm down."

"But those are Janice's," Millie whined.

The officer turned his back to place the boxes in the van, but Millie had already attracted Detective Troxell's attention.

"Who's Janice?" she said, approaching us.

I filled her in while Millie paced, throwing imaginary daggers toward the guy standing guard at the van.

"What's so important in these boxes?" she asked Millie.

"My daughter's school memories," Millie said defiantly. "Those can never be replaced."

Behind her back, I rolled my eyes. Like Janice gave a hoot about her childhood memorabilia.

"We'll keep them intact, and you'll get everything back at the end of the case," Troxell said.

"Why are you taking them?" I asked.

Troxell looked at me over the top of her glasses and lowered her voice. "Biologicals on the cardboard. Blood."

Millie had excellent hearing. "Oh, dear Lord. Blood on Janice's things."

"On the *boxes*," Troxell specified. "We need to collect samples at the lab."

I tipped my head toward the garage. "Sure you don't need to take *everything* in there to the lab?"

Troxell grinned. "No, thanks."

"Have you found anything else?"

Troxell knew I was asking about the dead man's hands. "Not yet, but I'm expanding the crime scene to include the house. Mrs. Shelton, you'll have to make arrangements for a place to stay."

Aunt Millie gasped. "You can't kick me out of my house. My daughter's coming to visit."

"I understand, but I can't release the scene until we search the house."

I recognized our golden opportunity to delay Janice's visit. *Afraid there's been a tragedy, Cuz. I'll be in touch as soon as the crime-scene tape comes down. How does April grab you?*

"You can come home with me." I put an arm around Millie's shoulders. "I'm sure Janice won't mind postponing her visit."

"She can't." Millie shook her head. "She said this weekend was the only possibility. She called it her window of opportunity."

How kind of Janice to find a "window of opportunity" for her mother.

"Detective," I said, "could you call us the second we're allowed back here to clean things up?"

Troxell hadn't seen the inside of Millie's house yet. The search could take days, and God only knew what shape the place would be in when they finished.

Troxell agreed, and I gave her my business card. She allowed us to enter the house under an officer's supervision to gather Millie's overnight necessities and round up her cat. I wasn't thrilled at the prospect of Jett coming to my house—he shed like crazy—but he and Millie were a team.

It was dark by the time I convinced Millie to get into my car, using my motherly, this-isn't-open-for-discussion tone. Jett had started complaining the second I put him into his carrier and probably wouldn't quit until we released him. I tuned out his howling and placed the carrier on the backseat next to the cat food and a bag of litter.

We took Highway 90 from Sugar Land into Richmond, where I'd bought my one-story bungalow located in town near the Jackson

Street courthouse shortly after my divorce was finalized. The house was on the small side, just right for one person, but I could put Aunt Millie up for a few days.

Millie sat in the passenger seat twisting the handles of her overnight bag so hard, I thought she might rip them off. I wasn't sure if she was more upset about the man who'd lost his life or the fact that we might not get the house ready for Janice's visit.

"As soon as Detective Troxell gives us the go-ahead," I said, "we'll haul everything to the storage units the way you wanted to."

"What if Janice gets here first?"

I didn't want to think about that. Janice was coming to see Millie, and Millie was on her way to my house. *Good grief.*

"We'll work this out. I promise." I'd solve the murder case myself if it meant Millie got back home in time for Janice to visit her there.

Millie worried the strap some more. "I wonder how long that poor man was out there."

The thought of my aunt sitting home alone while a killer stashed a body in her garage made me feel ill. "Try not to think about him. Everything will be fine."

"It will *not*. That man is dead, and they don't even know who he is." Millie unzipped her overnight bag and took out a prescription bottle.

"Someone will report him missing," I said. "He'll be identified."

"I hope it's soon." She opened the bottle and popped a pill, then dropped the bottle back into her bag and shuffled more things around.

My growling stomach reminded me I hadn't eaten since breakfast. I sped up, thinking about the leftover slices of turkey breast in my refrigerator. A turkey sandwich along with a nice hot cup of raspberry tea, then a steamy shower to wash away some of the stress—that's what I needed more than anything. I'd worry about Aunt Millie's house and the prospective Featherstone job, not to mention the murder, tomorrow. Tonight I needed peace and quiet.

Millie produced a roll of mints and offered me one. "It's not right, me getting kicked out of my house and the hussy across the street isn't. She's the one who probably caused this disaster."

"She who?" I stopped for a red light and looked at her.

"That Lori Gilmore. She has men coming and going like her

place is Grand Central Station. Thinks I don't notice, but I'm old, not blind. Goes on every day while her husband's at work."

I had noticed a redhead who'd come outside in a skimpy robe when the police arrived. "And how does that connect to the man in your garage? You think she killed him?"

"Not necessarily," Millie said. "But I wouldn't put it past that big bruiser husband of hers. Or one of the boyfriends. Men have that jealous streak, you know. Or . . ." She put a hand on her chin, thinking. "Maybe Barton Fletcher is involved."

She was too much. "Is he one of Lori Gilmore's boyfriends?"

Millie waved a hand. "No, no. He's a bigwig, or at least he thinks he is, with the homeowners association."

"And why do you think *he* could be involved?"

"He's a nasty, mean-tempered, foul-mouthed man," she said. "No telling what he'd do if somebody crossed him. Men like him oughta be banned from the golf course."

I was beginning to wonder what kind of fast-acting pill she'd taken.

"What makes you say that?"

"Golfers are crazy to begin with," she said, "and he's worse than most. I wouldn't be surprised if that man got killed on the course. Game's supposed to be fun, but there's plenty of cussing and throwing clubs. You'd be surprised what I hear."

"What did Detective Troxell think about these people?"

"Oh, I didn't mention them to her," she said, "but I will."

Troxell would be thrilled to hear Millie's crazy suspect list. I remembered the detective's questions about Wayne McCall and turned to ask Millie more about him, but like a baby in a moving car, she was sound asleep. I wished the howling cat would follow her example.

The rest of the way home, I wondered about McCall and whether Troxell had good reason to be suspicious of him. As I pulled into my drive, the headlights caught movement on the front porch. I squinted to get a better look.

My son, Kevin, sat on the stoop, one arm propped on a huge duffel bag. I felt happy and relieved to see him but irritated at the same time. It *had* been over a month with no contact. He'd refused to pick up the phone whenever I tried calling him. Darn caller ID. Maybe I was ready to accept some of the blame for our awful fight, but if he wouldn't even answer—

I homed in on the duffel bag. Dare I hope?

Scanning the shadows around the house, I half expected the girlfriend-from-hell to materialize. Grayson Sullivan, a career groupie, had somehow convinced Kevin to ditch his college education to start a rock 'n' roll band.

I checked on Millie. She was sleeping soundly, so I climbed out to say hi to Kevin without turning off the ignition. He stood as I approached, and I took in his wrinkled clothes, the misbuttoned shirt, his too-long sandy blond hair. He'd been a mess ever since he was a toddler, but I had sworn to stop nagging him.

"You're out late," he said.

"Hey, that's the mom's line." I laughed uneasily and caught him up in a hug. He felt thinner. "You okay?"

"Yeah." He hugged me back, all too briefly.

"Been waiting long?"

"An hour or so."

"You should have called me."

"Lost my cell phone."

The poor boy didn't have an organized bone in his body, but this wasn't the time to remind him how many phones he'd lost in his short lifetime. He scuffed a rubber-soled shoe on the concrete, looking as fidgety as the time he'd broken my Waterford flower vase when he was seven. Fourteen years ago seemed like yesterday.

"What's wrong?" I asked.

"Nothing."

Right. That's why you're here with your duffel bag. I waited.

"Mom, I need a place to crash for a while. Okay?"

"Of course." I unlocked my front door, suppressing a smile. I didn't know if Grayson had dumped Kevin or he'd dumped her. Either way, he'd be better off.

When I turned around, Kevin was staring at my car.

"Who's that with you?"

"Oh, I almost forgot Aunt Millie. She's spending the night. Jett too. Don't worry. I'll make room for all of you." I noticed his dusty, time-worn pickup, its dirty green finish camouflaged next to the neighbor's hedge. It bugged me that he didn't take better care of his belongings, but some things never change.

"Truck holding up okay?" I asked.

"I guess."

"You get those new tires?"

"Not yet."

"You know it's dangerous driving around on bald—"

"I know, Mom, you've told me a hundred times." He picked up his duffel, and his tired eyes met mine. "Could we please skip the twenty questions?"

"I'm making conversation. That's what people do when they haven't seen each other."

He released an aggravated breath. "All right. I know you won't quit, so here it is. I'm overdue for an oil change, haven't seen the dentist in years, I dropped my classes, and Grayson is still the love of my life."

I wanted to know more, especially about Grayson, but I didn't want Kevin to leave. He looked exhausted and obviously needed some space. At least he was here with me, and that would have to do.

"Okay," I said quietly. "Why don't you go on in and make yourself at home in the guest room? Aunt Millie can bunk with me."

"Thanks, Mom." He lugged his duffel bag over the threshold.

For now, taking care of Aunt Millie would have to satisfy my mothering instinct. I went to wake her, remembering how excited I'd felt when I left home this morning. Eager to help Millie turn her life around so things could be calm, organized, and in order—like my life.

Wait a second. My life wasn't peaceful and controlled anymore. All of a sudden I had two houseguests, a cat, the Featherstone meeting, a potential big bonus, and Janice coming to town. Not to mention the handless corpse, cops, and crime-scene tape.

A chill ran up my spine, and I looked around nervously.

Better get Aunt Millie inside—you never knew where a murderer might be lurking.

Chapter Four

No matter how long you know a person—forty-something years in this case—there's always something new to learn. Turns out Aunt Millie is quite the snorer. I'm not talking a soft, snuffling sound. Hers is a bone-jarring snore, like a freight train rattling through the room. She had slept quietly in the car, so what had brought on this racket? Was it the big meal right before bed?

Over our late supper, Millie had told Kevin all about the man found in her garage while I shoveled food into my mouth to keep from asking him about his relationship with Grayson. In fact, I'd eaten a lot more than Millie had—so maybe I would snore, too, *if* I ever fell asleep.

I tossed and turned and buried my head beneath pillows for what seemed like nights on end before giving up and moving to the living room couch—which didn't solve the problem, since the racket carried through the whole house, even with the bedroom door shut tightly. Not to mention Jett, who joined me as soon as I settled on the couch and proceeded to knead my tummy, his purr running a close second to Millie's snore.

It didn't help that I couldn't get my mind off the murder victim. What circumstances could have possibly led to the man ending up dead in Aunt Millie's garage? How long would it take the police to identify him? Was this a random murder or premeditated?

Jeez. How could I clear my mind and get some sleep? Music might help. I went to fetch my portable CD player with headphones and ran a finger down my alphabetized media rack to a soothing George Winston selection. I settled back on the couch. Winston's piano wasn't quite so soothing at the volume I had to play him to drown out Aunt Millie, but I fell asleep sometime before the music ended.

I woke at five in the morning, and Millie was still sawing logs. *Good grief.* The snoring hadn't seemed to bother Kevin, but then he'd probably slept through worse during his short tenure living in a fraternity house.

I threw back my blanket, disturbing Jett, who had slept at my feet. I felt exhausted after the restless night filled with nightmares about the handless corpse, but I reminded myself that worrying about things I couldn't change was a waste of time and energy. I had none to spare. So I got up, took a quick shower, and looked in on Kevin. Seeing him cocooned in the blankets sent me back in time and tugged my heartstrings. I hoped Grayson hadn't hurt him too badly—and that they wouldn't patch up whatever had sent him here last night. At the moment, Kevin believed she was the love of his life, but he'd get over her. There was a young woman out there somewhere who was perfect for Kevin. Grayson wasn't the one.

Back in the kitchen, I fed the cat, then took out my pre-printed grocery list, designed to save shopping time. Of course, the list only contained essential-food-group items I normally buy for myself. I tossed the list back into the drawer and made a comfort-food run.

By seven-thirty, I'd stocked the kitchen. Frosted Flakes, chocolate-iced doughnuts, English muffins, and Kraft Macaroni & Cheese in the pantry. Waffles, frozen pizzas, and Blue Bell Homemade Vanilla ice cream in the freezer. A huge bowl of fresh fruit on the kitchen table provided a nutritious facade for the empty calories hiding behind closed doors.

I ate three doughnuts while writing a note asking Kevin and Millie to call me once they woke up so we could make arrangements to pick up Millie's car. Then I gave Jett a good-bye pat on the head and left for the meeting with my prospective new client.

My approach to the Featherstone house took me right past Aunt Millie's, where crime-scene tape flapped in the early-morning breeze. Today was cold and drizzly, a thirty-degree temperature drop from the day before. Typical Texas winter.

If the weather had stayed cold and if I hadn't entered that garage yesterday, no telling how long it would have been before the body was discovered. Which made me think the killer knew Aunt Millie well enough to know she wouldn't find anything, even a dead body, in that mess anytime soon. *Hmm.* I didn't see any police cars around, so the cops weren't out canvassing the neighbors. Surely they would. But it *was* kind of early in the day to go knocking on doors.

I pulled my SUV into the Featherstone driveway behind a white Ford Taurus with an Enterprise Leasing frame around the license plate and shifted my focus to the job at hand. The house was a two-story Tudor and bigger than I'd realized from a distance. If Steve's grandmother was half as messy as Aunt Millie, I could be in over my head.

Remember that bonus, I told myself. *You can do this.*

I grabbed my tote, then climbed out and pasted on a confident smile. Steve opened the front door before I reached the porch, and I had another chance to admire his physique in close-fitting jeans and a white knit shirt.

"Good morning, Poppy. Glad to see you're punctual."

He glanced at his watch, a Tag Heuer.

"I aim to please."

He turned around, and I followed him into the musty foyer. I checked out what I could of the old house from where I stood. The place was big, all right, but it seemed like more organized clutter, not a disaster zone like Aunt Millie's.

"I need to put this project behind me," Steve said, "and get back to work ASAP."

"What kind of work do you do?" I asked.

"I'm behind-the-scenes in the film industry. Lighting director."

I flushed, remembering Aunt Millie's asking him if he liked movies. I looked down to pull a folder from my tote.

"What's that?" he said.

"My new-client packet. Inside, you'll find my Organizer/Client Engagement Terms, my Tips for Killing Klutter, business cards so you can refer me to your friends, and—" I hesitated, self-conscious because Steve was staring at me. "If you decide to hire me, that is."

"There's no question," he said. "You're here. The work needs doing. Let's cut to the chase."

He pulled a money clip from his pocket and unfolded a wad of bills. He peeled off ten hundreds and handed them to me.

I wondered if all Hollywood types dealt in cash.

"Will that cover your retainer?" he said.

I hadn't even seen what I was up against, hadn't agreed to take the job, and I don't usually collect up front. But who turns down cash? I accepted the money, smiling.

"Certainly." I zipped the bills into the side pocket of my tote. With this much cash I could hire contract help if I needed to. "Why don't you give me the tour, so I can make my game plan?"

"No need." He snatched a sheet of paper from the hall table and handed it to me. "Your copy."

I looked down at typed columns that outlined room by room, closet by closet, shelf by shelf, precisely what he wanted me to do. And I thought *I* was detail-oriented.

"Any questions?" he said.

What was with these people making their own game plan when *I* was the professional? First Aunt Millie, now this guy. I looked up from the instructions, but he didn't wait for a response.

"If not, I'll show you around, and then you can get started. Here's the dining room."

I followed him into the room to our left. Featherstone flipped on a spiderwebbed chandelier that illuminated tall stacks of myriad patterned dishes covering an immense cherry dining table. A collection of teapots lined the enormous hutch against the far wall and the windowsills. Looked to me as if the lady of the house had a china fetish.

Four of ten chairs were pulled out from the table and held stacks of folded linens of various colors and holiday designs, the whites yellowed with age. At least a dozen ancient cardboard boxes sat in one corner.

"Found these in the attic," he said, indicating the boxes. "More dishes. Some may be antiques. I've arranged for an appraiser to view the china. Crystal and silverware too, which you'll find inside the cabinet. Take special care with the silver tea set behind the glass—it's eighteenth-century, I believe, which grandmother brought from London when she was a girl."

I nodded my understanding, but Featherstone didn't appear to notice.

"As you'll note on the list," he went on, "you need to unpack the boxes and group like items together to prepare for the appraiser's visit. Day after tomorrow."

"Two days from now?" Was he serious? And where did he expect me to put all this stuff?

"Right. Thursday." Steve crossed the foyer to French doors.

I closed my gaping jaw and followed him.

"Grandmother was an artist." He opened the doors, and the smell of paint and thinner hit me before he flipped on the light.

I entered the room, awestruck. Easels sat around the perimeter, holding paintings at every stage of completion. Still lifes. Landscapes. Portraits. Her supplies filled a large table. Oil paints, acrylics, blank canvases, paintbrushes, scenic pictures ripped from magazines.

Landscapes of every season, obviously done by the same artist, graced the walls. I walked over to inspect a dazzling spring scene and saw the name *Featherstone* scripted in the lower right-hand corner.

"Your grandmother was very talented," I said.

"Yes, she was," he said. "The appraiser will take a look at the artwork as well, see if it's worth anything. The rest needs to go. Paint's probably dried up anyway. If you can find a needy artist who'd use the brushes or canvases, be my guest."

I turned from ogling the paintings. "You're not getting rid of them, are you? I mean, they're gorgeous."

Steve sighed. "You probably think I'm one cold so-and-so, but Grandmother and I weren't close. Fact is, I hadn't seen her in a very long time. I figure guilt prompted her to leave me everything."

"Guilt?"

"Long story," he said. "Short version—Grandmother had one child, my father. She never accepted my mother when they married, which is a great understatement. She *hated* my mother. Tormented her. One day my mother couldn't take any more. She committed suicide."

A deadly mother-in-law? How odd.

"I know what you're thinking. There must have been other problems." Featherstone looked me square in the eye. "There weren't. She belittled her. You had to be there."

"What about your father?" I said.

"My father disowned his mother. We moved away, and he died of a heart attack years later." Steve's shoulders sagged, and he looked at the floor.

"I didn't mean to pry."

He straightened and inhaled as if gathering resolve to go on. "Don't worry about it. Happened a long time ago."

I tagged behind as Steve showed me the rest of the first floor. I felt awful for bringing up the bad memory, which reminded me of my own childhood tragedy, not nearly as profound as Featherstone's, though I'd let it affect me more than his seemed to affect him.

But his story had struck another nerve with me. The mother's disapproval of the son's wife hit too close to home. I'd said some harsh things to Kevin about the woman he claimed to love. As we headed upstairs, I vowed to keep my mouth shut in the future. Kevin was a grown man now, capable of making his own decisions.

In the master bedroom, Steve dispassionately gave me permission to dispose of his grandmother's clothes however I saw fit. Looking at the old dresses, shoes, and handbags, I felt like I'd been transported back in time. I made a mental note to check with the Fort Bend Playhouse first to see if they were in need of costumes.

I was drawn to boxes of jewelry in the dresser drawers—more than a hundred, I guesstimated, some bearing names of department stores long since out of business.

"The appraiser will look at the jewelry too," Steve said, "so I'd like you to make sure it's all gathered in one spot."

"Okay." I walked over to a chifferobe and opened the double doors. More clothes hung on the right side. I pulled out a drawer on the left and found several bundles of photographs wrapped in soft cloth and tied with grosgrain ribbon tucked in beside yet more jewelry boxes.

Steve reached around me to pick up the bundles. "I'll take those. Thought I'd already collected all the pictures."

After the depressing story he'd told, I was surprised he had an interest in them.

We went down the hall, and he opened a bedroom door just wide enough to reach in and leave the photo bundles on a dresser top before closing the door again. "My room. I've gathered everything I want to keep in here."

"Okay." *Good. One room down.*

"That's probably enough to keep you busy today," he said. "I have some catching up to do while I'm in town, so I'll be going out. I hope that's not a problem."

"Not at all." I was accustomed to people staying to work with me on my jobs, and I sure could have used the help here, but that was his decision.

Steve pointed out a row of garbage cans he'd lined up out back to hold the enormous amount of trash he expected to collect. He showed me where to find coffee and soft drinks and told me to help myself, then left me alone with the work.

I was eager to get started. Any client as generous with cash as Steve Featherstone deserved top-notch treatment. First priority— make sure everything's ready for that appraiser. The dining room headed Steve's instruction sheet and seemed as good a place as any to start.

I began by sweeping the spiderwebs from the chandelier, then started unpacking boxes of dishes. Two hours into the job, the china, crystal, and silver were all sorted according to pattern and type, and I had convinced myself that I needed to hire a subcontractor to get through the week. As a member of the local National Association of Professional Organizers chapter, I knew just where to go for help. I put in a call to our chapter president, Bailey Devine, but got her voice mail and left a message.

I consulted Steve's list. The family room was next. He had directed me to discard all silk and dried flower arrangements but to make sure to keep the containers, as some of them were Depression glass and might be valuable. The curio cabinet, packed with miniature glass and porcelain figurines, should be left intact until the appraiser looked them over. Magazines and books could be tossed, except for first-edition hardbacks that might be collector's items. I hoped Aunt Millie didn't get wind of this, or she'd haul all the discards over to her place.

Steve had already emptied the antique barrister's bookcases that stood against one wall, and his grandmother's books were strewn across the Persian wool carpet. Glad for a chance to give my legs a rest, I sat down cross-legged next to the pile.

I was no book expert, but in my opinion these were all in excellent condition and would be welcome donations for the library's used-book sale. I opened each one anyway and, after finding a couple of first editions from the fifties, started a separate pile for them. Within half an hour, my eyes were getting heavy, and I decided to go in search of coffee. Groaning, I stretched my legs and grabbed the sofa arm to pull myself up.

But I didn't make it as far as the coffeepot. On my way to the kitchen, I passed a bay window. Out on the golf course, police officers scurried around like ants in a field of bread crumbs. What now?

I grabbed my jacket and hurried across Steve's backyard toward the course. Detective Troxell was front and center, standing near a small lake, talking with a man in thigh-high wading boots.

The rain had stopped, and a slight breeze ruffled my hair. The temperature had risen enough to bring out golfers, who were being directed away from the vicinity by the cops. Once again, neighbors congregated in a nearby yard to watch the action. I glanced over, then did a double take when I realized Aunt Millie was among them.

"Poppy!" she called out to me, waving wildly, so I headed in her direction.

"How did you get here?" I asked when I got closer.

"Kevin brought me."

"I'm surprised he was up before noon." I checked the street for his truck. "Where is he?"

Millie shrugged. "Dropped me off and left. Do you know that nasty detective still won't let me into my house? Has an officer guarding the place."

"She said she'd call us when you were allowed back in. You need to be patient."

"I didn't sleep a wink last night for worrying about this," Millie said.

I raised my eyebrows, but she went on before I could comment.

"Then I get here, and things are worse instead of better."

"What's going on?"

"They found something," said the woman next to Millie. "While they were dragging the lake for golf balls this morning. Some kind of weapon is what I heard."

The gun, I thought, tossed into the water after the killer left the body in Aunt Millie's garage.

Detective Troxell turned around, holding something carefully between gloved fingertips. Something long. Not a gun.

Aunt Millie sucked in air and grabbed my arm.

I looked at her. "What is it?"

"My machete," she whispered.

"Your *what*?" I could see the neighbor straining to listen. I backed away from the woman, pulling Millie with me, my eyes glued on the cops as Troxell handed the weapon to another officer and marched in our direction.

"How can you tell it's yours?" I asked quickly.

"Mine had a red handle like that."

"What do you mean *had*?"

"Well, I bought it to get rid of that pampas grass taking over my yard, but then the thing went missing."

"When was this?"

"I just thought I couldn't find it," Millie whined.

"When's the last time you saw it?"

"Two days ago or, I don't know, maybe longer. Whatever day Wayne started painting the living room."

"Did he see the machete at your house?"

"Sure did. He used it to hack down those plants for me. Man's got one heckuva swing."

Chapter Five

I prepared for Troxell to quiz us about the machete, but a barrel-chested man in a black windbreaker waylaid her. The man's buddies waited on the path, where golf carts were stacked up like cars at the Sam Houston Tollway booths during rush hour. I couldn't hear their conversation, but the red-faced man waved his arms as if the wrath of God was about to come down on the cops for delaying his game.

"Who *is* that guy?" I said.

"Barton Fletcher, the mean-tempered jerk I mentioned last night," Millie said. "Looks like the kind who'd commit murder, doesn't he?"

I rolled my eyes. "More like the type who'd sue if he heard you say that."

Fletcher rattled on, but from what I'd seen of Troxell in action, she wouldn't put up with his behavior very long.

"Get ready to answer questions about the machete," I told Aunt Millie.

"I have nothing to hide," she said.

"I know *you* don't, but what about your friend McCall?"

Millie couldn't have looked more shocked if I'd told her I worked nights at a strip club. "What are you insinuating?"

"Nothing." I didn't want her to realize that Troxell and I had discussed McCall.

"Wayne didn't hurt that man," Millie said.

"I'm not saying he did, but if that *is* your machete, you might want to start thinking about what you'll tell the police. Who else had access to your house and garage besides you and McCall?"

Millie chewed her lower lip in silence.

"How long ago did you hire him?" I asked.

She answered immediately. "A month. Six weeks maybe."

Fletcher still had the detective's ear. He pointed, first toward the street, then to several areas on the course, as if he was giving directions while Troxell scribbled in her notebook. I turned back to Millie.

"Does McCall live near here?"

She grinned. "I knew you'd like him. I thought of you that day in the store, even before the purse incident. Noticed Wayne in the frozen-food section picking out TV dinners and thought, now there's a man who needs someone nice like Poppy to come home to."

"Aunt Millie, quit that. Yesterday Featherstone, now McCall. You know the last thing I need is a man to complicate my life."

She gazed at me like someone expressing condolences at a funeral. "You don't know what you need. Wayne could—"

"Aunt Millie, please!" I lowered my voice. "I think it'd be better if you don't act as if you two are close."

"Why? He's a nice man."

"Just keep an open mind, and when Detective Troxell questions you, tell the truth."

"You think I would lie?"

I shook my head, frustrated. "Just tell her whatever she wants to know. If she asks where Wayne lives, tell her."

"I don't know where he lives."

"Where's he from?"

She frowned. "We never talked about that."

"What *do* you know about him?" I asked.

"If you're trying to get me to say something bad about Wayne, I don't want any part of it."

"Avoiding questions seems suspicious, Aunt Millie. Don't act this way in front of the detective."

"I'm not acting any way. I'm leaving." Millie turned on her heel and took off across the course.

"Wait. I didn't mean to upset you." I ran after her. "You need me to take you back home?"

"So you can grill me some more?" she said, keeping her pace. "Accuse my friends? Forget it."

"But you don't have a ride."

"That's what you think, missy. My car's right there in my driveway, and I'm taking it. I don't care what anybody says."

Troxell and Fletcher had been joined by a group of neighbors.

Didn't look as if I'd get a chance to ask the detective about getting back into Millie's house anytime soon—which meant I'd be dealing with my aunt's cold shoulder *and* her snoring tonight.

Millie power walked toward her house. Either the officer Troxell had stationed there would let her take the car or not. I decided I'd better stay out of it. If she didn't get her way, she might come looking for me. If she got the car, I'd see her later. Maybe she'd settle down if I left her alone.

Most of the neighbors had tired of the golf-course scene, like bored moviegoers at a third-rate show, and were headed home. I had a job to get back to.

When I turned toward Featherstone's house, I noticed that a blond toddler in blue overalls had escaped his mother, laughing with delight as he ran toward the street. The mother, balancing a smaller child on one hip, was doing her best to catch up with him. Her fashionable tan mules weren't made for running, and she lost one of the shoes in the grass.

"I'll get him." I took off and, since I was much closer than she was, easily caught up with the child. He wasn't fazed by my practically sitting on him to keep him in one place and was still laughing when his mother reached us.

After giving him the evil eye and clamping a hand around his wrist, she turned to me. "Thank you so much. I swear this one's gonna be an Olympic sprinter."

"Glad I could help." I introduced myself as Millie's niece and explained that I was doing some work for Steve Featherstone. Better to know who's who when there's a murderer on the loose, I figured.

"We live next door to Steve." She indicated the house with a swing set in the backyard. "I'm Vicki Rhodes. My little escape artist here is Dylan, the baby is Tyler. I knew Ida Featherstone better than I know Steve, since he's only been here a week or so. What kind of work are you doing?"

I told her about Klutter Killer as we headed across the lawn.

"Organization?" Vicki glanced down at her kids. "With these guys? Impossible."

I grinned. "I remember how hard it was when my son was little, and he's an only child."

"Actually, I have two more boys," Vicki said. "Cooper's eight, Harris six. They're in school right now." She stopped walking and looked at me. "You know, I could use your help too."

She had to keep ducking her head to stop Tyler from grabbing a dangling earring. Dylan was squirming, trying his best to make another escape. I hoped she wasn't talking babysitting.

I must have looked scared because she laughed. "I mean, I need to hire you. We'll suffocate under clothes and toys if I don't do something soon—like have the Super Bowl of yard sales. No way I can handle that by myself with the kids running around. My husband travels two, three days a week."

"Just the kind of job I love to sink my teeth into," I said, "and I have some great tips for teaching kids to be organized. Never too early to start. Unfortunately, I can't get to you right now."

"No rush. In fact, I wouldn't consider doing this until—" She looked at Dylan, then lowered her voice. "After they catch the bad person."

I nodded my understanding.

"I hope they find him soon," she said. "Should be easier now that they have a suspect."

"They do?" I said, surprised.

"You didn't hear?"

"Guess I'm out of the loop, since I don't live in the neighborhood. Who is it?"

"They don't have a name yet, but several people have seen the perp hanging around, or so I'm told."

"Where did you get this information?" I said.

"From my dad," Vicki said. "He's taken a personal interest in the case since his grandsons live so close. He lives on the richer end of the subdivision, but he's always over here keeping an eye on things."

"That's what fathers are for."

"That and antagonizing their kids. Believe me, he's an expert." She motioned toward the golf course. "That's him in the dark Windbreaker, talking to the detective."

Barton Fletcher. Sounded like Vicki might agree with Aunt Millie's take on the man's personality.

"Dad's one of the witnesses," Vicki went on. "Gave a detailed description, and two other people reported the exact same man lurking around."

"That's great news," I said. "I'll feel a lot better once they have him in custody."

"Me too," said Vicki. "In the meantime, watch yourself. They say the kid's twentyish."

Not McCall, then.

"He has blond, shaggy hair," she continued.

McCall had dark hair.

"Drives an old Ford pickup."

My heart rate quickened. There had to be a million of those around, didn't there?

"Green, so dirty you can hardly read the plates."

No way. She couldn't be talking about my Kevin.

"Dad got half of it."

"Half of what?" I said.

"The plate number. It ends in YNS."

I felt like somebody had clamped my windpipe shut. Kevin's truck plate ended in *YNS—ya numbskull*—Kevin's acronym.

"They had another sighting this morning," Vicki said, "so the perp couldn't have gone too far."

Kevin had dropped Millie off—what, thirty minutes ago? Where was he now?

"Anyway." Vicki shifted Tyler on her hip and struggled to keep a hold on Dylan. "It's lunchtime. I'd better get these little monsters inside where it's safe."

"Right," I said, not sure if my voice was audible. "Be careful."

"You too." Vicki headed for her house, Dylan in tow.

Before they were out of earshot, I heard him shout, "Perp. Perp."

Just what Vicki needed. A toddler using police lingo.

Chapter Six

The last thing I wanted to do right now was draw attention, so I forced myself to walk, not run, back to Featherstone's house.

They had it all wrong. Somebody saw Kevin in the neighborhood this morning, but connecting him to the murder was a big leap. Maybe the killer drove the same kind of truck Kevin drove. Every other vehicle on the road these days was a Ford pickup, right? I had to put an end to this ridiculous misconception before the cops did something stupid.

But first I had to talk to Kevin.

By the time I reached Featherstone's back door, I was close to hyperventilating. I stepped into the kitchen, flipped my cell phone open, and nearly jumped out of my shoes when Featherstone entered the room.

"Whoa," he said. "You okay?"

"I'm fine." My mouth felt as dry as chalk dust. "You surprised me, that's all."

"Stopped in to check on progress," he said. "How's it going?"

"Steady." I slid my phone into my pocket. No way I could talk to Kevin in front of my client. "Hard to see a difference this soon, but I've been a busy bee."

"Good." He glanced through the family-room window. "Seems you're not the only busy one. Nasty business out there."

"Sure is." I smoothed my windblown hair with a shaky hand.

"They know whodunit yet?" he said.

"I haven't heard." My mind raced for an excuse to leave the house. I couldn't concentrate on work until I'd talked to my son.

As if Featherstone had read my mind, he said, "You have lunch plans?"

"Lunch? No. I mean, yes." I checked my watch. Twelve-fifteen. Where was Kevin now?

37

Featherstone eyed me curiously. "You *sure* you're okay?"

"Positive, but I have to run an errand. I mean, during my lunch break."

"I hope this won't affect my deadline," he said.

"Don't worry." I snatched up my purse. "I'll make your deadline. May have to bring in a subcontractor, another professional organizer, if that's okay."

"Whatever it takes." The concern on Featherstone's creased brow didn't match his light tone, and I could feel his eyes on me as I headed out. I was acting as edgy as a cat in a day-care center. No doubt I'd aroused his curiosity.

As soon as I left the subdivision, I pulled into a strip mall parking lot. I dialed Kevin's cell number and got his voice mail before remembering he'd lost the phone. I tried my home number, and it rang until the answering machine kicked in. After the beep, I pleaded for Kevin to pick up if he was there. No response.

Much as I wanted to avoid Kevin's girlfriend, I pulled out my organizer and found the number for the apartment they shared. I dialed, trying to come up with a plausible reason for calling when I had never called them before. But I didn't need a reason because that number, too, was out of service. I checked to see if information had a listing for Grayson Sullivan or Kevin Cartwright. They didn't.

Good grief.

I sat there feeling like a miserable excuse for a mother because I had no idea where Kevin spent his days. Or his nights for that matter—up until last night. Maybe he'd gone back to my place and crawled into bed after he dropped Millie off. Worth a shot.

I headed home, plotting what we should do after I found Kevin. We'd go talk to Troxell—face the problem head-on. Explain why he'd been in the neighborhood. She'd see he had nothing to hide. Simple.

My heart sank when I turned onto my street and saw that his truck was nowhere in sight. I went inside anyway and erased the pleading message I'd left for him on the machine because it was the type of panicky message he would ignore. Instead, I'd leave him an innocuous note to call me. Throw in a bribe—free steak dinner at Outback tonight if he called in time. I'd never known him to turn down a meal.

I scribbled my note with a blue Sharpie on a large piece of paper. Jett was winding through my legs, rubbing against my pants, and purring loudly.

"Where'd he go, Jett?" I asked. "Where the hell did he go?" The cat answered with a yowl that told me nothing.

I turned to stick my note under a magnet on the refrigerator door where Kevin couldn't miss it. That's when I saw the note he'd left there for me.

Mom, I'll be out of town for a while. Don't worry. Kev.

I stared at the note. Out of town where? How do I find you? Didn't I teach you better than this?

I ran down the hall to his room. His duffel was gone. Everything he'd brought with him last night was gone. Even more scary, he'd made the bed. Kevin *never* made the bed. I took deep, even breaths, blew them out, told myself to stay calm. There was a perfectly reasonable explanation for everything.

The ringing phone jolted me.

Kevin.

I raced back to the kitchen and grabbed the receiver. "Hello."

"Penny, what the devil is going on?" Doug, my ex, who insisted on aggravating me every chance he got by using the nickname I detested.

"With what?" I said, trying to keep my voice level.

"Kevin just went flying through town like a bat out of hell. As if he doesn't have enough speeding tickets. Tried to call him, but his stupid phone's not working."

Cartwright Realty, Doug's real estate office, was located on the main drag through Richmond, and his office window faced the street.

"Which way was he going?" I said.

"What difference does that make?" Doug said. "If the cops catch him—"

"Were cops chasing him?" My heart thudded so hard, I had to grab onto a bar stool to steady myself.

"Nobody was *chasing* him," Doug said, using his are-you-an-idiot-or-what tone. "Not yet. But this is a thirty-mile-per-hour zone. He's had enough tickets to paper the walls of the Galleria."

"I'm not worried about a traffic ticket, Doug."

"Why should you? I always end up paying the freight."

I bit my lip. He didn't want to go there with me—not after my pitiful divorce settlement. I said, "Are you sure it was Kevin?"

"Of course I am. Who could mistake that dirty heap of—"

"Okay, let's say it *was* Kevin."

"I'm telling you, it was him, and I've spent enough on that kid—"

"Stop harping about money!" I yelled. "He's not a kid anymore, and worse things are going on."

Doug lowered his voice. "What's wrong with you, Pen?"

"Are you at your office?" I said.

"Yeah."

"Stay put. I'm coming over. It's important."

Ten minutes later, I pulled into the parking lot behind the real estate office. A gray BMW occupied the reserved spot that had belonged to me during the twenty years *I'd* run the place. I parked, hurried around the building, and barged through the front door.

Doug's thirty-something girlfriend—more specifically, the woman he'd slept with while we were married—looked up from a cluttered desk and gave me her best fake smile.

"If you aren't the last person I'd *ever* expect to see come through those doors," she drawled, "I don't know who is."

"Hello, Brandi." I closed the door behind me. "Nice to see you too. Doug's expecting me."

"He is?" She stood, knocking over a pile of file folders stacked on the floor next to her desk.

Brandi's curly red hair normally hung halfway down her back, but today she wore it up—twisted and fastened haphazardly in a clip. Her lipstick had worn off, and her tanning-bed complexion had faded. No doubt the price of becoming the woman in Doug Cartwright's self-centered life.

I scanned the messy room. Her taking my place here, in what used to be my immaculate office, bothered me a thousand times more than her sleeping in Doug's bed. Not wanting to dwell on the disarray, I crossed to his office quickly and rapped on the door, then went in without waiting for an invitation.

He was on the phone but hung up when he saw me. "Whatever's so all-fired important, make it quick. I have a two o'clock."

I plopped into a blue-striped visitor chair. "Cancel it."

"No can do." He looked like he wanted to rail on, but my expression must have stopped him. "What is it?"

So I spilled the whole awful story, beginning with my discovery of the body in Aunt Millie's garage and ending with the news that the cops thought they had a likely suspect for the murder—namely, our son, Kevin.

"My God." Doug pushed his chair back from the desk. "You think he's running from the law?"

"No." I ran my hands through my hair. "I don't know. Why's he running at all? Why did he have to leave town now, all of a sudden?"

"Have you talked to Grayson?"

"No, and since he spent the night with me, and their apartment phone is disconnected, I figure that relationship is over." *Thank God.*

"Too bad," Doug said. "She sure was a nice gal."

I glared at him. "Wipe that smirk off your face. I came here for help, not for you to fantasize about a girl young enough to be your daughter."

He did his best to look offended. "What do you expect from me?"

"I can't believe you don't care what's happening, or what might happen to Kevin if we don't do something."

Doug smacked his palm on the desk. "I care, but what in God's name do you want me to do?"

"Help me think. Who can we call? Who would Kevin confide in?"

"The guys in his band," Doug suggested. "Why don't you call them?"

"Duh," I said. "Because I don't know who they are. Do you?"

"No." He slumped in his chair, then perked up. "Wait a minute. I might know somebody who can help." He picked up his phone, dialed a number, and walked to the window.

After a couple of seconds, he said, "Hey, how're you doing?"

He turned away, but not before I caught the smarmy grin on his face—the same grin he used to wear during his "secretive" talks with Brandi. He'd lowered his voice, so I got up and edged closer.

"—when we saw the band the other night? Did you ever get with them about the publicity?" He waited a beat. "Good girl. You have a phone number?"

He turned around abruptly, came back to his desk for a pen and paper, then scribbled a number on his pad.

"Thanks a bunch," he said into the phone. "Listen, I'll call you later."

He hung up the phone and glanced at me, looking embarrassed. A new expression for him.

"Who was that?" I asked.

He cleared his throat. "Friend of mine. She's in publicity. Mother of one of the band members asked her to do some work for them on her dime. This is mom's number." He dialed the phone again.

I decided to leave it alone. What goes around comes around, and if Brandi didn't know enough to keep both eyes on her man at all times, who was I to clue her in?

Doug's next conversation was short, and he was smiling when he hung up.

My heart pounded in my throat. "You found Kevin?"

"Not yet." He snatched his sports jacket off the back of his chair. "But I'm on my way to Austin. Kid's mom says the band's been talking about going to some festival up there. A slew of agents coming to town. She figures they got an early start."

I frowned. Last night, Kevin sounded like he planned to spend several nights with me. Why would he suddenly be in such a hurry to go to Austin that he had to race through town? But he *had* left me the note.

Doug stopped halfway to the door and turned around to look at me. "You wanna go along?"

I shook my head. "No. You go. Let me know the second you find out anything. I'm heading back to my job. Kevin didn't kill that man, but someone did, and I have a better chance of finding out what the cops know if I stay here."

"Okay, I'll be in touch." Doug flung his door open, and I heard him say, "Brandi, cancel my two o'clock. I'm going out of town on urgent business." A pause. "Sorry, hon, not this time. I need you to stay here and man the shop."

This time it was an innocent trip, I thought. Next time Brandi might not be so lucky. I hurried through the front office while they were talking, not wanting to look her in the eye.

Chapter Seven

I grabbed a quick lunch so I wouldn't pass out from hunger while I worked and returned to Featherstone's before two. I planned to stay into the night if that's what it took, unless my client objected. I didn't think he'd care, as long as the job got done.

The golfers were back in full swing with no cops in sight, though crime-scene tape surrounded the lake where they had recovered the machete. Did that mean the police were out looking for Kevin now? No, they hadn't identified him yet. At least I hoped they hadn't, and sitting around worrying wasn't going to do anyone any good. Doug may have been a schmuck as a husband, but he'd always been a great dad. He would find Kevin, and we'd straighten everything out.

For now I needed to boot my organized and efficient self back into action. I was relieved that Steve Featherstone's rental car wasn't in the driveway. No need for explanations about my long lunch. I'd get straight to work and impress him with how much I could accomplish in one afternoon.

I carried some boxes from the stash in my Durango into the house and packed up the books I'd sorted for the library's used-book sale. I put the few remaining first editions back on the shelves, hauled the old magazines out to the garbage, cleared all surfaces of knickknacks, and tossed all silk flowers as instructed.

My hand hovered over a pile of the old lady's half-finished crossword puzzles. I imagined her rambling around this big house by herself after alienating her family. Sitting in the armchair doing crosswords. Painting beautiful pictures. Sad.

I shook myself out of the daydream, threw the crosswords away, and looked around the room. The furniture was old and dusty but sturdy. Goodwill would be glad to have it. The drapes were goners, the lining threadbare from years of Texas sun beating on the windows.

43

I made a mental note to ask Featherstone if he wanted me to take them down and throw them away. On to the next room.

Standing in Ida Featherstone's crowded artist's studio, I surveyed the room. This would take a while. Not to mention, I felt like I was about to destroy the woman's sanctuary. I let out a sigh, then opened the wood shutters covering the windows. Sunshine always made a chore seem less overwhelming and, in this case, less depressing.

First I segregated the blank canvases and paints that had never been opened—things that a school might put to good use. Then I brought an empty garbage can inside and placed it next to the table holding the used paints. I was about to sweep the whole mess—tubes, bottles, and cans—into the trash when my cell phone rang.

I knew by the caller ID it was Bailey Devine, my organizer friend.

"Hope you have good news," I said without a hello.

"That bad, huh?"

"Not necessarily bad, it's just there's a ton of work here and a short time frame to do it in."

"Tell me what you've got."

"Client's grandmother passed away and left him the house," I said. "He's selling and needs the whole place cleared out by this weekend."

"Better than my job." She lowered her voice. "We're doing a garage. Client's a hoarder with a capital *H*. He's collected hundreds of hubcaps from the side of the road. And I swear he has every car part he ever bought—new, used—don't even get me started. You should see it."

"No, thanks," I said. "So what do you think? Can you recommend a subcontractor?"

"Matter of fact, you're in luck," Bailey said. "I have the perfect guy. Talked to him this morning, so I know he's available."

"A man?"

"Don't get all feminist on me."

"No offense, but it's not that guy who comes to our meetings— Ricky?" I'd met the rail-thin, geeky twenty-year-old and wasn't sure he was operating on all circuits.

"Not him," she said. "I don't think Ricky will go the distance. No, the guy I have in mind has muscle. Sounds like you'll need some if you're emptying a whole house in a few days."

"And he's experienced? I won't have time to supervise every move he makes."

"Trust me. Now tell me where you're at."

I gave her the address without asking whether she had a pen and paper to write it down. A good organizer *always* has a pen and paper nearby.

"When do you want him to start?" she asked.

"Now would be great."

"I'll give him a call—"

She was interrupted by a loud crashing sound on her end. "I'm gonna wring my client's neck. I gotta go."

She clicked off. I stared at the phone for a second, then put it back into my pocket. There were definite benefits to working without the client around. I felt lighter knowing help was on the way. Had Bailey mentioned a name? If she had, I hadn't caught it.

I swept Ida's old paints into the garbage can. I had planned to fill the can halfway, then drag it back outside before it got too heavy. I didn't have to worry about that with Mr. Muscle on his way. So I worked fast and tried not to dwell on the fact that Ida Featherstone's favored possessions were being pitched like common garbage.

Used brushes, cans of solvent, and assorted scraps of paper— into the can. After the table was cleared, I moved on to a corner cabinet that held piles of art magazines and yellowed sketch pads. All trash. The cabinet itself was gorgeous mahogany with glass doors. Probably antique. I brushed a decade's worth of dust bunnies from the empty shelves and closed the doors.

What next? A row of department store bags filled with more paper stood in a corner. I couldn't in good conscience throw them out blindly. People often hid valuables in the least-expected places. I'd once found lumpy sofa cushions stuffed with ten-dollar bills inside a thin foam liner.

I checked the weight of the bags and hoped the old paper wouldn't give way as I carried two of them outside. I placed the bags next to a garbage can and brought over a patio chair so I could sit and enjoy the nice afternoon while I sorted.

I had just taken my seat and lifted papers from the first bag when a plump woman walked around the corner of the house. Short with blond helmut-cut hair and round wire-framed glasses, she wore a navy pants suit with a plain white shell underneath and scuffed pumps.

"Poppy," she said, smiling. "You sure look busy. I knew you would be."

She didn't seem the least bit familiar. "Do I know you?"

"Oops. I guess you don't. I'm Dawn Hurley." She extended her hand, and we shook. "I work for Allen Tate. Maybe you don't know Allen. Some people don't, but most do, especially those who had their will done, since he's the probate attorney in town, but you've never been to our office, so maybe you've never heard of him. Anyway, that's who he is, and I'm his secretary, legal assistant, paralegal, accountant. All of the above."

"Nice to meet you." I felt out of breath from listening to her.

My confusion at her being there and knowing my name must have shown, because she went on. "Seems like I've known you for years from your Aunt Millie. She always has such nice things to say about you."

Guilt stabbed at me for fighting with Aunt Millie earlier.

"Bless her heart," Dawn said, "I know she's upset about the poor man who showed up in her garage. Anyone would be, and I can't believe they can't figure out who he is. I mean, if he was from around here, we'd know by now, wouldn't we?"

"You would think," I said.

"I know most everybody around town," she continued. "Lived here all my life. I know all about your business too. Klutter Killer sounds like a name Allen might have invented. He's always telling me to clean up the office, but he doesn't understand. There's a *ton* of paper. It keeps coming in and coming in—a lot more comes in than goes out—until you feel like you're gonna drown, and there's not enough time to keep up with it all."

I nodded, sympathizing with her plight, though I hoped she'd come to the point of her visit soon so I could get back to work.

She shook her head. "The man can never find anything, even if it's staring him in the face, and he blames it all on me. Well, you know how attorneys are. Or maybe you don't know, but believe you me, they are a handful. I've worked for plenty in my time, and Allen's a nice guy, but he shouldn't harp on me like he does. I know where every piece of paper is in that place. Not my fault he can't find anything and . . ."

She droned on, and I decided she'd never stop talking if I didn't interrupt. I assumed Allen Tate must have been Ida Featherstone's attorney. I put my stack of papers back into the shopping bag and stood.

When Dawn paused to take a breath, I said, "You must be here to see Steve Featherstone."

"No, not exactly," Dawn said. "I saw him earlier today—that's how I knew you were working here, which is a good thing, since he's planning to sell the house real quick-like, and I know you'll do a great job for him. Anyway, I told him he needs to be patient, but you know men have a problem with patience. I always tell Little Joe—that's my brother—he needs to take a big dose of patience. Like Little Joe on the *Ponderosa*—you remember him, which is how my Little Joe got his name, 'cause that used to be our daddy's favorite show. Anyway, where was I?" She held an index finger to her mouth, thinking.

"You told Mr. Featherstone he should be patient," I prodded.

"Right. Probate only takes a couple of weeks if everything's in order, and if anybody kept things in order, it was sweet Ida. I already miss seeing her, you know. She was like the grandmother I never had, seeing as how my grandma passed when I was only three years old, and the other one I never even knew 'cause she lived in Detroit, so Ida kind of filled those shoes for me, you know what I mean?"

"I do," I said, nodding. Her description of Ida was the mirror opposite of Steve's, but then, he hadn't lived here since he was a kid, and some people *do* change as they get older.

"Is there a message you'd like me to give Steve when he gets home?" I asked.

She considered the question for a split second. "No, I don't think so."

I wondered if she'd stopped by just to meet me. "So you're here because—"

"Oh, silly me." Dawn giggled. "I came to see Ida's paintings. She always told me I should stop in, but I never got around to it, and when I mentioned this to Steve, he said come on by and check them out because they won't be here much longer. I didn't like the sound of that, but he didn't say what he meant. Do you know what he meant?"

I told her about the scheduled appraiser's visit.

"Surely he's not going to sell her paintings," Dawn said. "I mean, not with how torn up he is about everything. He's like a breath of fresh air, you know, compared to the clients we see fighting while their loved one's barely in the ground. Like the sisters we had once who sued each other over who got their mother's purse. A purse—can you believe that?"

"I can," I muttered, still stuck on her comment about Feather-stone's being torn up. I hadn't seen any of that, but he might be putting on a macho front for me. Dawn had actually stayed quiet for two seconds, so I said, "Why don't I show you where the paintings are so you can take a look while I'm working?"

Her eyes twinkled as if I was about to show her King Tut's tomb. "Oh, goody."

I probably should have cleared this with my client, but he'd invited her over, or so she'd said. It wasn't as if she could steal a painting without my noticing. So I took her inside where I sorted through a bag of papers while she oohed and aahed over Ida's work in between telling more stories about cases. So much for attorney-client confidentiality.

I had finished a bag that held no surprises and moved on to the next when I realized Dawn hadn't spoken for more than a minute. I'd just met her and already knew that silence was abnormal. The woman probably even talked in her sleep.

I looked up. Dawn stood across the room, where canvases were stacked against the wall. She'd flipped to the third one and paused. I walked over to her.

"Find something interesting?" I peered over her shoulder at the group portrait she was studying. Two women, one man, and a child in front of a fireplace.

She wiped at her eyes, and I noticed they were wet. "This must be Ida's family," she said. "That's her in the middle, and it's just sad she was alone and so lonely during her last days."

"I'm sorry," I said.

"That's why she tried so hard to find Steve. I mean, we had the private eye, the whole nine yards, but when he finally tracked Steve down—" She blinked rapidly to ward off tears.

"What?" I said.

"Ida had passed away before we found him. I took care of her funeral arrangements myself. She'd already planned everything, and we had the service. Then the PI contacts me two weeks later. Says guess what, I found your guy, and I told him our client had died already but we'd need the grandson's address."

"That is very sad," I said, "but I'm sure Ida was glad for your friendship."

Dawn smiled through the tears. "Thanks for saying that." She glanced at her watch. "Oh, boy. I'd better get back to the office. I'm sure Allen is having a fit. Sent me out to notarize something for a client, but I wanted to stop here on my way back. Do me a favor?"

"Sure," I said, feeling sorry for her.

"I don't know what Steve has in mind for these paintings, but if he's getting rid of anything, would you ask him to give me first dibs?"

"I'll be sure to let him know."

The doorbell rang, and I suppressed a groan. At this rate, I wouldn't accomplish much work. We headed toward the front door.

"I'll get out of your hair," Dawn said. "Maybe you could come by the office sometime, give me some organizational pointers."

"Will do." If Tate was willing to pay, I'd stop by weekly and do whatever he needed done.

"Thanks for everything," she said, as I opened the door.

Wayne McCall stood on the front stoop. He was more dressed up than he'd been the day before, wearing a knit shirt with starched khakis and black athletic shoes.

Dawn stared at him. "Wayne McCall, you sure do clean up nice. What are you doing here?"

Good question.

"Yes, Wayne," I said. "What *are* you doing here?"

He focused on me. "I thought you needed help. Bailey sent me."

Chapter Eight

Dawn said her good-byes, and after she left, I turned to McCall.

"Bailey sent you?"

"Yes, ma'am."

"Call me Poppy." *Ma'am* made me feel about a million years old, which was kind of how I felt after being slugged with the surprise of finding Wayne McCall on the doorstep. Never in my wildest imagination—

"Poppy?"

I jerked to attention. "Yes?"

"Should we get started?" he said.

"Right. But first, I'm curious. Tell me how you and Dawn know each other."

"We don't," he said, "not really. Ran into her a few times around town."

"Oh. Sounded friendlier than that."

"She's very outgoing."

Couldn't argue there.

McCall looked past me into the house. "Where do you want me, boss? Point the way."

I forced a smile, though I felt as enthusiastic about this working relationship as I would if Doug proposed remarriage.

"What's going on here, McCall?"

"I don't follow," he said. "You need a subcontractor? Or did I get the wrong message?"

"Right message, wrong experience," I said.

He grinned. "Think I can't handle the job?"

"I didn't say that."

"You one of those women who assumes all men are disorganized slobs?"

"I *meant,* this is no remodeling project." *Not to mention that a*

50

couple of hours ago I was picturing you as a machete-wielding murderer.

"You always been so narrow-minded?" he said, his brown eyes twinkling.

"I thought Bailey was sending an experienced professional organizer, that's all."

"And you've decided I don't fit the bill."

"There's a big difference between being a handyman and being an organizer," I said.

He chuckled. "Narrow-minded *and* jumps to conclusions."

"Excuse me?"

"Are you going to stand there and tell me you've never painted a wall or hung a shelf?" he said.

"What on earth are you talking about?"

"Organizers are multitalented. We have to be."

"We?"

"Guess Bailey didn't give you my background," he said. "I'm one of her students."

"Is that so?" I knew about Bailey's online organizer-training classes, but McCall had omitted this little detail yesterday when we met. The man annoyed the heck out of me.

"Already learned decluttering and prioritizing," he said proudly. "Next week's classes will cover motivation and finding your niche."

If he wanted me to ask about *his* niche, I wasn't biting. "Then you're new at this."

"Relatively new," he admitted. He retrieved a business card from his wallet and handed it to me.

The card said, *Wayne's Way—Organizing, Cleaning, Refurbishing* above McCall's name and a phone number. No address. The man had to be in his forties, maybe late forties. I looked up from reading the card.

"What did you do before?"

"This and that," he said. "Some desk work. I'm enjoying the organizing. Lots of variety."

"Taking a class is a lot different than real-life experience." I slipped his card into my apron pocket.

He grinned. "There's that narrow-mindedness again. Bet it's been a problem all your life."

"Let's just say I wasn't impressed by your on-the-job judgment at Aunt Millie's." Standing here on the stoop was feeling awkward, but McCall didn't seem to mind, and I wasn't sure I wanted him coming inside.

"Maybe you don't know the Bailey Devine Rules of Organizational Success," he said. "Number one—listen to your client. Number two—listen to your client. Three—"

"Give me a break," I muttered.

"In other words," he went on, "don't force the client to do anything she doesn't want to do. Millie wanted me to paint her walls and hang bookshelves. And does she have what she wanted?"

"The bookshelves aren't finished," I said.

McCall raised his eyebrows. "My work was interrupted. Goals tend to change when dead bodies turn up."

"You have a lot of experience with that, do you?" I watched his face closely for any sign of guilt. The only change I noticed was that the twinkle had left his eyes.

"You want me to leave, or you want the help?" he said.

I didn't know what to think. Bailey *had* recommended him. I *did* need the help. Those heavy, filled garbage cans were inside. I debated, telling myself that I trusted Bailey completely and that she trusted Wayne McCall. She obviously knew him better than I did.

"The help," I said.

"Then let's cut the chatter and get to work."

"All right. C'mon." I turned and headed to the art studio.

The door closed, and McCall followed me in. He appraised the room in two seconds. "Way I see it, this job's easier than most."

"That's because you missed the 'before' version," I said.

"All I'm saying is, we can skip a couple steps. Client wants the place cleared out, right?"

"Except for the valuables. Your point?"

"We sort and purge, then we're done. No assigning a home for stuff. No containerizing."

Okay, Mr. Smart Aleck, you know the lingo. Let's see your stuff. I pulled Featherstone's list from my apron pocket and handed it to McCall.

"I *listened* to my client," I said, "and these are his priorities."

"Okay." McCall scanned the list. "Good."

I smiled sweetly. "So why don't you finish in here, take these garbage cans to the curb, then tackle the kitchen?"

Kitchens are a *huge* undertaking, but McCall didn't blink. He looked me square in the eye.

"Whatever you say, boss."

We quickly came to an agreement about fees, and I told him how to approach the kitchen detail. Then I headed upstairs to the master bedroom. With Bailey's word that McCall was good at this, I'd leave him be without watching over his shoulder. The more distance between us, I figured, the better we'd work.

But I couldn't help thinking about Detective Troxell's questions as I pulled Ida Featherstone's clothes from the closet and spread them across the bed. Where was McCall from? Why had he come to the Houston area? Why couldn't she find any information about him?

The fact that he'd taken Bailey's classes didn't tell me much. He could have done that online from anywhere. The only thing I knew for sure was that the man downstairs wasn't the same McCall my imagination had conjured up. I couldn't picture him as a murderer any more than I could picture him as an organizer.

Praying that the cops found the real culprit soon, I made myself get down to the business of sorting clothes—the majority of them in shades of red. Deep garnet. Scarlet. Burgundy. Obviously Ida Featherstone's favorite slot on the color wheel. I felt sad for dismantling her wardrobe, but it had to be done.

Worn and ratty pieces in the throwaway pile, those in good condition in another for the women's shelter, and the quality pieces that had brought the theater to mind in a third.

This closet job was a lot smoother than those where I dealt one-on-one with a client trying to decide what to keep, what to toss, what fit, and what didn't. Easier—just like McCall said. I felt as dumb as a wire hanger for not catching on immediately.

I finished the closet quickly and stuffed the discardables into garbage bags. Filled boxes with the clothes to donate. Then I called information for the phone number of Fort Bend Playhouse and had a short conversation with the wardrobe manager. She was excited about getting Ida's clothes and handbags and especially costume jewelry from the fifties. Since the clothes in question were already on hangers, she preferred that I keep them that way and deliver them any weekday between one and five in the afternoon.

In the Durango I kept a clothes rod that attaches to the hooks above the back side doors. I grabbed an armload of future costumes and headed down the stairs. Pots and pans clattered in the kitchen. Sounded like McCall was into his work.

He had parked behind me. I made a short detour around his white pickup to peer inside. You can tell a lot about a man by how he keeps his truck. The interior was clean and, I hated to admit, very organized. The backseat held crates of office supplies. No empty cups or discarded wrappers. The front console held only a tin of Altoids mints.

The clothes were getting heavy, so I hit my unlock button and placed them on the backseat before retrieving the clothes rod. As I struggled to put the rod up, I noticed a dark unmarked van down the street, backing into a driveway. The van was still maneuvering for position when I finished hanging the clothes. I stood behind my open door, stalling as I watched three young men pile out.

They were at the house Aunt Millie told me belonged to Lori Gilmore. She'd said Lori entertained men at the house while her husband was away, but *three* men at a time?

The garage door rose, and a fourth man came outside to greet the others. He was tall and hefty, dressed for business in slacks with a white shirt and tie, while the first three wore jeans and T-shirts. Probably Lori's husband—home for a change—which might mean no hanky-panky for Lori today, but I had enough problems without worrying about theirs.

I closed my door and turned back to Featherstone's house. Mc-Call was rolling a garbage can to the curb on a hand cart he might have brought with him. His focus was on the men I'd been watching.

"You know them?" he asked.

I shook my head. "Nope."

The men carried stacks of small oblong boxes from the garage to the open back doors of the van. White boxes with no noticeable identifying marks—at least none I could see. Of course, we were several house-lengths away.

"Third time this week," McCall said. "Every time, more boxes. Something weird's going on."

"Weird like what?" I asked.

"I don't know, just a feeling I have."

"You get these feelings often?"

He looked at me. "Yeah, matter of fact."

"What's your batting average? You usually right or wrong?"

"Right, nine times out of ten."

I glanced back to the men. Funny how before the murder I never would have noticed them, but now everything seemed suspicious.

"They probably sell stuff out of their home," I said. "Maybe they have an eBay business."

McCall nodded. "A lot of that going on these days."

"You ever meet the Gilmores?"

"I've seen them come and go," he said. "Never officially met. Husband works long hours away from home, except for these box pickup days, whatever that's about."

"You're pretty observant."

He grinned. "Look who's talking."

I frowned, wondering if he meant that as a compliment.

"Did my truck pass your inspection?" he said.

I put a hand on my chest and pasted on my best whatever-are-you-talking-about expression.

"Just giving you a hard time," he said. "Tell you the truth, I don't blame you for checking me out. Especially not with this murder happening right under our noses."

I nodded. *Yeah, that's the reason.* "Do the cops know that it, uh, happened, near here? I mean, have they found the actual site?"

McCall shrugged. "Haven't heard, but they're narrowing the suspect list."

"They have a list?" I said.

"They *had* one. Thanks to yours truly it's now a very short list."

"How short?"

"Far as I'm concerned, a list of one. Saw the guy myself. Blond, five-ten, a hundred seventy-five, give or take ten pounds."

My heart pounded so hard, I was sure McCall could hear it thudding.

"He's been lurking around the golf course the past two weeks," McCall continued.

"Lurking?"

"Lurking, stalking, whatever."

"For two weeks."

"Right. Troxell said she'd call me as soon as they have him."

"How close were you to this person?" I concentrated on taking even, steady breaths.

"Close enough," he said. "I could pick that sucker out of a lineup."

I hadn't liked thinking of McCall as the murderer, but I liked this neighborhood-informant persona even less.

"Seeing someone on the golf course isn't exactly suspicious," I said. "Droves of people go out there every day. And you know how golfers can act kind of crazy." I attempted a laugh.

"Yeah, but the guy I'm talking about isn't a golfer," he said. "First off, he didn't have clubs. And I just had this feeling about him."

Screw McCall and his feelings.

"Standing around and speculating isn't getting our work done," I said.

"You're right." He looked back at the men and said, "*Could* be an eBay business. Never know." Then he turned and headed for the house.

I followed on shaky legs and checked my watch. No point calling Doug this soon. He hadn't been gone long enough to make it to Austin. But he'd better find Kevin. Fast.

Chapter Nine

$\mathbf{B}$y seven that night I had handled enough outfits to dress the Red Hat Society of Greater Houston. After removing everything from the closet rod and the dresser drawers, I'd discovered vacuum-packed clothing under the bed, behind the TV, in the cedar chest, and stuffed in the guest bath cabinets. Ida had used the storage bags that convert a big pile of clothes into a skinny packet when you suck the excess air out with a vacuum cleaner. I wanted to strangle whoever invented the nifty, space-saving packets when I opened them and found myself knee-deep in yet more apparel.

After designating every stitch of clothing for either the theater, Goodwill, or the trash, I moved straight to jewelry sorting. Ida had a unique collection, and I might have enjoyed the task if I'd been in a decent mood. But between the clothing overload and Doug's call a few hours earlier, I was physically and mentally exhausted. Worry gnawed at my gut.

In Austin, Doug had learned that the music festival activities wouldn't kick off for two more days. He had talked to the other mother again, but she couldn't reach *her* son either. I couldn't imagine where he would begin to look for Kevin in a city overflowing with UT college students.

Work hadn't taken my mind off the problem, but at least I'd made progress. The costume jewelry was packed up in boxes, and Ida's nicer pieces rested on the dresser top for the appraiser to view.

I sat on the edge of the bed and inspected the open closet from a distance. Mangled wire hangers lay on the floor along with dust bunnies, lint, and broken buttons. The closet's upper shelf held a mountain of handbags—every color, size, and material imaginable. I pulled them out and dumped them onto the bed. Had the woman kept every purse she ever owned or what? I'd have to go through them all before disposing of them—you never knew what might be hidden inside—but I could hardly move and wasn't sure I should tackle the project tonight. If Featherstone remarked about the mess I'd made of this room, I could explain that in the professional organizing business, things always got worse before they got better. He'd see more results tomorrow.

McCall had been banging up a storm in the kitchen, and I headed downstairs to check his progress. Voices drifted out to me as I got closer. Steve Featherstone was home.

I entered the kitchen and blinked hard to make sure I wasn't dreaming. The gray-speckled Formica countertops were cleared. Most of the white cabinet doors stood open to reveal empty shelves. Empty and *clean* shelves. I might have let out a subconscious gasp, because the men turned toward me.

"Your colleague does good work," Featherstone said. "I'm impressed."

Me too. "Where *is* everything?" I glanced around the room and noticed that several items sat on the kitchen table.

McCall read from Featherstone's priority list. "Says right here, dispose of kitchen paraphernalia unless antique." He pointed at the table. "Those things might fit the bill. The rest is outside, either in the Goodwill pile—by the way, I've scheduled a pickup with them for tomorrow at ten—or in the Dumpster."

"What Dumpster?" I said.

"You didn't hear it arrive?" McCall said. "I contacted Republic Waste. Two hours later, we had our very own Dumpster. Figured we'd need one."

"Good thinking," said Featherstone.

I went to the kitchen window and, in the glow from the floodlight illuminating the driveway, saw the Dumpster. I moved away from the window and scanned the empty pantry shelves. Rings from canned goods marred the shelf liner. *Jeez.* Why hadn't McCall bleached out the stains while he was at it?

He opened a cabinet door next to the refrigerator and addressed the client. "Here are the essentials you might need during your stay. A few dishes, glasses, pots. Should tide you over."

"Great." Featherstone turned to me. "I understand you concentrated on Grandmother's bedroom. If it looks this good—"

I held up a hand. "Not quite ready for an inspection. Tomorrow. I'm calling it a night." Now that I knew what McCall was capable of, we didn't need to work overtime.

"Sure, sure," Featherstone said. "I understand. How's your aunt holding up? I noticed cops are still running around her place. Doesn't seem right to push her out of her house."

"She's doing fine staying with me," I said, "and she'll be back home soon."

"What're the cops doing over there?" Featherstone said.

"Looking for evidence, I suppose."

"They find anything?"

I shrugged. "I'm not in the loop."

McCall said, "Standard operating procedure, I'd guess. Doesn't mean they suspect her of anything."

"I hope not," Featherstone said. "Couldn't find a sweeter lady. Reminds me of a gal runs errands for us on the set."

McCall started asking questions then about Featherstone's career in the movie business. I interrupted long enough to tell them I was going to head out and that I'd be back around eight in the morning. McCall said he'd meet me then.

On the way home, I checked my cell phone, but there were no new messages. No progress on finding Kevin, or Doug would have called.

I was glad to see Aunt Millie's Taurus in my driveway but puzzled by the white Crown Victoria parked out front. I was in no mood for company. I parked beside the Taurus and climbed out. If Aunt Millie had invited a friend over, I'd say hi and go on to bed. I hoped Millie had gotten over our little tiff.

I entered through the back door into the kitchen. The place smelled like a bakery, a warm, sweet aroma hovering in the air. I stopped short at the sight of Detective Troxell sitting at my kitchen table eating a piece of chocolate cake. She wore a long-sleeved white shirt, and a black tweed jacket hung on the chair behind her.

Aunt Millie stood at the kitchen counter. "There you are, Poppy. Glad you made it home before Rae had to leave."

Rae?

I waved hello to Troxell, but I couldn't take my eyes off Aunt Millie, who had flour on her cheek and down the front of her blue paisley blouse. Baking supplies lined the countertop. Baking powder, soda, salt, cupcake papers, measuring cups, and spoons sat in a mess of flour and chopped nuts.

As I scanned the room, I noticed Jett sitting on top of my refrigerator wearing a smug, feline, I'll-sit-wherever-I-want-whenever-I-want expression.

A loaf of something—banana nut bread, if I had to guess—sat on a cooling rack next to a mound of freshly baked peanut butter cookies. Millie picked up a mixing bowl and stirred vigorously as she turned to me. "You always work this late?"

"No. Aunt Millie, what's going on here? You holding a bake sale you forgot to mention?"

"No, silly. I always bake when I'm nervous."

I knew that, but what was she nervous about? I looked at Troxell. Had she already discovered something about Kevin?

"Your aunt bakes a mean chocolate cake," Troxell said.

"Yes, she does." I slid my gaze over to the kitchen desk where framed pictures of Kevin sat next to today's mail. I placed my purse in front of the photos. "Did you need to see me, Detective?"

"Not really." Troxell picked up a napkin to wipe a dab of chocolate frosting from the corner of her mouth. "I've said what I came to say, but I wasn't about to pass up the cake."

So what had she said? I was afraid to ask.

"You want another piece, Rae?" Millie put down the mixing bowl. "I have another cake in the oven."

Troxell grinned. "I could probably force another slice."

I went to the oven, my shoes sliding over gritty spilled sugar, and peeked inside at a pineapple upside-down cake. This aunt of mine was plumb crazy.

I faced Troxell. "What was so important that you came over here in person?" I held my breath, waiting for her answer.

"Wanted to let Millie know she can get back into her house now," Troxell said. "Thought she'd want to know ASAP."

Not about Kevin, but my heart kept tripping over itself anyway. "Thank you, Detective. That's great news."

I looked around the messy room. *Would have been nice to know before Aunt Millie destroyed my kitchen.*

"I'll go home tomorrow." Millie brought Troxell another slice of cake. "After what happened, I'd rather not go back in the dark."

"Don't blame you." Troxell picked up her fork and took a bite.

I reached for a long plastic bag to Troxell's left, sitting next to the day's newspaper. "Aunt Millie, what's in here?"

Millie glanced over her shoulder but kept mixing the batter for God-knows-what-else she was planning to bake. "Oh, that's the case for my machete."

I yanked my hand back as if I'd been burned.

"Found this in her garage," Troxell said, watching me. "We believe it's the sheath that came with the weapon we retrieved out on the golf course earlier today. Probably the same weapon used to sever the victim's hands."

"How awful." I put a hand on my chest and felt my heart beating ninety to nothing.

Millie stood with her back to us. "We went over everything I can remember since the day I bought the machete at Wal-Mart," she said. "Rae's gonna have it checked, so I told her everybody I knew who had touched the thing. You know, so she can rule out prints."

"You're going to fingerprint the sheath?" I said.

Troxell swallowed a bite of cake and chased it with a gulp of milk. "That's right."

Millie began pouring yellow batter into two round pans. "Besides my prints and the Wal-Mart checker, whoever she is, they'll find Wayne's and Kevin's fingerprints. Any others might belong to the killer—can you believe that?"

I opened my mouth and hesitated, then blurted out the first thing that popped into my head. "Has Kevin been helping you with your yard work again?"

Millie looked confused. "No, *Wayne* helped with the yard work."

"Oh." From the corner of my eye, I could see Troxell chowing down on the cake. Didn't mean she was missing a lick of our conversation.

Millie scraped out the last of the batter and set the bowl aside. "But I remember clear as a bell that day Kevin stopped by to visit. I'd just brought the machete home, and it was outside on the picnic table. He was all upset, and he picked the thing up and kept turning it over and over while he told me all about his problems with Grayson."

I nodded, my mind racing. Neither Millie nor Kevin had mentioned this visit to me. What had led to his discussing his girl problems with Aunt Millie? He never discussed them with me. I turned to Troxell and forced a smile.

"Kids," I said, shaking my head. "Date somebody a few times and they think it's the real thing."

The doorbell rang before I could come up with something more to say that might draw Troxell's attention *away* from Kevin. Could things get any worse? I excused myself, hurried to the door, and flung it open.

My cousin Janice stood on the front stoop.

Holy God—things *could* get worse.

Chapter Ten

I watched in disbelief as Janice marched into my living room. She'd aged ten years in the three since I'd last seen her despite her multitude of cosmetic surgeries. She wore her hair very short, dyed a harsh black. In her fine wool business suit, my cousin looked like she'd come straight from the office. Except Janice's office was over twelve hundred miles away.

She glanced around the room like royalty who couldn't believe she'd lowered herself to entering my hovel.

I closed the door behind her and found my voice. "Janice. What a surprise."

"Where in *hell* is my mother?" she said. Her diamond tennis bracelet glinted in the lamplight as she raked her hair with blood-red fake nails.

"Nice to see you too," I said.

"Cut the crap. That annoying blabbermouth from the attorney's office told me Mother is staying with you."

Talk about "annoying."

"I'm holding her hostage in the kitchen," I said.

"Mother?" Janice's voice rose and changed to baby talk as she crossed the room. "Where are you? I smell cookies."

Gag me.

I entered the kitchen behind her, in time to catch Millie's shocked reaction.

"Janice!" She ran to hug her daughter, throwing a look of sheer panic at me over Janice's shoulder. "I didn't expect you yet. It's only Tuesday."

Janice patted Millie's back. "Don't you worry about a thing, Mother. *I'll* take care of you now."

"But why are you here so—so early?" Millie sputtered.

Janice pulled back to look her in the eye. "I came as soon as I heard the news."

Millie looked confused.

"About the murder," Janice continued. "You know I wouldn't leave you to handle this all by yourself."

What am I? Hanging meat?

Between my worry about Kevin and having a cop questioning my loopy aunt, I was in no mood to put up with my snotty, two-faced cousin.

"Right," I said, "just like you helped her through the last family crisis."

Janice glared at me.

"Who wants coffee?" Millie said.

Off to their left, Rae Troxell pushed back her chair and stood. She picked up the evidence bag containing the machete sheath. "I need to get going. Don't want to horn in on y'all's reunion."

Millie said, "Don't be silly, Rae. You stay as long as you want. Have some more cake."

"Now, Mother." Janice glanced at her Rolex. "I think it's time I get you home. You look like you need a good night's rest."

"I *can't* go home," Millie said. "I—I have a cake about to come out of the oven and more to bake."

"Penelope can handle that," Janice said crisply.

"But I need to clean up," Millie said. "I won't leave my mess for Poppy."

"Let's make quick work of it, then." Janice slid her watch and bracelet into a pants pocket and shed her jacket. "Where's the dish detergent?"

My jaw dropped when she turned to the sink. Janice, doing dishes? I'd pay to see that.

Millie was shaking her head. "We're not going home."

Janice spun around. "Why ever not?"

"Police orders," Millie said. "Can't go into that house until they give me the go-ahead. No way, no, ma'am. Isn't that right, Rae?"

Millie looked at Troxell, her expression hopeful.

Janice gave Troxell the evil eye. "Who are you anyway?"

I jumped in and made introductions, then said, "Detective Troxell, I'm sure my cousin will understand when you explain that the crime scene *cannot be released yet.*"

I hoped Troxell would go along with this. Millie's house was sure to be an even bigger disaster after the cops had sifted through the place. We couldn't keep Janice away forever, but Millie was clearly not up to facing this new problem tonight.

Troxell smiled and turned to Janice. "They're right, ma'am. Can't allow civilians to traipse around my crime scene."

Relief washed over Aunt Millie's face.

"How much longer?" Janice spat.

Troxell shrugged. "Too soon to know."

Millie touched Janice's arm. "It's okay, honey. You can stay here with me and Poppy."

"Or at the Doubletree," I blurted. "Don't you and Conner usually stay there when you're in town?"

"Conner's not with me." Janice sidled closer to Millie. "And I wouldn't dream of leaving Mother at a time like this."

I rolled my eyes.

"Conner's my son-in-law," Millie told Troxell. "He and Janice are investment bankers on Wall Street."

"Impressive," Troxell said. "Much as I'd like to stay and chat about life in the Big Apple, it's getting late."

"Let me send some cake home with you." Millie slapped a piece of aluminum foil over the remaining chocolate cake and shoved the plate at Troxell. "Thank you *so* much for everything."

Troxell tucked the evidence bag under one arm and took the cake, then mocked a salute. "I'll be in touch."

Already needing a break from Janice, I fell in behind the detective as she headed for the door. "I'll walk you out."

In the driveway, a red Mercedes sat behind Millie's car. Of course, Janice would rent nothing less.

Troxell turned to me. "What was *that* all about?"

"Aunt Millie told Janice on the phone that she's turned over a new leaf—that she is now the epitome of organization."

Troxell laughed. "No, seriously."

"I *am* serious. Even worse, she wants her house to *be* totally organized before Janice sees it."

"Then the jig is up," Troxell said. "Your cousin strikes me as a woman who doesn't take no for an answer."

"They don't call you detective for nothing," I said. "But that's only one of Janice's bad traits. She's a snake in Bloomingdale's clothing. I'm not sure why she's here."

"To support her mother?" Troxell said.

"No way," I said. "She's up to something."

"I could pull her in, put her under the bright light."

"How about locking her up for, say, a week?"

"That's asking too much." Troxell headed for her car.

I followed. "Did you find anything interesting at Aunt Millie's?"

"Only this." Troxell indicated the evidence bag.

"And you came here to quiz her?"

Troxell stopped walking and turned around. "I came to tell her she's free to return home."

"That's all?"

"Should I have another reason?" She raised one eyebrow.

"No. Seems like you could have called her, sent an assistant, something. You know, to save you the trouble."

"No trouble." Troxell watched me, her face bland.

What if she'd come to my house fishing for information about Kevin? My shoulders tensed. Had she noticed the photos sitting in plain sight in the kitchen? Was she acting friendly to throw me off guard?

Asking more questions might make her suspicious, so I forced a smile. "Well, enjoy that cake."

"I will. Have fun with your guests."

"Yeah, right."

She got into her car and drove away. I watched until her taillights disappeared, then rubbed my temples.

This was too much. Kevin. Millie. Now Janice. And why hadn't Doug called? I unclipped my cell phone and dialed his number. I had almost given up when he answered on the sixth ring.

"Hey, Pen, you get my message?" He had to shout for me to hear him over the noise on his end—loud music, laughter, clinking glasses.

"What message?"

"I talked with your aunt an hour ago."

I groaned. "You didn't tell her about Kevin, did you?"

"I'm not an idiot, Pen, despite what you think. I asked her to have you call me."

"Where are you?" I found myself yelling because he was.

"Club Armadillo," he said.

"Is Kevin there?"

"No, I haven't seen him yet."

"Can you go somewhere quieter to talk?" The rock music that passes for country these days was giving me an even bigger headache than I already had.

"Hang on."

I paced the sidewalk for a minute that seemed like an hour. The noise coming over the phone line receded.

"That better?" he said finally.

"Yes, where's Kevin?"

"I don't know."

"Is he coming to the club?"

"Huh? No, I don't think so."

"I thought you were there to meet him."

"You must have read something into what I said, 'cause I never said that. Bad habit of yours, Penny."

"If Kevin's not there, then what are *you* doing there?"

His heavy sigh came over the line. "I needed a drink. And before you get your panties in a knot, listen to me. I found Kevin's friend Jojo, the band's bass player. He talked to Kevin this morning and invited him to lunch tomorrow. I'll be there too."

I let out my breath. "Thank God."

"It'll be okay," Doug said in a softer voice. "No matter what anyone says, no matter what they think they heard or saw, our boy had nothing to do with that guy's murder."

"I know," I said.

"You sound stressed."

"I am. Janice just showed up on my doorstep."

"Cripes," Doug said. "Maybe you should knock back a few yourself."

"Maybe I will."

My front door opened, and light beamed across the lawn. Aunt Millie stood in the doorway.

"Psst. Poppy? Poppy, where are you?"

"I have to go, Doug. Call me the second you see Kevin."

"I will."

"Call my cell, *not* the home phone."

"Gotcha."

"And, Doug, thanks." I clicked off.

"I'm here, Aunt Millie." I met her halfway up the walk. "Where's Janice?"

"In the bathroom." Millie was wringing her hands. "Oh, Poppy, what now? I can't believe she's here—not that I'm not thrilled to see her. I am, but, oh, my God. I almost wish Dawn wouldn't have told her anything, but then—"

"Hold it. Are Dawn and Janice friends?" I couldn't imagine.

"I wouldn't call them friends," Millie said. "Dawn knows Janice, of course. Her boss did my estate planning."

"That doesn't naturally lead to Dawn calling Janice to gossip about the body found in your garage."

"Dawn *does* like to talk," Millie said.

"I know. We've met." None of this made sense to me.

"I don't *care* how she found out," Millie said. "I care that she'll know I lied, and she's going to hate me when she sees the house, and she'll probably turn right around and go home before we even have a chance to visit."

"She won't hate you, Aunt Millie." I put an arm around her shoulders. "No one would expect your house to be in good shape now. Not after a police search. Of *course* they messed everything up. That's what we'll tell her."

"Janice will know the truth," she said.

I wanted to say, *Who cares what Janice thinks? She can turn around and go back where she came from, and good riddance.* But the dejection in Millie's voice broke my heart.

"Don't worry. I'll figure something out."

"Like what?"

"Like you and Janice *both* stay at the Doubletree the whole time. You can visit there."

Millie shook her head. "She was just saying how excited she is about staying in her old room, taking a trip down memory lane."

"Janice?"

"Yes, and it sounds wonderful, but she's not very patient, and then I saw her drop my house keys into her purse when she thought I wasn't looking—"

"Wait." I held my hand up like a stop sign. "She stole your keys?"

Millie reached into her pocket and came out with a fat ring of keys. "I took them back as soon as she went into the bathroom."

"I can't believe her." I grabbed the keys and stuffed them into my jeans pocket. What was her rush to get to the house?

"What are you going to do?" Millie said.

I ran my hands through my hair and paced some more. "I don't know. Maybe hire some moonlighting movers."

Millie's face lit up. "What a good idea. They could take my things to the storage units."

I put up a hand again. "Don't get too excited. I was thinking out loud. We'd need an eighteen-wheeler to haul that much stuff, and I don't know if movers work twenty-four-seven."

"They might." Millie pulled an envelope from her pocket and handed it to me. "My storage unit keys. There's a card inside with the address."

Had she set me up? I was exhausted, and part of me wanted to tell her to keep her danged keys. Then I pictured Janice gloating, saying how she never believed a word Aunt Millie had said about cleaning up her mess. I was too wired to sleep anyway. Work would keep my mind off the cops' search for Kevin.

I took the envelope.

"I'll go see about the house," I said, "as soon as Janice turns in for the night. But you know she's not likely to sit still. You keep her here, no matter what. Can you do that?"

Millie grinned as she reached into her pocket for a third time and came out with another set of keys.

"What are those?" I said.

"Keys to Janice's rental car," she said. "She's not going anywhere."

Chapter Eleven

I spent the rest of the evening avoiding Janice by busying myself around the house—changing bed linens and cleaning up the kitchen after Aunt Millie's baking extravaganza, a chore in which Janice was no longer interested. Instead, my cousin took a shower long enough to use a month's worth of hot water, then emerged complaining that my cheap soap would ruin her skin. One look at her makeup-free face told me she was in for the night. Janice *never* went out in public without her war paint.

She nosed around the kitchen and whined that I didn't have the right coffee or the yogurt she liked for breakfast. I was certain my sheets wouldn't be the proper thread count for her highness.

After finishing in the kitchen, I took a brief, lukewarm shower and pulled on my most comfy sweats and tennis shoes. Around eleven, Janice finally turned in. I clipped back my hair to keep it out of my way while I worked. Then I grabbed my purse and told Aunt Millie good night.

"Be careful, Poppy," she said as I was leaving. "There's a killer on the loose."

"Thanks for the reminder."

Since Doug had a line on Kevin, I had shoved worrying about him to the back burner and wasn't focused on the murder. Even now that she'd brought up the dead man, I didn't think I had anything to worry about. Whoever killed him was long gone, or so I hoped.

I climbed into the Durango and dropped Millie's and Janice's keys on the console. I wouldn't want to be Aunt Millie when Janice realized the keys were missing, but she had dealt with Janice's tantrums before, and she could handle whatever came. Pulling out of my driveway, I grinned. Janice would probably think she could snap her fingers and get a taxi. Fat chance out here.

I usually start winding down at this time of night, but the prospect of cleaning up my aunt's place without her around to protest energized me.

My game plan was set. Don't waste time on decision-making or scrubbing. Pick up and straighten. Toss newspapers and magazines. Pack the junk Aunt Millie thought she needed into boxes and stack them outside for hauling to the storage units later. I wasn't fooling myself—this would be a long, hard haul.

With no time to spare, I sped past road construction barrels on the freeway. In Aunt Millie's neighborhood, the streets were deserted and most of the houses dark. Since it was a school night, families with kids were snoozing peacefully. Odd that Vicki Rhodes' house was lit up like a Christmas tree. I didn't envy her wrangling with those four little boys every night, trying to settle them down for bed.

The cops had left crime-scene tape around Aunt Millie's house. Good. Whoever stashed the body wouldn't be inclined to return if it appeared the cops were still around. Plus, it would support the story we told Janice.

Odds and ends from the garage sat in the driveway. Fitting everything back inside would be like putting together a jigsaw puzzle with too many pieces, and the cops had passed on that challenge. I might set the stuff by the curb—looked like garbage to me.

I parked on the street and went to the front door with a supply of garbage bags under my arm, then scooted under the crime-scene tape to go inside. I locked the door behind me and turned on some lights. Surprisingly, the place didn't look any worse after the police search, which said a lot for the state of Aunt Millie's housekeeping. I plunked my purse onto a living room chair. With the new coat of paint, this room would show improvement the fastest. Good place to start.

McCall's cardboard boxes stood inside the back door. I began by assembling two dozen, then hit the room like a Tasmanian devil. I filled the new bookshelves, tossed junk into garbage sacks, and packed anything Aunt Millie might actually look for one day. I unearthed an envelope holding the estate-planning documents she had hoped to find and set them on the kitchen counter where she couldn't miss them.

I finished in the living room, then hit the breakfast area and the kitchen, clearing a path as I moved along. After I tossed the expired foods in the pantry, there was room to store groceries that had accumulated on the counter. I unearthed the Mr. Coffee and decided to make a pot. While the coffee brewed, I wiped off the countertop with a soapy rag. Even though I'd vowed no scrubbing, I couldn't ignore dust-caked Formica that probably hadn't seen the light in years.

Looking out over the wet bar into the living room, I felt a swell of pride. After the garbage bags and boxes were out of the way, I would arrange the furniture and line the coffee table with a few current magazines. Janice wouldn't believe her eyes.

I opened the back door and hauled the filled boxes out to the covered patio, stacking them where they wouldn't be visible from the living room windows. The night air was nippy but felt refreshing, given the sweat I'd worked up. I stood in the doorway. What to do with those bulky garbage bags?

I remembered the Dumpster at Featherstone's. Perfect, except driving the bags down there and dumping them would likely wake him, and it was far too late to call unless he happened to be a night owl. Still, I was on a mission, and I wanted them gone.

I poured a cup of coffee and went outside, walked to the edge of Aunt Millie's yard, and looked in the direction of Featherstone's. He was four houses away, too far to carry the heavy load. I couldn't tell from here if his lights were on or off. I walked out to the golf cart path and headed that way.

Out there in the open, the air felt colder. I sipped hot coffee to stave off goose bumps prickling my neck. A half-moon peeked from behind the clouds, giving me enough light to see the path ahead. I veered into the grass, hoping to spy Featherstone's windows without going all the way to his house. That's when I heard a clicking sound and noticed rustling in the bushes behind Vicki Rhodes' house.

I froze as Aunt Millie's words came back to me. *There's a killer on the loose.*

The figure in the bushes moved, and I could see the outline of a tall man. He appeared to have his back to me. The Rhodes house wasn't as bright as it had been a few hours ago, but downstairs windows were still lit.

I hesitated, not sure what to do. If the man turned around, he'd see me no matter which way I went. Running would catch his attention.

He moved before I decided, angling so that I caught his profile. He had his hands up to his face, holding something.

Another click.

A camera. The man was taking pictures of the house. This didn't fit my image of the killer. There was so much in the news lately about crimes against children that it seemed more likely he was a pedophile interested in Vicki's boys.

On this still night, if I called 911, the man would hear me. I took one step backward, then another. A floodlight flicked on behind Vicki's house, and the man turned abruptly. He rushed straight toward the cart path, then stopped in his tracks when he saw me.

"Who are you?" he barked.

Something about the guy seemed familiar, but I couldn't place him.

"I'm taking a walk," I said, avoiding his question. "What are you doing out here?"

"None of your business." The camera swung from a wide strap around his neck.

"You're spying on those people, aren't you?" I said. "I think I'll just call the police."

"No, you won't."

His hands were empty, and I didn't see any bulging pockets. No weapon in sight. I pulled out my phone to make good on my promise.

"You're a pervert spying on innocent children," I said.

"What?" He shook his head and chuckled. "You are one delusional individual."

"You're hiding in bushes and taking pictures," I said. "What am I supposed to think?"

The man stepped closer.

I stood my ground.

He jabbed a thumb over his shoulder toward the house. "My daughter lives there."

I remembered him now. "Barton Fletcher?"

He came closer, squinting. "Do I know you?"

I ignored his question. "Why are you taking pictures?"

"Like I said, that's none of your business."

"It sure as hell is Vicki's business," I said. "Does she know you're out here?"

"Keep Vicki out of this," he growled.

I took that as a no.

"I've heard about you." I remembered Vicki's comments about her father. "And apparently what I've heard is true."

"Show me some ID," he said. "I'm president of the homeowners association, and I know everyone. You don't look familiar."

"I don't carry my ID when I take a walk, Mr. Fletcher. See you around." I turned and headed back toward Aunt Millie's. If it had been daylight, Fletcher might have seen angry steam rising from my head. I didn't care if he was President of the United States—he shouldn't be trespassing in the dead of night.

Back in Millie's kitchen, I poured a fresh mug of coffee and retrieved the package of fudge cookies I'd stored in the pantry. Enough fresh baked goods to feed the Fort Bend County Sheriff's Department for a week were going to waste back home. These would have to do. I tore into the cookies and ate half a dozen before coming up for air.

Aunt Millie was right—Barton Fletcher was a mean-tempered jerk. He sure had rubbed me the wrong way. I wouldn't bother Vicki Rhodes with this tonight, but she deserved to know about her father skulking around her house in the middle of the night.

I gulped down more cookies, dropping crumbs on the dusty floor. I fetched a mop from the broom closet and pushed the crumbs and dust bunnies into a pile. Then I leaned on the mop and told myself to focus. There was no point in wasting energy on Barton Fletcher. I'd made a big dent in my project, but there was a lot more to do. I could take the garbage bags to the Dumpster at daybreak—if I didn't collapse by then.

I entered the crowded dining room and looked around. That's when I heard a noise coming from Aunt Millie's first-floor bedroom—located opposite the dining room, on the other side of the foyer.

The back door had been unlocked while I was out of the house. Anyone could have come inside. Maybe I was paranoid, translating creaking old house noises into something more. Just in case, I tiptoed into the kitchen and armed myself with the mop. Back in the dining room, I flattened myself against the wall, listening.

No doubt about it. A door creaked open, then closed. I heard a slight shuffling sound. Had the killer returned?

My mind raced. He'd come back for something. No, he came back to leave something. To plant evidence. No, that's crazy. But he wouldn't risk being spotted for no good reason. So why was he here?

Aunt Millie. He thought she knew something. He'd come for her. *Stop it, Poppy. Do something.*

I should leave. Go out the back door before he saw me. But *I* wanted to see *him*. I couldn't let him get away. There might not be another chance. I inched through the dining room, across the foyer. He was still moving around in there, though I could barely hear above the blood hammering in my ears.

I reached the bedroom, holding the mop like a baseball bat, ready to beat this jerk to a pulp. I tiptoed across the carpet toward Aunt Millie's dressing room and screamed bloody murder when a man rounded the corner.

Chapter Twelve

I was already swinging my makeshift weapon when I recognized the intruder.

Wayne McCall grabbed the mop handle in the nick of time.

"Whoa there," he said. "That could be lethal."

I stared at him, my pulse racing. "What in the world are you doing here?"

"Looking for you," he said. "Your truck's parked out front. Saw lights on, but you weren't here."

"I *was* here."

"Not when I showed up. And the door was open."

"I *know*. I left it open when I went outside."

"Bad move," he said. "In case you forgot, there was a murder in the neighborhood."

"Smart aleck." I lowered the mop and propped it against the wall. "The cops don't know *where* the murder actually took place."

"Come on. That's a technicality."

No doubt some women would be thrilled to have Wayne McCall looking out for their safety. I wasn't one of them. I didn't appreciate his scaring the bejeebers out of me, though I had to admit he looked good—freshly shaved and wearing starched jeans with a soft yellow sweater.

"Now that you know I'm alive and well," I said, "you can leave. I have work to do." I headed for the kitchen.

"Work?" he said, trailing behind me. "It's after one in the morning."

"So?"

"Enough's enough," he said. "You'll run yourself ragged."

I stopped in the living room and turned around. "It's one A.M. on your watch too."

"What has you all riled up?" A grin flickered at his mouth.

"You," I said.

"I think this mood started before you saw me."

"It's not a 'mood.' I didn't ask you to look out for me. You have no right to come prancing in here as if you own the place. *And* none of what you've said explains why you were in the neighborhood to *see* that the lights were turned on in the first place."

"Whew," he said. "That was a mouthful."

I blew out a breath. "Do you live nearby?"

"No."

"Then I'll repeat my question. What are you doing here?"

"Making the rounds," he said. "Looking for a killer lurking in the shadows. I've spotted him before, out on the golf course."

"Who are you? The self-proclaimed watchdog?" The last thing I needed was for McCall to stick his two cents in before Kevin had a chance to come home and explain himself. "Just because you saw someone doesn't mean he's guilty."

"He was *acting* guilty," McCall said.

"In your opinion. Ever consider you might be wrong?"

"Not about this. The guy was up to something."

My heart was still beating too fast, and McCall's innuendo about Kevin wasn't helping. "I've had more than enough aggravation for one night. Please go."

He looked around the room, making no move to leave. "Place looks good. Millie have you working the night shift?"

"What's between me and Millie isn't your business," I said.

He stepped closer and lost the mocking tone. "Listen, sorry I scared you."

I started to deny it, but I was trembling as if I'd just come from a face-to-face meeting with Hannibal Lecter. I looked down, avoiding his gaze, and rubbed my temples. My hair came loose from its clip and fell across my forehead. McCall tipped his head and tucked the hair behind my ear so he could look me in the eye.

"You okay?" he asked.

The intimate gesture had me momentarily tongue-tied. Finally, I managed, "I'm fine."

"Did something happen here tonight?" he said. "I mean, before I showed up?"

To turn the conversation away from his personal observations, I told him about my run-in with Barton Fletcher.

"Fletcher's an oddball," McCall said. "To him, those homeowners association rules are as serious as the Ten Commandments. Guy probably takes pictures of everything. Flagpole too close to the street, trailer parked in a driveway more than a day—he'll nail you."

"How do you know all this?" I said.

"I spend a fair amount of time in the area, doing odd jobs. Some of them fixing problems Fletcher reported."

"I don't think that explains why he was out there tonight," I said. "A father wouldn't turn in his own daughter."

"This one might," McCall said.

I was curious about the reason behind Fletcher's late-night photography, but I already had enough on my plate.

"I guess rules are rules," I said.

"Speaking of rules," McCall said. "Cops won't look favorably on your violating their crime scene."

"I'm not. Troxell gave us the go-ahead. They're all finished here."

"So where's Millie?"

"At my house with her daughter."

McCall crossed his arms, nodding. "Now I get it. The infamous Janice arrived, and she hasn't seen the house."

"Not yet. Which is why I need to get back to business."

"You can't work all night," he said.

"Yes, I can. Wouldn't be the first time."

"What about the Featherstone job?"

"Don't worry about that. I'll show up. Over there, I have you to help me."

"I'm here too."

We stared at each other for a few seconds. McCall had intense dark eyes, and I found it difficult to look away.

"Go home," I said.

He shook his head. "I'm not leaving. Wouldn't get any sleep knowing you're here alone."

I decided right then that there's a time to stand your ground, and a time to give in and accept help. And I needed help. I ran down the game plan for McCall over a cup of coffee, then he attacked the dining room, and I took on the master bedroom.

My approach to this bedroom would differ from Ida Feather-stone's, where my goal had been to empty the room. But after look-ing at some of the clothes overflowing from Aunt Millie's closet and piled all around the room, it was obvious that three-quarters of them had to go. I didn't see Aunt Millie fitting into her size tens anytime soon.

I went through the mindless chore of packing all clothes marked size fourteen and under into storage boxes, my thoughts on Wayne McCall. Working with him might not be the smartest move. He could be the killer for all I knew—a skillful liar with a hidden agenda.

Get real, I told myself. *You're delirious from lack of sleep. You want a reason to keep your distance from the man.* No self-respecting mur-derer would put up with this job, no matter what his agenda. That's if I seriously thought of McCall as a suspect, which I didn't.

I wouldn't let myself think about the real reason being close to McCall bothered me, so I turned off my inner critic and concentrated on moving faster. Still, it took me nearly two hours to get through Millie's clothes. By 3:00 A.M., all sixteens, eighteens, and Triple X's were on the closet rod, the hallway lined with boxes stacked three high.

I blasted through Millie's bathroom and tossed everything that looked grungy. Didn't leave much, but the room looked two hundred percent better. If Millie freaked out, I'd take her on a Wal-Mart spree to replace the necessities.

I splashed cold water on my face to revive myself, then pasted on a businesslike facade and went to check on McCall. He had packed as many boxes as I had—his filled with excess dishes and Aunt Mil-lie's endless bric-a-brac. He stood in the now-pristine dining room, closing up his last box.

"What's next, boss?"

"These boxes need to go," I said. "There's no other way. You have your pickup here?"

He did. We loaded up his truck and the Durango and headed for Millie's storage units. I figured we could make the round trip in an hour, before starting on the upstairs.

The streets were deserted—a good thing, since my eyelids kept trying to slam shut. We made it to Simply Storage in First Colony without mishap. No other crazies were accessing their unit at this ungodly hour, so we had the place to ourselves.

Lucky for us, Millie had rented side-by-side spaces we could access by driving right up to them. Each roll-up door was illuminated by a small light fixture. Weak beams shone on the driveway, and McCall parked his truck so his headlights would shine on our work area.

Under ordinary circumstances, I would have labeled each box with the precise contents, but to save time I'd made do with *D* for dishes and *C* for clothes.

Millie's units were empty, and we unloaded and stacked boxes in comfortable silence. The first unit was filling quickly, and I wondered if we'd have enough space for all the junk we'd eventually bring.

I yawned and decided to worry about that another day. For now, just get this stuff inside. I picked up two boxes marked *D* and was heading into the unit. But I lost my footing when a wave of dizziness passed over me.

McCall was right there to take my elbow and keep me from keeling over. He grabbed the boxes. "I got 'em. You sit."

I backed up to a stack and sat. I closed my eyes and leaned against the cartons behind me.

"What is it?" McCall said. "You hot, too cold, thirsty? What can I do?"

"Nothing. I'm just tired." I opened my eyes and looked at him.

He wore an expression that reminded me of the one I saw sometimes in the mirror. The one that said you're pushing too hard—take a break.

"Don't say it," I said. "I'm not as young as I used to be."

"You're plenty young," he said, "but you work too hard and too long."

I moved to stand. He put his hands on my shoulders and pushed me down, then sat beside me. "We'll both sit if that's what it takes to keep you down for a few minutes. Have you eaten anything lately?"

"Cookies," I said. "Fast and nutritious."

"You wanna keep at it all night, you need gas in the tank," he said. "Premium, not regular. That's what I always told the guys."

"Where was that?"

"At work," he said. "A million years ago."

"I mean where? What city?" I tried to place his accent. Somewhere south of the Mason-Dixon line, I'd bet.

"Nowhere close," he said. "You grow up around here?"

"Yeah. In Houston." Was he purposely changing the subject?

He leaned forward and checked my face. "Feeling any better?"

"I think so." The dizziness had passed. "Let's finish up."

"Give it a few more minutes," he said. "While we're waiting, I'm curious. What drew you into the organizing business?"

"I could ask you the same question."

"I asked first." He grinned. "Bet you're the type who could never stand a mess. I can see you as a kid, alphabetizing your Little Golden Books."

"You're close." I looked away, remembering that horrible day so many years ago. I spoke in a near whisper. "I was eighteen when my mother's house burned down. She died in the fire."

"Poppy." He put a hand on my arm. "I'm sorry. I shouldn't have pried."

"It's okay." I turned to him. "I made my peace with this a long time ago. And even though I was an orderly kid, the event turned me into an anal neat freak."

"How so?"

"My mother and I were complete opposites. She never put anything away, spent her life collecting junk, piled up papers in every nook and cranny. And she smoked. In bed."

McCall grimaced.

I went on. "Spent my whole childhood trying to keep the place neat. Did a decent job. But then I went off to college. A month into the semester . . ." I let the sentence die.

McCall wrapped his arms around me. "You don't have to go on."

I relaxed against him, too exhausted to cry. He smelled of outdoorsy cologne and spearmint. "Guess that was more information than you asked for."

"Not too much," he said.

After a while, he released his hold and backed away. "Now I know why you want to help Millie. Is she your mom's sister?"

"No, my dad's." I let out a rueful giggle. "I have this mess on both sides of the gene pool. No wonder my son—"

I stopped abruptly.

"He a messy kid?" McCall said.

"Kind of." I stood. "Thanks for that shoulder. I'm feeling much better. Let's get this show on the road."

"Okay, boss."

Chapter Thirteen

McCall and I got back to Millie's house in the wee hours of the morning and started working on the upstairs. It had been years since I'd stayed up all night, but I felt energized by our progress. In Millie's home office, I straightened her desktop first. Then I picked up papers cluttering an armchair and sat down to flip through them. The next thing I knew, McCall was shaking me awake. Sun streamed through the window, hitting me in the eyes.

I squinted at McCall. "What time is it?"

"Seven," he said.

"Jeez." I jumped up, spilling the papers in my lap onto the floor. "What hit me?" My back felt like one big knot. Every muscle complained. Self-conscious, I rubbed sleep out of my eyes.

McCall smiled. "You'll feel better after breakfast. I have scrambled eggs, bacon, toast. How's that sound?"

"Great, but you shouldn't have let me sleep." I followed him down the hall, looking into neat, orderly rooms as we passed. "You finished the whole upstairs?"

"Best I could," McCall said. "Closets aren't perfect, and don't open any drawers. At least the place is presentable."

"More than presentable. You're a miracle worker." I followed him downstairs, thinking I should always wake up completely before speaking. I didn't need to start fawning over McCall. It was bad enough I'd let him see my weak side last night.

"You did a good job yourself," he said.

"I need to do more in that office."

"I say leave it. Realistically, everyone has a junk room."

I don't, I thought, but I didn't comment.

McCall had changed to khakis and a button-down shirt. I carry a change of clothes with me, and I guessed he did too. In our business, you never know what kind of mess you might run into. Or maybe

84

McCall made a practice of spending the night away from home. I wondered if he always looked so chipper in the morning, even when he hadn't slept.

The kitchen sparkled, and breakfast smelled delicious. McCall was something else. I sat at the breakfast table and attacked my food while he stood at the counter eating toast piled with jelly.

"I'll make sure Millie knows what a huge part you played in this home makeover," I said, "but send *me* your bill."

"There's no charge," he said.

I looked at him. "We'll discuss this later. Time to work my own miracle. Make myself presentable for Featherstone. He's probably looking out his window already."

"Guy likes to stick to his agenda," McCall said.

I gulped my coffee. "That reminds me. I've got to get Millie's keys back to her."

"It's a done deal."

"Huh?" Was he a magician too?

"Millie sent a friend over to pick them up an hour ago."

"What friend?"

"Dawn Hurley."

I frowned. "From the attorney's office?"

"That's the one," McCall said.

"And she's not still here talking?"

McCall laughed. "Dawn knew Millie was in a hurry to get the keys."

"So Millie and Janice might show up here any second," I said.

"It's still early."

"We need to clear out pronto to pull this off."

"We will," McCall said. "I kept the storage unit keys, and my pickup's loaded with more boxes. I'll head over there first, drop them off, then meet you at Featherstone's. You going home?"

"I'd rather not." I finished the last bite of eggs and pushed my chair back. "Let Janice think I leave for work at the crack of dawn."

I stood and looked around, smiling. Millie would save face in front of her daughter. Her house was in good shape. Didn't know how long that would last, but I'd discuss maintenance with her when I came back to go through the closets and drawers McCall had mentioned.

McCall made quick work of washing the dishes and putting them away. I grabbed a sponge to wipe up crumbs around the toaster and noticed a cell phone on the counter next to Millie's legal documents. My phone was clipped to my waistband.

"Don't forget your cell," I told McCall.

"Got it," he said.

I frowned and leaned over the counter to inspect the phone—one of those new thin models with a blue face.

"Then what's this?" I said. "Did Dawn leave hers?"

McCall came over, drying his hands on a towel.

"No. Found that upstairs."

"Upstairs where?" Aunt Millie didn't have a cell phone, yet this one looked familiar.

"In the guest room," McCall said. "Figured the sheets should be changed, with Janice in town. So I pulled the dirty sheets off, and the phone fell out."

I nodded, like no big deal, but my heart rate picked up. I knew who was missing a cell phone, but I had no idea why he'd have lost it here. Or why Aunt Millie had never mentioned his staying with her.

I waited until McCall left for the storage units, then opened my phone. I dialed Kevin's cell number and watched the phone on the counter vibrate.

My first instinct was to call Millie and find out what else she'd kept from me, but I didn't want Janice listening in on the conversation. And then I thought about Kevin. Grown up, in charge of his own life, capable of making decisions. Aunt Millie didn't have Alzheimer's. If she hadn't mentioned Kevin's visit to me, it was because he'd asked her not to. I had to respect that and keep quiet—for now. Besides, I had a job waiting for me.

When I rang Featherstone's bell at eight sharp, he didn't immediately answer the door. While waiting, I looked at the Chevrolet Caprice in the driveway and wondered if a relative had come to visit. When he finally opened the door, I noticed that his brow was creased, the usual smile absent.

"Am I too early?" I asked.

"No, no." He motioned for me to come in and closed the door behind me.

My eyes hadn't yet adjusted from the sunlight, when someone else greeted me.

"Hi, Poppy. We meet again."

I recognized Dawn Hurley's voice.

"Hello, Dawn," I said. "What brings you here?"

Featherstone wore a relieved expression, as if he was glad I'd arrived to save him from entertaining Dawn alone.

"I was in the neighborhood," Dawn said. "Not that I planned to be, but something came up." She winked at me. "You know how that goes."

"I do."

I mentally traced Dawn's path this morning. She'd come to pick up the keys, then drove out to my house and returned here to drop in at Featherstone's. Didn't make sense unless his house was on a direct path to her job. That wasn't the case.

Dawn had kept talking while I worked out the details in my mind. "So I thought it would be a shame to come so close and not stop by," she said, "to catch Mr. Featherstone at home and make sure he knew about my interest in the paintings."

"I would have passed on your message." I turned to Featherstone. "Dawn was here yesterday while I was working and expressed her interest in buying one of your grandmother's paintings if they're for sale."

"She told me that," Featherstone said, "among other things."

Dawn giggled. "I know I talk too much. Everyone says so, but Mama is the same way, and sometimes I think it's just a trait I inherited. Do you think that's possible, Mr. Featherstone, that a person can inherit something like being talkative?"

Featherstone shrugged. "Never gave it any thought."

"Seems like family members always have a lot in common," she said. "Like Andy Axelrod and his son. They're the opposite of me and Mama. Can't drag two words out of 'em to save your life. And there's old Mrs. Webber and her daughter—they sing like birds. See what I mean? I'll bet you and your grandmother had a lot in common too."

"I'm sure we did," Featherstone said.

I jumped in to put a stop to the character sketches. "You seem to know a lot about the people in this area, Dawn."

"Sure do," she said. "Lived here all my life. I love dealing with people, and I'm a really good listener."

Featherstone, behind Dawn, put a hand to his head like a fake gun and pulled the trigger. He was able to joke about this nosy woman, but with the little sleep I'd had, she was getting on my nerves. I remembered that Janice's early arrival was due to a conversation with Dawn, and I wanted to know exactly how and why that had come about.

Featherstone said, "Dawn, if there's a particular painting you're interested in, I'd be glad to set it aside for you."

"That's so thoughtful, but I'm not sure which one I'd pick." She screwed up her mouth, thinking. "The florals sure are pretty. Maybe I should pick the painting of her favorite flower. You know the one." She paused, watching Featherstone.

He smiled. "Whatever you like."

"That family portrait of you, Ida, and your parents really touched me," Dawn said, "but I'm sure you don't want to part with it. That portrait meant so much to her."

Featherstone was nodding, though he seemed to have drifted off while she talked.

"Where was that done?" Dawn said.

"What?" Featherstone said.

"The family portrait. I'll bet you were at Ida's daddy's home in Abilene. She talked about that house so often, I feel like I've been there myself. What was it they called the place? I forget. The old Sapperstein place? No. Steigerwalt? That doesn't sound right either. It was something with an *S* though, wasn't it?"

Featherstone smiled. "You're getting warm."

"Sauerwine," Dawn said. "No. I give up. What was it?"

"Hate to ruin your fun," he said.

At this rate, we'd never accomplish anything. Featherstone was being too nice, so I interrupted. "You know, Dawn, we have a full day ahead of us, and we need to get to work."

"Oh, me too," Dawn said. "Mr. Tate is probably pacing the office as we speak. Sorry for taking up so much time. Just wanted to make sure Mr. Featherstone knew to save a painting for me."

"I will," Featherstone said.

"I'll stop by again sometime," she said.

"Looking forward to it." Featherstone looked at me and crossed his eyes.

Dawn turned to the door.

"Be right back," I told Featherstone. "I have a quick question for Dawn."

We went outside, and when the door closed behind us, I said, "You know my cousin Janice is in town?"

"Yes, that's why the keys—"

"We don't need to get into that," I said. "Do you and Janice talk often?"

"I called her a few times," Dawn said, "and, tell you the truth, I was kind of sorry each time I called. She's not very sociable."

"You called to tell her about the murder." It wasn't a question. I was annoyed at how much pleasure Dawn took in gossip.

"I told her, yes," she said, "But that wasn't the reason for my call."

"What was the reason?"

"I needed her correct address."

"Janice lives on East Seventy-third in New York City." I'd heard more than I wanted to know about her wonderful apartment in the city.

"She used to," Dawn said. "I didn't mention this to Millie because I knew it would upset her—Janice not keeping her informed and all. But it took me a couple of weeks to track her down."

"Did you try calling her at work?" I said.

"Sure, but she doesn't work there anymore."

"She doesn't?"

"Nope. They told me she left right after Christmas."

"Interesting," I said. "Why were you so eager to find her?"

"I mailed her a power of attorney Millie needed her to sign. If I'd known she was coming to visit, I'd have just waited, but I didn't know. So I mailed the document, but then the mail came back undeliverable. And now I know why."

"Why?" I said.

"Because Janice moved to Parsippany. That's in New Jersey."

Ordinarily, I wouldn't give a flip about where Janice worked or lived, but after the way she'd shown up, acting so concerned, I was downright suspicious of my oh-so-perfect cousin.

The door opened behind me, and Featherstone stuck his head out.

"Excuse me, Poppy?" He tapped the face of his watch, stretching my last nerve to the breaking point.

Dawn might have more interesting tidbits about Janice if I let her talk herself out, but that wasn't on Featherstone's agenda.

I told her good-bye and went inside to work.

Chapter Fourteen

I love organizing when I'm in the right frame of mind. My attitude this morning didn't qualify, but Steve Featherstone wouldn't wait around until I had a drastic mood swing.

I forced myself to pay attention as he ticked down his list of today's top priorities and reminded me that tomorrow was the big day for the appraiser's visit. When he finished, he grabbed a leather tote stuffed with documents that I guessed he'd gathered from around the house. He was on his way out to run errands and expected to return by midafternoon. I was glad to know he didn't need me to handle the papers Ida had left behind and happy to have him out of my hair.

After he left, I trudged upstairs to pick up where I'd left off the day before in the master bedroom. McCall and I could divvy up the prioritized list when he arrived.

I sat on the floor in front of Ida Featherstone's massive oak dresser and emptied drawers, piling things on the floor beside me. Nightgowns, belts, slips, girdles—thank God we didn't wear those anymore. I worked on autopilot, my thoughts on family—gullible Aunt Millie, scheming Janice, and especially Kevin. I sighed.

What the heck was that boy up to?

We'd know soon, but not soon enough to suit me. And now that the meeting time was so close, I worried about Doug's seeing Kevin without me there to act as a buffer. I hoped Doug wouldn't arrive in attack mode, though I knew good and well that's how he'd handled issues in the past.

Assume the worst—that was Doug's child-rearing motto.

Kevin stayed out past curfew—he must be on drugs. Kevin didn't say how a test went—he must have flunked. Kevin left town after discovery of a dead body—he must have killed the man.

No. Doug didn't believe that. And I had to admit that he *had* matured some in the thirty-odd years I'd known him. He could handle this without going off half-cocked. I leaned back, propping my hands behind me and wondering if the police had found any information that would lead their suspicions away from Kevin.

One way to find out.

I retrieved a business card from my purse and punched in the number on my cell.

Three rings, then, "Detective Troxell. Talk to me."

As we exchanged greetings, I realized I'd acted on impulse. How could I approach this without sounding suspicious? Troxell took the lead.

"Glad you called," she said cheerily. "I was about to phone *you.*"

Hope sparked in my chest. "Really? Have you found the killer?"

"Wishful thinking. No. I need you to come by the sheriff's office for a meeting."

My heart rate kicked up. "A meeting? Why? What's going on?"

"I'd rather do this in person," she said.

"When? My schedule's pretty tight." I paced the bedroom. Troxell *had* spotted my photos of Kevin after all, and now she wanted to drag information about him out of me.

"I understand you're working," Troxell said. "So am I. How about six?"

"Tonight?"

"That work for you?"

"I, uh, think so. Sure." I swallowed and tried to sound casual. "What's this about? Have you identified the victim?"

"Not yet."

"You have a new development?"

"More like continuing developments. We'll meet at the Ransom Road facility. You know the place?"

"Yes, but can't you give me some idea why—"

"Not now," she said. "But you called me. Something I can do for you before then?"

I hesitated, sorry I had called. How would I survive until six without knowing exactly what Troxell wanted? "Aunt Millie is going home this morning," I said, making up a plausible reason to have called her. "Are you sure that's safe?"

"Can't guarantee safety. Wish I could. Tell her to stay inside, keep the doors locked. Same advice I'm giving everyone."

"You've talked with all the neighbors?"

"Some of them."

"Oh. I thought you would canvas the whole neighborhood." I'd seen plenty of movies where cops pinned the blame on the first suspect to come along. I couldn't let that happen.

"You trying to run my case?" Troxell's tone had a slight edge.

"No. I didn't mean—"

"As a rule, citizens aren't shy about reporting every quirky detail when it comes to catching up with a killer," she said. "We're getting plenty of calls."

"Really?" I said. "Has anyone reported on Barton Fletcher's quirks?"

That stopped her for a second. "What would those be?"

I told her about my run-in with Fletcher the night before.

"Sounds like he was on private property," Troxell said.

"But not on *his* property."

"You're assuming the daughter didn't know he was out there. Can't assume anything. Man could be into night photography. Could be studying the nocturnal habits of geckos for all I know." She chuckled.

"This isn't funny."

"You're right." Troxell sobered. "And I thank you for the information. I'll add your report to all the other trivia we're gathering. Gotta go. See you at six."

She disconnected, leaving me both perturbed and frightened at the prospect of our meeting. Even if Kevin could attend the meeting himself and give Troxell his perfectly innocent reason for being in the neighborhood, would that put an end to her suspicions? What we needed were some other suspects.

I dialed Doug's cell number and got his voice mail. Probably still fast asleep in some plush hotel room. I closed the phone and paced some more. What to do? If only I didn't have this darned Feather-stone job to deal with. I looked out the window facing the street. No McCall.

I glanced over at a blue Astro van parked in Vicki Rhodes' drive-way. Maybe Vicki had known about her father hanging out in the shrubbery last night, but maybe she didn't. I turned quickly, almost stumbling over the piles of undergarments I'd made on the floor, and went to find out for myself.

I expected the shrieks of little boys to greet me at the Rhodes' front door. Instead, lively Latin music—Ricky Martin if I had to guess—emanated from behind the walls. I rang the bell and was surprised when a middle-aged Hispanic woman in a Fiesta Texas T-shirt over bright turquoise spandex pants answered the door, a can of Lemon Pledge in one hand, a rag in the other. She had the hip movements of a teenager, gyrating to the rhythm of the music. She waited for me to say something, as if speaking would cause her to lose the beat.

"Is Vicki home?" I asked.

"Come in, come in." She smiled broadly. "Sorry the music so loud. I like to—how do you say?—knock over two birds with one rock. Houseclean and exercise together. You see?"

I nodded. "Good idea. I should try that." I really should—either that or appropriate one of Ida's girdles. I'd need one soon if I didn't make exercise a priority.

"One minute." She held up an index finger and hurried into the other room. The music subsided, and the woman returned.

"So sorry. How may I help you?"

"I'm looking for Vicki," I said. "Is she here?"

"Not this minute." The woman offered her hand. "I am Blanca Sandoval. I clean house for Miss Vicki, a very long time. Since before babies."

I introduced myself and explained that I was working next door, including a rundown of the type of work I did so Blanca wouldn't think I was the competition.

"I know that house," she said. "I work for Miss Ida too, even longer than Miss Vicki. Very, *very* long time."

"I heard good things about Ida," I said to make conversation.

"Good sometimes." Blanca nodded, and her gaze took on a faraway look before she focused back on me. "I guess Mr. Steve is back."

I had the impression Steve Featherstone had left the area so long ago that he and Blanca never would have crossed paths, but I didn't know how old she was when she'd first worked for Ida.

"He's in town now," I said. "Probably not for long."

"Then I must speak with him soon. To see when I may pick up my silver."

I didn't know how to respond.

"I admire for years when I am polishing," she went on, "and Miss Ida says, one day it shall be yours Blanca, for all your good work."

"It?" Maybe Ida had promised Blanca some small inconsequential piece.

"The set." She pantomined pouring, then outlined a rectangle with her hands. "It is on a tray. You know, for tea."

Steve hadn't mentioned any special bequests in Ida's will, and I couldn't imagine him giving up the eighteenth-century English silver to this lady.

"I don't know anything about that," I said, "but I can ask Steve about it later today if you like."

"Please," she said.

"Okay," I said, "and would you tell Vicki I need to speak with her? She can call my cell phone." I handed Blanca a business card.

She studied the card, frowning. "Killer," she said.

"It's just a turn of phrase," I said. "I clean up junk. You know, get rid of stuff. Kill clutter. Nothing to worry about."

"There is much to make me worry," she said. "Everyone talks about the man who is dead."

"What do you know about him?" I asked.

"Me? I know nothing, except he is dead."

"You said everyone is talking about him. Does anyone know who he is?"

"I do not know who he is." Blanca shook her head.

"What have you heard?"

"So many things." Blanca's hands fluttered. "I cannot remember. How do you say? My brain, it is like a sink."

I didn't correct her. "Have the police spoken to you?"

More head shaking. "Police no talk to me."

"Do you spend much time in this neighborhood?" I asked.

"Every day."

Blanca was exactly the type of person Troxell should be focusing on instead of calling *me* in for a meeting.

"I'm trying to help the police," I said. "If you remember or hear anything important, I'd appreciate your giving me a call. We want the neighborhood to be a safe place for everyone."

"Yes. Is important to be safe."

"So you'll call me?"

"I can call you," she said, "or you can talk to Miss Birdie. She knows *everything*."

"Who is Miss Birdie?"

"Birdie Peterson," Blanca said. "She lives two streets over. I think she is the oldest lady around here."

"How old is she?" I said.

"Almost ninety," Blanca said. "But her mind is—how do you say?—smart as a tack."

Chapter Fifteen

I wanted to go straight to Birdie Peterson's house and chat about neighborhood gossip, but Wayne McCall hadn't made it to Featherstone's yet. Not a good idea to leave the house unlocked, and he didn't have a key. I felt selfish and ungrateful for wanting McCall to work while I was out asking questions. The man *had* stayed up all night helping me. But this was about Kevin, and I couldn't be in two places at once.

Maybe McCall had run into a snag at the storage place. I'd give him more time. It was early to pop in unexpectedly at Birdie's anyway.

Reluctantly, I went back to work in Ida's room. I segregated some nice garments—nightgowns and sweaters that might find a second home—and pitched the rest into a garbage bag. That done, I checked the drawers to make sure I'd gotten everything. The floral paper lining one drawer bulged in a corner.

Under the paper were a few wallet-sized school pictures—those that parents often enclose with Christmas cards so friends and relatives can be amazed at how much the kids have grown. One larger group shot had been taken in a classroom, the students lined up in rows. I doubted Steve Featherstone would have an interest in the photos, but I'd leave them in his room so he could have a look.

I trudged down the hall and opened his bedroom door far enough to leave the photos with those we'd found the other day. The dresser top was empty.

I pushed the door inward and peeked into the room. Not only were there no photos in sight, but the place looked like a vacated hotel room with the haphazardly made bed and a lump of dirty towels on the floor. Empty water bottles and balled-up trash lay in and around the wastebasket.

Curious now, I entered the room. Nothing personal in sight. No clothes. No shoes. Nothing.

I checked the empty closet rod and pulled out a couple of empty dresser drawers. This *was* the room he told me he was staying in—I was sure of it. Was he living out of his car or what?

The more I thought about this, the more I realized I shouldn't be surprised. I'd run into plenty of anal personalities working in the real estate business with Doug. Featherstone seemed the type who'd think that personal belongings would taint prospective buyers' viewing of the house. He may have already had them shipped home.

Which reminded me how much work I had to do before those buyers showed up.

I left the photos on the dresser top—in my mind, this was *the* spot designated for photos until I was told otherwise—and closed the door behind me. I went to a window to see if McCall had shown up.

He hadn't. What was taking so long?

I opened my phone and found McCall's cell number, glad that I'd had the foresight to program it in, and punched SEND.

Three rings, and then I heard a woman talking a blue streak in the background even before McCall could say hello. Janice. I'd recognize that condescending tone anywhere.

"What's going on?" I asked.

"Met your cousin," he said. "She's everything I heard she would be. And more."

"What's her problem?"

"I'm not sure," he said slowly.

A sound like falling boxes came over the line. I cringed.

"What is Janice doing?" I asked.

"You don't want to know," McCall said.

"Try me."

"Says she wants to help."

"Help with what?"

"I'm not clear on that."

"Where are you?"

"Your aunt's place."

I closed my eyes. "I thought you were coming to Featherstone's."

"That was the plan," he said.

"What went wrong?"

"As luck would have it, I drove by when Janice pulled into the driveway."

"Where's Aunt Millie?"

"She pulled in right behind Janice. Appeared to be chasing her."

"Oh, God."

"Exactly."

"And you got involved how?"

"Millie spotted my truck and flagged me down. She's calm now, but it's forced."

"I'll be right there."

I ran down the stairs and grabbed my purse, locked up, and pocketed Featherstone's house key. I'd been wanting to knock Janice upside the head my whole life. Today might be my lucky day.

Aunt Millie's place was so close, it seemed silly to drive, but I wasn't wasting any time. With three vehicles already parked out front, it looked as if she was hosting a Tupperware party over breakfast. I slid to a stop at the curb, jumped out, and jogged up the sidewalk.

McCall opened the door. "Good morning," he said with false cheer. "Glad you could join us."

I shot him a look. "Where are they?"

He raised his eyes to look at the ceiling as bumping and knocking noises sounded above us.

"You want me to get to work," he asked, "or stay and referee?"

"Go." I pulled out Featherstone's key and slapped it into McCall's palm. "I'll handle this."

He left, and I took the stairs two at a time, then stopped on the landing to determine exactly where the noise had come from. They were in the room that had been Janice's bedroom eons ago.

I stopped in the doorway, speechless at the sight before me. Boxes, shopping bags, stacks of clothes—things that were packed away in the closet a few short hours ago—littered the floor. Aunt Millie stood at the foot of the bed, her back to me, wringing her hands. Janice was inside the walk-in closet. I saw only her arm when she tossed a pair of tiger-striped slippers out to the floor.

"But, Janice," Aunt Millie was saying, "I don't want you to spend your vacation working so hard."

"This isn't hard work," Janice said. "You need somebody to help you get organized."

I growled.

Aunt Millie turned around, her eyes wide. "Poppy, honey," she whispered. "I'm sorry."

"Not your fault," I snapped.

"What was that?" Janice poked her head out and wrinkled her nose when she saw me. "What are you doing here? I thought you were at work."

"I was." *Matter of fact, worked all night.* "My job's right down the street."

"You didn't need to take a break on my account," Janice said. "I *am* capable of taking care of my own mother, you know."

She was so aching for me to slap her.

Aunt Millie put a hand on my arm, squeezing gently.

"What are you looking for, Janice?" I asked.

"Nothing," she said. "I'm going to help Mother get rid of some junk."

"You're going about this all wrong." I wasn't willing to admit her method was actually the best way to clean and organize a closet. Empty the entire closet, then put back only those items you need to keep. "What exactly is your goal here?"

"My goal?" She rolled her eyes.

"Right. What's your plan? Your goal?" I was talking too loudly, but I didn't care. "In other words, why are you ripping apart your mother's closet when the room was already neat?"

"The room *did* look nice," Millie said. "Very nice. Whole house looks nice, or at least I thought so."

"Until Janice came along," I said. "Who does this to her mother? I don't get it."

"Poppy," Millie said.

"I'm sorry Aunt Millie, but something is up here."

Janice came out of the closet and stepped over her mess to approach me. She was wearing designer sportswear accessorized with diamonds—not exactly closet-cleaning attire. She needed better concealer to cover the dark circles rimming her eyes.

Janice shook her head as if I was some poor, misguided soul.

"The only thing 'up' seems to be your temper, cousin. You should see your doctor about getting some Prozac."

"I don't need drugs. I need—"

"You're jealous," Janice said. "Admit it. You don't want me spending time with my own mother."

"That's ridiculous. What are you looking for?"

"Girls, girls, girls," Millie said. "Why don't we go downstairs and have some coffee and blueberry muffins?"

"You two go on," Janice said. "I don't like getting interrupted in the middle of a project."

Like she had ever done real work with those inch-long fake nails. I wasn't finished speaking my mind, but Millie took my arm and dragged me from the room.

"We need to talk," she said in a low voice. "Downstairs."

I bit my lip to keep from ranting to Aunt Millie, but when we reached the kitchen, I couldn't keep quiet any longer.

"You can't honestly believe she wants to help you clean house," I said. "She's—"

Aunt Millie put up a hand. "Of course not. I'm old, Poppy, not stupid."

"I didn't mean—"

"You and I both know that Janice has an ulterior motive. I wish she'd tell me what's on her mind, but she never has before, and I don't know why I expected she'd change after all these years." Millie's eyes misted.

"Sorry if I've upset you." I put my hand on her shoulder.

"It's not you," she said. "That's Janice's specialty. But truth be told, I'm happy to have her here no matter what. Better here than in New York City."

I bit my lip again, harder. Aunt Millie didn't know about Janice's move to New Jersey. I wasn't surprised.

"Something's wrong," Aunt Millie said. "I can't tell what, but maybe I can get her to open up while she's here."

Fat chance, I thought, but I smiled for Aunt Millie's benefit. "That would be nice."

"I know you're busy," she said, "but there's something I need you to do for me. Something important."

"Name it," I said.

She took my hands in hers. "Not that you haven't already done enough. I nearly fainted when I walked in here this morning—thought I had the wrong house. You must be exhausted."

"Don't worry about me, Aunt Millie. What do you need?"

She let go of my hands and opened a kitchen drawer. She pulled out the papers I recognized as those from the lawyer's office. She ripped the documents in half and handed them to me.

"Get these back to Allen Tate's office. I don't want Janice to see them. Tell Dawn these aren't going to work after all. You know Dawn, don't you?"

"Doesn't everyone?" I said.

"Tell her I need to discuss estate planning alternatives. I'd call, but Janice might overhear."

"Why the big secret?" I said.

"Because I have no idea what's going on with my daughter," Millie said, "and I'm not leaving her in charge of the money your Uncle Hal worked so hard for until I understand what's wrong."

I didn't blame her for that.

"Tell Dawn I'd like an appointment toward the end of next week. Maybe by then I'll know what Janice's problem is."

If Aunt Millie didn't have a will in place, Janice, as an only child, was likely to inherit everything—but that was between Aunt Millie and her lawyer. And, God willing, that wouldn't become an issue anytime soon.

Aunt Millie looked so serious that I stuck the torn documents into my purse and promised to deliver her message immediately.

Halfway to Tate's office, I remembered finding Kevin's phone in Millie's house and how I had wanted to ask her about the time he'd spent there.

That discussion would have to wait. I wasn't going to add to poor Aunt Millie's problems. With Janice on her mysterious rampage, Millie had more than enough aggravation for one day.

Chapter Sixteen

On days like today I wonder why I waste time planning my schedule. Between Kevin, Janice, and dealings with the police, my stable—sometimes boring—life seemed to be whirling out of control. I'd enjoy a little boredom about now.

I was having trouble keeping myself on track, but somehow I had to maintain Featherstone's rigid schedule. I'd get back to that as soon as possible—right after a quick visit to Dawn Hurley. I'd deliver Aunt Millie's message and her papers first. Then, if I was lucky, Dawn might shed more light on Janice's odd behavior.

I had some trouble finding a place to park in the heart of busy downtown Richmond. Must be some media-driven case going on over at the courthouse that brought everyone and their brother out to watch. I didn't pay much attention to such things, but apparently lots of people with nothing better to do did. I discovered a small parking lot behind the old three-story building that housed the Law Offices of Allen Tate on Morton Street and parked there. Inside, I took the sluggish elevator to the top floor, tapping my fingers impatiently on the handrail.

Tate's office door chimed when I opened it into a small waiting room decorated with tasteful upholstered furniture and subdued art on the walls. Copies of *The Texas Lawyer* and *Texas Bar Journal* lined the end tables, as if clients would have an interest in reading them.

There was no receptionist desk, and no one came to greet me. I crossed the room toward a short hallway off to my right and called out.

"Dawn? Hello?"

No answer.

She could be on the phone, in her boss's office, or typing dictation and unable to hear me, so I went to the first door and peeked in. The clutter might have made a weaker person run for cover.

I sidestepped Office Depot delivery boxes to approach the desk, drawn to the mess like a rubbernecker to a traffic accident. How could anyone work under these conditions? The nameplate teetering on the desk's edge said Dawn Hurley. *Jeez.* The woman clearly didn't have time for all the visiting she'd been doing.

Haphazard mountains of paper lay on top of, under, and around the desk. A stack of unclaimed printed documents sat on the laser printer. Multicolored Post-its with scribbled reminders framed the computer monitor. Three miniature stuffed cats sat atop the monitor as if they'd jumped up there to escape suffocation.

Behind the desk, a bank of file cabinets lined the wall, doors standing open to reveal masses of sloppy folders that wouldn't fit in all the way because the shelves were too packed. More folders sat on the floor in front of the cabinets.

I couldn't bring myself to add Aunt Millie's documents to the heap on the desk, even if she did want them redone. I retraced my steps and went farther down the hall to peer into a space that obviously doubled as a kitchenette and supply closet. This room was a little neater than Dawn's office, but not by much.

Behind me a man said, "Dawn, the Flemings are due here any minute, and we need—"

I turned around.

He stopped in his tracks when he realized I wasn't the person he'd expected, and he pulled off his reading glasses. "Excuse me. I was looking for my secretary."

He was a handsome, sixtyish gentleman in a starched white shirt and red-striped tie. His cheeks dimpled when he smiled, and I mentally forgave him for mistaking me for Dawn, who was twice my size.

I smiled in return. "So was I. Looking for Dawn, that is. You must be Mr. Tate." I introduced myself, and we shook hands.

"Allen," he said. "Mr. Tate was my dad."

I told him why Aunt Millie had sent me, and he invited me to sit down in his neat and orderly office. I looked around appreciatively, then sat in one of his guest chairs. But I was perturbed by Dawn's absence. Where *was* she?

Allen cleared his throat. "You have those documents?"

"Yes, right here." I grabbed my purse and fumbled through it for Aunt Millie's papers. Annoying, since I usually keep things where I can pull them out at a moment's notice. Finally I got my hands on the papers and slid them across the desk to him.

He glanced down but didn't pick them up. Pages ripped in half pretty much told the story. "Your aunt had a change of heart about the bequests in her will?"

"She's faced some new developments and isn't sure how to proceed. She'd like to meet with you and discuss her situation."

"I can do that." He turned to the computer and, with a few clicks of the mouse, brought up his calendar. We set an appointment for a week from Friday. He jotted the date and time on one of his business cards and handed the card to me.

"This have anything to do with the body found on her property?" he asked.

"No, no," I said quickly. "More to do with her daughter. My cousin, Janice. She's visiting from up north."

"Hell of a thing, finding that man," he said. "Strange they haven't identified the body yet. Or have they?"

"Not that I've heard," I said.

"Millie didn't recognize him?"

"No."

Allen leaned back, rocking his chair. "This could make a good *Law and Order* episode. Love that show. Figure most of 'em out before the end, but sometimes they stump me. The dead man nobody knows. You didn't recognize him either?"

I shook my head.

"Huh. How about Janice?"

"Janice wasn't even here when it happened."

"To your knowledge."

I raised my eyebrows, surprised. "That's right."

"But she's the estranged daughter, isn't she?"

"You could say that." What was he getting at?

"I remember Millie telling me about her. Hasn't been around in a while. All of a sudden she is."

"What are you saying?"

"Nothing. Ignore me." Allen straightened, and his chair popped back to an upright position. He showed me his dimples again. "Imagination gets carried away sometimes. Escaping the reality of running this place, I guess."

"Oh." I smiled and took advantage of the opening by handing him one of my business cards. "If you don't mind my saying so, you could use some extra help organizing the office."

"What I could use is a secretary who shows up for work on time." Tate checked his watch.

"Does she do this often?" I said.

"What's that?"

"Just blow off work. I mean, she should have been here by now. Hope she didn't have car trouble."

"By now?" Allen said.

"I ran into her earlier this morning," I said, then hurriedly added, "before work hours."

"Where was that?" he said.

"At Steve Featherstone's place. I'm doing some work for him now."

"Steve's a nice fellow," Allen said. "Would have liked the chance to chat with him about the movie business, but he's in a hurry to get back home."

"Seems to be," I said.

"What was Dawn bothering him about?"

"I'm sure he wasn't bothered," I said. "She's interested in his grandmother's paintings."

Allen shook his head. "Woman knows more about my clients than I do—maybe more than their own families know."

Given the amount of talking Dawn did, I suspected he was right. I figured Dawn for a lonely single woman and hoped I didn't grow more like her the longer I lived alone.

"If she spent half as much time doing her job as she spends befriending the clients," he went on, "her office wouldn't be such a dog-gone mess."

I nodded, allowing him to vent.

"She's like a mother hen, taking people under her wing, offering advice, fighting for justice if they won't fight for themselves."

"She's a nice person," I said.

"Yeah," Allen said grudgingly, "if she wasn't so damned nice, I'd have fired her years ago."

"Well, I'm not a secretary," I said, standing, "but if you need someone to help straighten the papers and update the filing, let me know, and I'll give you a quote."

He studied my card for a moment before putting it into his top desk drawer. "Just might take you up on that offer."

"Great."

The front bell sounded, and Allen got up. "That's probably the Flemings." He shook my hand, then said, "If you run into Dawn again, tell her to get over here. I've got a law practice to run."

"Will do," I promised.

He went to greet his clients. I stopped at Dawn's desk, unearthed a Post-it pad, and wrote her a note to call me. I stuck the note in the middle of her computer screen. I already had proof that Dawn had more information about my cousin than I did, and I wanted to know every little tidbit.

Much as I hated turning my back on a mess, I had other work to tend to. Allen and his clients were chatting in his office when I slipped out. Since I *did* want to get back to Featherstone's before dark, I bypassed the slow-as-molasses elevator and jogged down the back stairs.

On the road, I called Doug again, and this time he answered.

"I *said* I'd phone you when I see Kevin," he told me when I asked about his lunch meeting. "Quit calling me."

In the background, the low buzz of conversation and the clinking of silverware against plates told me he was having brunch, probably at some four-star hotel.

"Are you *eating*?" I said.

"Yeah. So?"

"I thought you and Kevin were meeting for lunch."

"We are, but I'm hungry *now*."

I mentally counted to ten, but it didn't help. "You are such a jerk."

"I'll ignore that 'cause I know you're worried. But you need to chill, lay low, and wait for *me* to call *you*. Okay?"

"Don't tell me what to do or not do," I said. "You're not the one facing the heat."

"Heat." He chuckled. "I thought you'd finally outgrown that melodramatic crap."

My temper flared. "The cops want me to meet with them tonight at their office. Still think I'm being melodramatic?"

He was silent for a second. "You think they want to grill you about Kevin?"

"What else would they want?" I snapped. "Just make sure you call. Don't forget."

"I won't forget," he shot back. "Keep your phone on."

"Fine." I punched END and threw my phone onto the console.

Jeez. That was childish, but I couldn't help myself. I was exhausted and more stressed than I'd ever been. And facing a full day of work. I checked the dashboard clock. Make that three-quarters of a day.

I was actually eager to get back to Featherstone's. Weird as it sounded, working relaxed me. I'd already had too many personal confrontations for one day, and clutter didn't talk back. I'd dig right in, and my client wouldn't even have to know I'd skipped out part of the morning.

I should have known by now that this wasn't my lucky day.

When I pulled up at Featherstone's house, I immediately noticed that Wayne McCall's pickup wasn't there. Even worse, Steve Featherstone's rental car was in the driveway. Just beyond the car, Steve and a twenty-something tall blond kid in tattered jeans and a grease-smeared shirt stood next to the Dumpster. It didn't take a genius to tell they were in the midst of a heated argument.

Chapter Seventeen

The last thing I needed was more conflict in my life. I quick-stepped toward the front door, hoping to escape Featherstone's notice. He and the kid stood facing the open garage, but their voices carried. I could tell they were discussing the car parked inside—an ancient, dust-coated yellow Impala convertible.

"Car belongs to me now," Featherstone said. "End of story."

I stopped walking to catch the kid's reaction.

"C'mon, man," he said. "Your grandma promised me the wheels."

Featherstone grabbed the garage door handle and rolled the door down. "That promise is as good as the paper it's written on. You have something in writing?"

The kid backed off, and I got a look at his reddening complexion. Girls probably thought he was cute with his long hair and pierced eyebrow. He tried to stare Featherstone down, and for a second I thought he might throw a punch. Featherstone didn't act concerned. Then he spotted me and seemed to forget about the kid.

"Nice of you to show up," he said. "You plan to work today?"

The kid waited, watching us, apparently not ready to give up on what he'd come for.

"I had an emergency," I said. "Didn't take long."

"Your cohort have an emergency too? I'm paying you people good money to get this job done, not to run around town."

I wondered myself why McCall wasn't here, but Featherstone's attitude irritated me. I marched over to him.

"The job *will* get done," I said evenly. "There's no need to be rude to me, my *cohort*, or to this young man." I turned to the kid and smiled. "Hi. I'm Poppy."

"Deke," he said. "I work over at the Chevron."

"Nice to meet you, Deke."

109

Featherstone cleared his throat. "Maybe I *was* rude, but you wouldn't like dealing with these people either."

"What people?" I looked around and didn't see anyone except Deke.

"People trying to get something for nothing," Featherstone said. "It's amazing the house wasn't looted before I got here."

Blanca Sandoval must have hit him up for the silver tea set. Or maybe there were others I didn't know about wanting to get their hands on Ida Featherstone's things.

"Look, man," Deke said, "I'm not trying to pull anything. Your grandma *gave* me the freakin' car."

"No, she didn't," Featherstone said, his voice level. "The car is in *my* garage. I'm not giving it away. Doesn't matter *how* many hours you claim to have spent under the hood."

"Hey, guys." I stepped between them, my arms up like a referee holding prize fighters apart in the boxing ring. "Why don't you call the lawyer and ask him instead of fighting over this?"

"Because I already know the answer," Featherstone said. "She left me with everything, and I'm not going to let her down. I won't—" He stopped talking and looked at the ground, closed his eyes, and inhaled deeply, as if he was trying to summon strength to go on.

Poor Featherstone. He was going through a lot. I glanced at the kid, trying to get a read on whether his story about the car was true.

When Featherstone raised his head, his scowl had softened. "Maybe I'm overreacting. You have to understand, I'm under a lot of stress."

"I can pay something," Deke said, holding out his hands. "I need a car bad."

"This car is a classic," Featherstone said calmly. "Might be out of your price range, but I can check the market value and get back to you."

The kid sniffed and said, "Isn't worth much, the shape it's in."

"We'll see," Featherstone said. "I'll call you. Okay?" He stalked up the driveway and around the corner. The back door to the house slammed.

I wasn't sure what to make of this situation. Featherstone's selfish reaction didn't make a lot of sense to me, but for all I knew he might have plans to donate the whole estate to charity after getting top dollar.

Nah, he was selfish.

"Dude has a burr up his butt, don't he?" Deke said.

I shrugged and asked Deke if he needed a ride somewhere.

"No, thanks. Girlfriend's pickin' me up."

I was glad he'd turned down the offer. Featherstone would have a cow if I left again.

"Did Ida Featherstone actually say she'd give you the car?" I asked.

"Yeah," Deke said in a what's-it-to-you tone.

"Okay. None of my business anyway. I just work here."

I went to my SUV for a fresh apron and my water bottle, then decided to phone McCall before going inside.

"What's the big deal?" he said when I asked where he'd gotten off to. "Attic's on my agenda today, and I needed a few things. Be back in ten."

"Make it five," I said. "Featherstone's on the warpath."

"Will do."

We hung up. I checked the time. Another hour or so before I'd hear from Doug and get a chance, finally, to talk with Kevin. Until then, I would focus on cleaning up the back bedroom.

I shut my door. Deke was already being picked up by a car that looked familiar—a red Miata. I watched him climb in, then caught a clear view of the girlfriend as she pulled away.

Even if I hadn't recognized the car, there was no mistaking the driver. The hennaed, punk-cut hair, black-framed glasses, dark red lipstick.

Deke's girlfriend was none other than Grayson Sullivan. Last time I'd seen her, she was practically drooling over Kevin. What was she doing way out here in Richmond?

I was still staring after the Miata when McCall pulled up. He rustled around in his backseat before getting out with a Home Depot sack, from which he extracted a pair of work gloves.

"All set for the attic." He pulled on the new gloves. "You get your business taken care of?"

"Partly." I couldn't wrap my brain around the fact that this mechanic person, Deke, was with Grayson. He didn't seem to be her type, despite their common interest in body piercings.

"What's that mean?" McCall said.

"Huh?" I turned to look at him.

"You said 'partly.' "

"Oh. Dawn Hurley was out. I talked with her boss, but I wanted to ask Dawn more questions about Janice's moving."

"Janice is moving?" he said.

"She *has* moved. At least that's what Dawn told me. I had no idea, and I don't think Aunt Millie knows yet."

"Where'd she move to?"

"New Jersey."

"Really?" McCall said. "Where in Jersey?"

"Piscataway? I don't know. Something with a *P.* Parsippany maybe. I don't remember." I threw my hands up. "Never mind. Let's get to work."

We went inside, and McCall hit the attic while I delved into the bedroom Ida had used for storage. I was relieved that Featherstone left us to our work. I didn't think I could take another of his speeches today. My mind was on Grayson and Kevin, Grayson and Deke. I wondered how long Grayson had known Deke. Or if Kevin knew Deke. Not that it mattered. Bottom line, I was glad she had somebody else—anybody at all, provided his name wasn't Kevin.

The storage room had three old dressers, all stuffed full. I emptied drawer after drawer and found enough sewing supplies to go into the seamstress business. Fabric, patterns, thread, hooks and snaps, hem tape, a billion buttons.

I worked steadily for the next hour, checking the time every few minutes, eager to hear from Doug.

Noon came and went, and my stomach was queasy by the time my phone finally rang at quarter past the hour.

I punched the button to answer. "Doug?"

"Yeah, it's me."

"Put Kevin on."

He hesitated. "Can't do that."

"Why not?"

" 'Cause he's not with me."

My heart sank. "What do you mean? You had it all planned."

"I'm here," he said. "I'm at the restaurant, but Kevin's not. He stood me up."

"Where's Jojo?"

"Don't know. He's not here either, and I can't get him on the phone."

"Maybe you have the wrong place?"

"It's the right place, Penny," he said. "I'm not a total idiot. Don't worry. I'll keep looking."

"But my meeting with the cops is tonight. What am I supposed to tell them?"

"You don't tell them anything," he said. "You listen. If things get dicey, request that your attorney be present."

That advice sent my worry gene into overdrive. We talked for a few more minutes, but Doug couldn't answer any of my questions. We didn't know where Kevin was or what he was doing or what he planned to do.

I'd go into the meeting with Troxell cold.

Chapter Eighteen

I kept my hands busy through the afternoon, even though my brain wouldn't quit conjuring possible reasons for Kevin's leaving town. He might be out having fun right this minute, taking a break from his routine, unaware that we were looking for him. It had been years since we'd expected him to check in with us every day. Maybe he'd met a new woman. Or maybe he was sitting at a bar somewhere drinking himself stupid, trying to get over Grayson. I didn't care about that. I only wanted to know where he was.

Around four, McCall came to check on me. He'd been bumping and thumping around in the attic all day, and I felt absurdly grateful for his help. Though I regularly took jobs this size alone, I wasn't usually lugging so much personal baggage while I worked.

I stood in the hallway outside Ida Featherstone's oversized linen closet, thigh-deep in blankets, quilts, and yellowed feather pillows. The closet was still half full.

"How's it going?" McCall asked, handing me a fresh bottle of water.

"Slow." My throat felt as if cotton fibers and dust bunnies had lodged deep inside. I took the water and sipped gratefully. "Thanks, I needed that."

"Where's the client?"

"He went out again. I'm just as happy to work without him looking over my shoulder."

"I'll second that," he said. "Hear any more from Millie today?"

"Not a word."

"Guess your cousin settled down."

"Janice never settles down," I said. "She's obnoxious even in her sleep."

McCall shook his head. "Can't imagine living with that. What's her husband like?"

114

"Conner? I barely know the man. Not that I'm complaining. He's arrogant. Self-centered. A lot like Janice."

"He make the trip with her?"

"Hah. He wouldn't lower himself."

"I know the type." McCall eyed me with a serious expression. "You should call it a day. Go home and get a good night's rest."

"Yeah, I should." I glanced at my watch. In two hours I'd know what Troxell had on her mind.

"But you won't," he said. "At least take a break."

"Hate to stop when I'm on a roll." I put my water down and turned back to the closet. I pulled sheets from an upper shelf. There were more than I'd bargained for, and the stack toppled down on my head and knocked me back a step.

McCall tried to catch me, but I stumbled over a pillow and tipped him off balance. We both went down in the pile of bedding, laughing. It felt good to laugh, even better with McCall lying beside me, gazing into my eyes.

He moved first, sitting up and gathering the sheets that had landed on top of me. Then he gave me a hand and pulled me to a sitting position. He didn't take his eyes off me, though, and I felt self-conscious under his scrutiny. He brushed hair back from my face.

"You okay?"

"I'm fine."

"You seem different. Preoccupied."

I shrugged. "Just tired, I guess."

"You sure that's all?"

I smiled, feeling myself weaken. I needed someone to talk to, but not McCall. Not now.

His eyes were intent, focused on me. I wondered if he could read my mind. For a second I wanted to lean into him and let my worries and fears pour out. Then my common sense took hold, and I scrambled to my feet. Better to keep things on a professional level.

"You were right," I said. "I *am* beat."

He stood close, holding an armful of tangled sheets.

"You mind finishing up here?" I needed to get home and take a good, hot, calming shower before facing Troxell.

"No problem," he said. "I'll handle it."

"We're keeping the quilts for the appraiser to have a look," I told him. "Trash the pillows. Everything else goes to Goodwill."

"Okay," he said, still studying me.

It had been a while since I'd been kissed, but I recognized the body language as McCall leaned slightly toward me.

I stepped back. "Then I'll see you in the morning."

"I'll be here," he said.

I hurried down the stairs, wishing I could just once let go and give in to my emotions without my logical brain getting in the way.

Back home, I stuffed my face with banana nut bread Aunt Millie had left behind. She'd left Jett, too, and he rubbed against my legs, purring, as I pigged out. I was glad for the comfort the cat provided, even though he left a trail of black hair clinging to my beige slacks.

McCall had succeeded in taking my mind off Kevin for a little while, but now I was back in worry mode. I considered taking a nap, but too little sleep would probably make me feel worse instead of better. I opted for a long, steamy shower, then dressed in a navy pants suit that I rarely got a chance to wear and headed out.

The Fort Bend County Sheriff's office building sat in what not so long ago had been rural Richmond. Fields where horses and longhorn cattle once grazed peacefully had given way to buildings that housed JP, precinct, and tax offices, as well as the Gus George Academy and a larger jail.

I was plenty early, but a thin black woman immediately showed me to an interrogation room like the kind I'd seen on court TV. A tape recorder sat on the table. I waited for Troxell, doing my best to stay calm, but I was soon covered in a cold sweat. I wrapped my arms around myself and fidgeted in the chair.

Troxell arrived a few minutes later, her eyes droopy, her ponytail limp. She'd been working hard too. We exchanged hellos, and she gave me a brief update. They didn't have any suspects in custody yet, but she was aggressively working the case and wouldn't rest until they had the killer behind bars.

She paused to put a tape into the recorder and pushed a button. I could see the tape rolling. She stated the date and time and gave our names, then she leaned forward and propped her elbows on the table.

I braced myself.

"Ms. Cartwright, are you working with Wayne McCall?" she asked.

What? I hesitated for a split second, then said, "Yes, I am."

"Please tell me what kind of work the two of you are doing."

I described our project and gave her Featherstone's name. "Mc-Call is a big help," I added. "Don't know what I'd do without him."

Troxell raised her eyebrows. "Do you and Mr. McCall have a relationship outside of work?"

"No."

"Okay. How did you meet?"

"We've been over this before. My aunt introduced us." I had forgotten Troxell's quizzing me about McCall the other day. Her questions were coming back to me now, but I was still clueless about why she was asking them.

"And where did your aunt meet Mr. McCall?"

I repeated the story Aunt Millie had told me about running into McCall at Kroger's.

"So that led up to his working for her," Troxell said, "and now you've asked him to come and work for you?"

"Not exactly. A friend recommended him."

Troxell wanted to know all about Bailey Devine and my conversation with her about McCall. The more questions the detective asked, the more aggravated I felt. When she hesitated for a moment, I interrupted.

"I barely know Wayne McCall. If you need to know more about the man, you should talk to *him.*"

"I may do that," Troxell said. "He tell you why he's here in Richmond?"

"No."

"Or where he's from?"

"I have no idea where he's from," I said.

Troxell stared at me for a split second before saying, "Okay, let's move on. I need to get in touch with your son."

I gulped. "Kevin?"

"You have another son?" Troxell said.

I shook my head. "No."

"Can you put me in contact with Kevin?"

"Uh, I'm not sure."

"What does that mean?" she said.

"He's out of town."

"Where does Kevin live?"

I hesitated. This might sound bad, but it was the truth. "I don't have a current address. He lived with a girlfriend. From what I understand, they recently broke up."

"I see," said Troxell.

"Why do you need to talk to him?"

"I'm talking to everyone who might help—"

She stopped short at the ringing of her phone and punched the tape recorder off before answering.

"This is Troxell."

I watched as she listened intently to the person on the other end. My heart was racing. She was suspicious of Kevin, just as I'd feared.

"Who made the ID?" she said into the phone. Then, after a beat, "Yeah, I knew her. Be there in ten."

She hung up. "I gotta run. Find your son, and have him contact me ASAP."

"But can't you tell me—"

"No, I can't. I have an emergency to deal with." She left the room without another word.

The thin woman came back to get me and show me out. I made a pit stop at the ladies' room and spent some time holding my icy hands under the warm-air dryer to thaw them out. The meeting was behind me now, but I felt more nervous than ever. Troxell *was* looking for Kevin, *and* she was suspicious of McCall. What was that all about?

I got out my keys and looped my purse over a shoulder before pulling the restroom door open to leave. I heard Troxell's voice nearby, though I couldn't see her. The words "another murder" reached me, and I stopped to listen.

"Least we got an ID on this vic," Troxell said, "but damn, who'd want to kill *her*?"

"Maybe they wanted to off a lawyer," a man said, chuckling, "and got her by mistake."

"Can it, Roger," Troxell said. "You're not funny. Dawn Hurley was a nice lady. She didn't deserve this."

I slumped against the doorjamb and felt the blood drain from my face. Dawn Hurley, dead?

A young woman with a Speedy Couriers logo on her shirt charged around the corner, almost running into me.

"Oops. You okay? You're chalk white."

I nodded. "Just heard some bad news."

"'Bout that murder over in the Munroe building? I just came from there."

I straightened. "What happened exactly? Do you know?"

"Didn't see the body or nothin'. Talked to this lady who was leavin' work—one of my regulars. She's the one found the dead woman on the back stairs. Shook her up bad."

"Maybe it was an accident," I said. "Maybe she fell down the stairs."

The courier shook her head. "Not with that wire wrapped around her neck."

Chapter Nineteen

I left the sheriff's office in a daze, got into the Durango, and sat there watching people leaving for the day to go home. Something that Dawn Hurley would never do again.

Learning what had happened to her had set my imagination to racing. Why would someone kill Dawn? Was she in the wrong place at the wrong time? Was it a disgruntled client? Someone so angry about not inheriting that they'd commit murder? Stranger things had happened, but getting rid of the lawyer's secretary wouldn't change anything. More likely this was a burglary gone bad or, God forbid, a sex crime.

I was already a bundle of nerves worrying about Kevin, and now this. Too shaky to drive, I got out my cell phone and called Doug to report on what had happened in my meeting with Troxell. He told me he'd been calling every one of Kevin's friends he could think of to see if anyone could give him a lead on Kevin's whereabouts.

I hung up, somewhat heartened that at least I wasn't in this alone. But then my thoughts drifted back to Dawn—her happy and talkative demeanor that morning. Now she was gone. I wanted to know more about what had happened to the poor woman. The cops wouldn't tell me anything, but Allen Tate might. I dug out his business card and punched his cell number into my phone.

"Mr. Tate, Poppy Cartwright," I said when he answered. "I just heard about Dawn, and I'm so sorry."

"Thank you," Tate said weakly. "Such a tragedy."

"Do they know what happened?"

"All they have so far is an estimated time of death. Ten this morning."

I shuddered. Dawn must have been killed shortly after I left Tate's office.

"I bad-mouthed her all day," he said, "for not showing up for work. And all the while—" He stopped talking, and I could picture him trying to rein in his emotions.

"Is there anything I can do?"

He cleared his throat. "Not right now. I may contact you later, though."

"Please do," I said. "Does Dawn have family nearby?"

"Only her mother. Brother lives up north. You know, she considered my clients family. And all I did was complain about her talking instead of working."

"Dawn wouldn't want you to beat yourself up over this."

"No, she wouldn't," he agreed.

I told him to take care, and I disconnected the call, feeling ready to cry. I barely knew Dawn, but she'd been a friendly, caring person, and you didn't run into enough of those types anymore.

It seemed like days since Aunt Millie had asked me to return her papers to the law office. If Dawn had treated Millie like family, then Millie undoubtedly felt the same way. She'd be very upset at this news, but I could try to soften the blow. I flipped on my headlights, shifted into drive, and headed for her place.

It was just after seven when I pulled up in front of Aunt Millie's house. The porch light was on, and some windows were lit. Millie's car sat in the driveway. Janice's rental car, thankfully, was gone.

I walked to the front door, feeling a hundred pounds heavier under the weight of bad news, and rang the bell. I waited a while, then rang again. No one answered. I went up the driveway to try the back door and noticed a sliver of light shining across the patio. The side garage door was ajar, the light on inside.

My pulse raced. I approached the door, clutching at my waist for my cell phone. *Jeez.* I'd left it in the Durango. I took a deep breath and told myself not to jump to conclusions. There was no reason Aunt Millie couldn't be in her own garage. I wondered if she would come out here, though, knowing that a dead man had been found inside mere days ago. And at night, of all times.

I tiptoed to the door and heard a voice inside. But that tone wasn't

Aunt Millie—it was Janice, and she didn't sound happy. I hoped she wasn't delivering this tongue-lashing to her poor mother. I edged closer and waited, listening.

"Yes, I know you're in a hurry," she snapped. "*Patience* never was in your vocabulary." She paused. "I *know* what I told you."

Another pause. She must be on the phone. I inched into the garage. With all of Aunt Millie's junk inside, I couldn't see Janice, and I was in no danger of being seen.

"I *remember* what we discussed, but my obligations to work come first."

I bumped into a rickety hall tree and grabbed it to prevent a domino reaction.

"As soon as the job's finished," Janice went on. "Quit harping on me, Conner. I'll sign when I'm back in town."

Trouble in paradise? Things weren't all wine and roses with Janice's husband the way she always made them sound.

"I have work to do," she said. "Don't call me, I'll call you."

A snap that sounded like her cell phone shutting echoed in the silent garage. I went on in, not bothering to be quiet about it.

"Who's there?" Janice called.

"It's Poppy." I came around a heap of rusty lawn furniture to see Janice standing over a bunch of opened cartons. "What are you doing out here?"

She propped her hands on her hips. "What's it to you?"

I swallowed a sarcastic response and said, "I came to see your mother. Is she home?"

"No," Janice said.

"Her car's here."

"She took mine."

No way. Janice letting Millie drive the rented Mercedes? That, without any other weird moves on Janice's part, was suspicious enough. She must have read my thoughts.

"What?" she said. "I was parked behind her. It was easier. You come to check on her morning, noon, and night now?"

"Somebody needs to," I said. "Somebody who cares."

"What are you insinuating?" she said.

"Nothing. I'm stating a fact. You don't care. You never did. You never pretended to care. So what are you doing here now?" I motioned to the boxes. "You *helping* some more?"

"These are my things," Janice said. "I have a right to look at them if I want to."

I noticed then that some of the boxes in front of her were those marked with her name.

"Something in particular bring on this sudden nostalgic urge to play with your high school pom-poms?" I said.

"Mind your own business."

"I will, after you explain why you're here."

Janice glared at me, giving new meaning to the expression *if-looks-could-kill.* "I am visiting my mother," she said. "Maybe you don't get that, since you don't have one of your own to visit."

Of all the low blows. I took a moment to gather myself, then said, "Why aren't you *visiting,* then, instead of rifling through junk that I'm certain doesn't mean a thing to you?"

"Because she went out," Janice said.

"Where did she go?"

"To see some old lady." Janice shrugged. "Friend whose daughter got killed today."

My breath caught. "Dawn Hurley's mother?"

Janice bent over the boxes, pulled out an old scrapbook, and began leafing through the pages. "I think that's the name she mentioned."

"Millie was upset, wasn't she?"

Janice glanced at me. "She cried some."

"And you stayed here while she went out alone to visit a grieving mother."

She fixed me with the death stare again. "Look at you, Miss Family Values. Why aren't *you* spending time with *your* kid?"

"What?"

"Your kid," she said. "Kevin."

I wouldn't have thought she remembered my son's name. "What about Kevin?"

"He looks like hell," Janice said. "Something's eating at him. Anybody can see that."

"What are you talking about?" I said, hearing panic rise in my voice. "When did *you* see him?"

"This afternoon," Janice said. "He was out back, walking the golf course."

Chapter Twenty

Janice continued rifling through the cartons. Ordinarily, I would have raised Cain about the mess she was making, but after the bombshell she'd dropped, clutter was the last thing I cared about. Janice had seen Kevin. He was back in town.

The same day another dead body had turned up.

Of course, I knew Kevin had nothing to do with either one of the murders. And the two incidents were totally unrelated. Dawn Hurley couldn't be connected in any way to the unidentified man found in Aunt Millie's garage—or could she?

Murder wasn't a common occurrence here in Richmond, and the police might try to tie the two events together. What if they pinned the blame for both deaths on my son?

I stood frozen in place as the horrible possibilities washed over me. Janice didn't seem to notice my silence. If we had a normal relationship, I would bombard her with questions. Ask for her help to track Kevin down here and now. But my cousin wasn't normal or helpful. She was older, though, and her eyesight might have worsened over the years. It had been a long time since she'd seen Kevin. Maybe she was simply mistaken about spotting him.

I sidled closer. "Are you sure it was Kevin you saw?" I said, trying to sound casual.

She pushed a box aside and ripped the next one open. "Couldn't mistake him. He's like a clone of Doug."

She was right about that. "How long ago did you see him?"

"Three, four hours."

"I didn't realize he'd taken up golf."

"He wasn't playing," she said. "I didn't see any cart or clubs. That's why I noticed him, meandering around out there looking like a lost puppy dog."

Gooseflesh prickled my arms. "What did he have to say?"

She scowled. "We didn't talk. I saw the kid, that's all."

"Okay, okay."

I zipped my jacket to ward off the sudden chill in the creepy garage. The dead man was gone but definitely not forgotten.

Janice knelt on the dirty concrete floor, oblivious to her undoubtedly expensive slacks, and began pulling things from the box. I wouldn't get any useful information from her, so I turned to leave. I had to find Kevin, talk to him, before the police did.

Behind me, Janice said, "Where'd you put the rest of my stuff?"

I glanced at her, then at the school notebooks, scuffed cheerleader shoes, and debris from another lifetime scattered around her feet.

"I didn't touch your things," I said.

"That's bull. Mother didn't suddenly turn neat and tidy. I know how you are, taking things into your own hands. So where's my stuff?"

She stood and propped her fists on her hips. With the frizzed-out hair and dirty clothes, she looked very unlike herself. Maybe she was having some sort of bipolar episode.

"You heard about the murdered man, didn't you?" I said.

"What does he have to do with my missing boxes?"

"The cops were here searching for clues," I said. "They took a couple of cartons with them."

Her eyebrows flew up. "Why would they take *my* stuff?"

"For Pete's sake, Janice. They didn't take them because they're yours—they took them because they found blood on the cardboard. They're running tests, then you'll get them back."

"When?" she said.

"I have no idea."

"You should have asked—"

"People are getting killed, Janice. Nobody cares about your old high school junk."

I stomped out of the garage as best as I could while navigating around piles of garbage. Outside, I stopped and looked around. Where the heck was Kevin? Chances of my trolling the golf course and finding him were slim to none, but I had no better starting point. I retrieved the heavy-duty flashlight from my glove box and took off on foot.

While walking the course, I called Doug and told him to get back home ASAP, that Kevin had been spotted here in town. We hung up without voicing our fears about where this might be headed if we didn't find some answers soon. I even called Doug's house and talked to Brandi—the first time I'd willingly addressed the woman—and asked her to let me know if Kevin showed up there. Not that he would—he didn't care for her any more than I did—but I had to cover all the bases.

For the next hour, I power walked around the golf course, shining my flashlight into every backyard and inside every carport. My voice was hoarse from calling out Kevin's name—not hollering, since I didn't want to attract too much attention, but loud enough for him to hear me if he was anywhere nearby.

I was exhausted and bathed in a cold sweat by the time I had made it full circle and found myself on the section of the course behind Vicki Rhodes' house. Time to make some inquiries.

It was nearly nine, but the lights were still on at Vicki's place. I approached the house from behind, shining my flashlight beam into the bushes where I'd seen her father the night before. No skulkers tonight.

Nearing the back door, I could hear her kids yelling even before Vicki answered my knock. She was dressed in a hot pink sweatsuit and Nike running shoes with pink laces. Behind her, four small boys raced around the kitchen island. She probably needed the running shoes to keep up with them.

"Poppy," she said, putting a hand on her chest. "Blanca told me to call you, and I completely forgot. What did you need?"

It took me a second to remember I'd left a message with the housekeeper for Vicki to contact me. Maybe I could get some information without giving out too much.

"I was just wondering if the police ever found that suspect," I said. "I'm a little nervous working over at my aunt's house."

"I haven't heard any news," she said. "Come on in. Care for some coffee? I have fresh decaf."

"No, thanks," I said, stepping into the kitchen.

"I'm sure my father would have said something if there were any new developments," she said. "He's like a thorn in the cops' side. Everybody's side, actually."

"Have you noticed anyone hanging around the golf course lately? Besides golfers, that is."

"No, but I haven't been around much. I'm taking some night classes to get a break from the little monsters." She turned to the kids and said, "Boys. Go on up to your playroom. Skedaddle."

To their credit, she didn't have to repeat the request. They zoomed out of the room, arms outstretched and making airplane noises.

"Your father hasn't reported seeing any strangers around here?" I said.

She shrugged. "Here? Why would he have?"

I relayed the episode of finding Barton Fletcher with his camera in her bushes the night before. "I may be totally out of line," I said when I'd finished, "but his behavior seemed odd to me. Is he hanging around in hopes of catching a killer on film?"

Vicki laughed. "My father is a control freak. Thank goodness I'm not the target of his insanity this time."

"What do you mean?"

"I was in class last night, but my stepsister was here watching the kids. I'm sure she rues the day her mother married dear old Dad."

"He takes pictures of her?" I said. "That's disgusting."

Vicki shook her head. "It's not what you think. Dad's trying to protect her from the entire male population, and that's where the camera comes in, I guess. Personally, I can't make sense of it. I mean, unless he catches her with a married man, what good would pictures do?"

"Beats me," I said.

"Anyway, she's twenty-two, a grown woman, and capable of making her own decisions. Dad needs to let go."

"Sounds like it."

I thought of Kevin's depressed expression the other night when he'd asked me to stop questioning him, and I knew he'd agree with Vicki's assessment.

"The girl needs a life," Vicki went on, "but I might live to regret letting her visit with her male friends here."

"Why's that?" I needed to make a graceful exit, but Vicki seemed to be in a talking mood, and I didn't want to be impolite to any prospective witness.

"I'm concerned she and her boyfriend might behave inappropriately in front of my boys. I love the kid, but she's not exactly the ideal role model with her punked-out hair, tattoos—you know what I mean."

I nodded.

"Grayson may be twenty-two," Vicki said, "but sometimes she acts more like sixteen."

I perked up. "Your stepsister's name is Grayson?"

"Yeah. Grayson Sullivan. You know her?"

Chapter Twenty-one

I debated how much to share with Vicki. As a mother, she would understand my concern for Kevin. While she didn't seem terribly fond of Grayson, I had to remember that they *were* related. Better not voice my opinion of the girl when I needed information. Grayson may have broken up with Kevin, but she might know where I could find him.

"Matter of fact, I *do* know your stepsister," I said, smiling.

"Don't tell me," Vicki said. "You're a Starbucks fanatic."

"Starbucks?" I said.

"Where she works," Vicki went on. "I can't believe how many people I know have run into Grayson there. But then, she *does* stand out in a crowd."

"Yes, she does. Which Starbucks is she with these days?" It was hard for me to envision Grayson working anywhere, and this was the first I'd heard about a job.

"She's still at Sugar Land town square." Vicki walked over to a heaping basket of laundry sitting on the breakfast table. She picked up a miniature red T-shirt. "Do you have any idea how many shirts four boys go through in a week?"

I laughed. "Couldn't even guess."

"Hundreds." She folded the shirt and picked up the next one. "How long have you known Grayson?"

"Eight, nine months," I said. "She and my son are friends."

"Oh?" Vicki looked at me with raised eyebrows. "What's his name?"

"Kevin."

"Don't know that one." She shook her head and turned her attention back to the laundry.

"That one? How many are there?"

"It's easier to keep count of the kids' shirts," Vicki said. "I don't try staying current with Grayson's men."

Now I knew why I'd never liked that girl.

"As her boyfriend's mother, I don't like the sound of that."

Vicki frowned. "I thought Deke something-or-other was her latest. At least that's who was here with her last night."

"I don't know about him, but I *do* know she's been living with Kevin."

Vicki dropped the shirt she was holding. "What?"

"They lived together in an apartment near West U." She didn't need to know about Kevin's unexpected appearance at my house with his long face and the duffel bag.

"Grayson lived there with her friend Katelyn," Vicki said slowly, "'Til she moved back in with the folks a couple of weeks ago."

"It was Kevin, not Katelyn."

Vicki frowned. "That can't be right."

I shrugged. "Believe me or not, I was there when they moved in last fall."

"She said she was moving in with Katelyn."

"Well, she didn't," I said.

Vicki flopped into a chair and surprised me by bursting into laughter. "Dad would go berserk if he knew. He thought he was paying for her to share an apartment with a girlfriend."

"And she never invited family over to visit?" I asked.

"Nope." Vicki wiped her tearing eyes and tried to get the laughing under control.

"I understand he wouldn't necessarily like the idea," I said. "But why would he be that upset?"

"Never mind."

"Let me guess," I said. "No man is good enough for her."

Vicki shook her head. "That's not the reason. It's this weird bargain he made with Grayson."

"What kind of bargain?"

"I've been dying to tell someone. Dad came up with this harebrained scheme a couple of weeks ago." Vicki glanced over her shoulder as if she wanted to make sure we were still alone. "He doesn't know I know, and this can't get back to him."

"I'm not telling," I said.

Vicki lowered her voice. "Dad has this investor he's trying to impress, a prospective business partner."

What did that have to do with anything? I leaned closer. "And?"

"The man has a son, thirty or so years old, kind of plain but oh-so-rich. So Grayson wants the snazzy red sports car, expensive clothes, weekends at the spa. Dad *really* wants to cozy up to this investor." She stopped and raised her eyebrows again. "You get the picture?"

I straightened. "He wants Grayson to marry the guy's son?"

"He wants her to keep the son happy," she said, "in hopes that the father will agree to buy in on his newest venture. Dad calls it the one-big-happy-family principle."

I shook my head in disbelief. "And Grayson's going along with this?"

"She's doing a pretty good job stringing them both along," Vicki said. "Dad and the geek. I don't know how far she'll go, but I think it's lucky your son got out when he did."

Barton Fletcher sounded like a sicko to me. "Does her mother know about this?"

"I doubt it," Vicki said.

"And what happens if Grayson doesn't go along with the plan? Or falls in love with somebody else?"

"I'd tell that somebody else to watch his back," she said.

Was that a turn of phrase, or did Vicki seriously mean that any man who interfered with Fletcher's plan was in mortal danger?

A chill swept over me, and my imagination raced. Vicki had insinuated that Grayson strung along a lot of men. What if the dead man in Aunt Millie's garage had been one of them? A long shot maybe, but something I could check out when I went to ask Grayson about Kevin's whereabouts.

I reached Starbucks with minutes to spare before closing time and rushed through the entrance, surprised to see the place still hopping with customers. I spotted Grayson behind the counter to my right. She was chatting with a male co-worker, not working. Leaning over to give him an eyeful of her cleavage.

I glanced around to make sure Barton Fletcher wasn't hiding behind a column with his camera. Or a weapon. On the way over I'd come up with a new concept: the financier's son was a jealous maniac who'd committed murder to keep Grayson for himself. But the dead man wasn't my main focus at the moment. Each of the bizarre scenarios I'd concocted put Kevin in danger. I had to find him.

I walked up to the counter, watching Grayson in action. She must have felt my stare because she turned my way and approached me reluctantly.

"Get you something?" she said without enthusiasm.

"Yes. Some answers."

She smirked. "I meant coffee."

"I need to talk with Kevin," I said. "Have you seen him?"

"Not tonight." She glanced at her co-worker. "Hey, you seen that dude's been buggin' the crap outta me?"

He shook his head. "Not since yesterday."

She turned back to me. "Can't help ya."

Resisting the urge to reach across the counter and grab the lapels of her shirt, I lowered my voice. "I don't appreciate your talking that way about him, Grayson. Kevin *loved* you. He thought you loved him too. But I hear you're into playing around, using men to suit your purposes. And you know what? That bugs the crap out of *me*."

Grayson stepped back. "Like I care."

I straightened and took a breath. "Fine. You know where I can reach Kevin? Have a number I can call?"

"How about, like, trying his cell?"

"I already did that. Any idea where he's staying?"

"Why would I know?" she said.

"I called the apartment. The number's disconnected."

"We moved out."

"So I gathered. You know anybody who might know where I could catch up with him?"

She shrugged.

"How about your friend?" I nodded toward the co-worker.

"He doesn't even know Kevin's name," she said.

"And you have no helpful hints?"

"I'm not the helpful sort."

God, I wanted to wipe the smirk off her face.

"One more question." I leaned forward and whispered, "Have the police questioned you yet?"

Behind the dark-framed glasses, her eyes widened. "About what?"

"You heard there was a dead man found in your dad's neighborhood?" I said.

"Yeah."

"I thought you might have known him."

"That's a crock," she blurted. "I don't know any dead guy."

"How can you be sure?" I said sweetly. "Have you seen the crime-scene photos?"

"No way. I'm not looking at any pictures of a dead guy." She'd raised her voice enough so that customers turned to stare.

"The cops will need to rule you out," I said matter-of-factly.

"Me?" she screeched. "Why?"

"I heard he might be one of the men you dumped."

I stood there for a few seconds, enjoying Grayson's expression of sheer panic. Then I turned and walked out.

I should be ashamed of myself for scaring the girl for no reason, but I couldn't help feeling a perverse sense of satisfaction for giving the little twit something to think about.

Chapter Twenty-two

I drove away from Starbucks thinking that Grayson could grow up to be a lot like Janice if she didn't watch herself. The world didn't need two Janices. Thoughts of my obnoxious cousin led to thoughts of Aunt Millie and whether she might shed any light on Kevin's whereabouts. I drove over to her house but found no cars in the driveway—not Millie's or Janice's. The house was dark. I pulled to the curb and wondered where they could be at this time of night.

Janice might have run off to harass the police about her stupid boxes. If she threw one of her fits, they might have arrested her. That image made me smile, but I quickly sobered when I remembered Aunt Millie had gone to visit Dawn Hurley's grieving mother.

I was about to pull out when I noticed a white pickup parked two houses down on the opposite side of the street. I coasted to the truck. Wayne McCall's, if I had to guess. I shifted into park and got out to look inside.

The pickup definitely belonged to McCall. The same supplies I'd seen before were inside. The same Altoids tin sat on the console. So where was he?

I looked around, taking in the silent neighborhood. I could see Steve Featherstone's dark house at the end of the street from where I stood, so it wasn't as if McCall had decided to pull another all-nighter. Had he come over to go somewhere with Aunt Millie? That didn't seem likely—she'd been out all evening. Was he with Janice? I didn't even want to consider *them* together. I remembered too well the closeness of McCall earlier, the feeling of nestling with him in the pile of bedding.

I shook my head to chase the memory away and climbed back into the Durango. What I needed to do was call it a night—go home, sleep off some of this stress, and hope for a better tomorrow. For once, I took my own advice and headed home.

I pulled into my empty driveway after eleven and slumped in my seat. I'd have felt a million percent better if Kevin were waiting on my porch again tonight, but no such luck. Jett was peering through my blinds, watching me expectantly, so I climbed out and hurried inside. The cat greeted me by winding through my legs, nearly tripping me as I headed for the kitchen. He darted to his bowl and whined to be fed, but the light on my phone caught my attention, and I went that way instead. Three messages. I punched the play button.

"Hi, Poppy, it's Bailey. How are things working out with Wayne McCall? Can't wait to hear. Call me."

I didn't want to discuss McCall, but I had to admit that if Bailey hadn't sent him my way, I'd be working around the clock. I owed her a response, but it was too late to return the call tonight.

The machine stated the date and time of the next call. Aunt Millie. "Poppy, sorry I missed you tonight. Janice said you stopped by, but I'm with Mrs. Hurley. She's devastated. We all are." Her voice cracked, and she hesitated. I nibbled my lower lip, still unable or unwilling to comprehend what had happened to Dawn.

"Hope Jett isn't a bother," she went on. "Take good care of him." Her voice shifted to baby talk. "You hear me, Jett? You be a good boy for Auntie Poppy."

I rolled my eyes. The cat howled even louder. Either he'd recognized Aunt Millie's voice, or he was put out with me for ignoring him. I turned toward the pantry to retrieve the Meow Mix, then froze in my tracks at the sound of Kevin's voice.

"Hey, Mom. You there?" A pause. "Got a question. Guess I'll call back." Another pause. "Tomorrow, okay? Keep your cell on."

I let out the breath I'd been holding, disappointed that I'd missed him. Why hadn't he called my cell *this* time? And what kind of question did he have? The machine signalled that all messages were played back. I punched the button to replay Kevin's. He'd called around nine—probably thought I'd be home by then, which explained why he'd left a message instead of trying my cell. Maybe his question wasn't urgent—unlike *my* need to talk to *him*.

I checked the caller ID for the phone number he'd called from. Local. I dialed the number, but the phone on the other end rang endlessly. No answer. No machine.

At least hearing his voice was some relief. He'd sounded fine—calm, unworried, certainly not guilty of anything. He was going to call me back tomorrow. Jeez, it was almost tomorrow already. I called Doug's cell, got his voice mail, and gave him an update. Then I plugged my phone in so it would be fully charged tomorrow when Kevin called. Jett was nipping at my ankles now.

"Okay. Auntie Poppy's coming."

I poured food into the cat's bowl, made myself a scrambled egg sandwich, then sat down with the sandwich and pen and paper. Now that I'd heard from Kevin and had high hopes of talking with him soon, my mind raced with other to-do's.

Tomorrow afternoon was Featherstone's appointment with the appraiser. I had a lot to finish before then. I took a bite of my sandwich and jotted down remaining tasks. I'd get cracking early, just in case the conversation with Kevin took me away from the job. If that happened, McCall could back me up. Once I finished working for Featherstone, I'd offer to help Dawn's boss with office organization. But only if Kevin was home, safe, and no longer under suspicion by the police.

I wondered how the cops were coming with solving the murders. Had they identified the first victim yet? Determined whether the two cases were connected?

Maybe I should talk with Troxell again. Tell her everything I knew. About Grayson's boyfriend situation and Barton Fletcher's weird plot to close a business deal. About that other neighbor, Lori Gilmore, who had men coming and going whenever her husband was away. She certainly needed to be questioned. Not to mention Blanca, the maid, and Birdie Peterson, the elderly woman who reportedly knew everything that went on in the neighborhood.

I scribbled the names on a separate list. These people might know something important. If Troxell hadn't questioned them—and I didn't think she had—she needed to have this list. But the detective hadn't cared to hear my opinion during our meeting. She wouldn't care about my list. And maybe I was way off base. I crumpled the paper and tossed it into the wastebasket. Then I took a quick shower, snuggled into my bed, and promptly fell asleep with Jett curled up next to me.

My brain woke me shortly after five, long before my body wanted to move. I made myself get up anyway, mindful of the long to-do list I'd made the night before. Knowing Featherstone's mind-set, showing up for work early might earn me a few brownie points.

I was up and ready by six, my cell phone tucked in a buttoned shirt pocket where I couldn't possibly miss hearing if it rang and it wouldn't fall out while I worked. It was a little too early to show up at Featherstone's unannounced, so I had time for a quick load of laundry and to vacuum the cat hair that Jett had distributed in every nook and cranny. Then I packed a lunch consisting wholly of baked goods Aunt Millie had left and headed out into a chilly black morning that made me long for daylight savings time.

At Featherstone's I rang the bell, surprised when my obsessive-compulsive client didn't answer within a minute. I realized belatedly that the house was as dark as it had been last night, and there was no car parked in the driveway. After yesterday's scene with that kid Deke, I was pretty sure Featherstone hadn't given up the Impala so he could park his rental in the garage. Maybe he was already out for breakfast, or jogging five miles, or doing whatever Hollywood types did at this hour.

Good thing I had a key.

I let myself in, turned on some lights, and deposited my baked goods on the kitchen counter. I started a pot of coffee. Then I grabbed a box of garbage bags and headed upstairs to tackle the jam-packed bathroom cabinets.

As promised, McCall had finished clearing away the things from the linen closet, so there was nothing in the hallway to remind me of our close encounter.

I moved straight into the master bath and got to work tossing ancient toiletries and medications. Dozens of half-used tubes of everything from hand lotion to hemorrhoid cream. Rusty hairpins and nail files. I threw away all the junk, salvaging three unopened Avon cologne bottles in the original boxes, since I had once heard them referred to as collector's items. I couldn't see it myself—who wants a bottle shaped like a turkey?—but that decision was better made by Featherstone or his appraiser.

I was through the master bath mess in less than an hour and feeling industrious as I dragged the full garbage sack downstairs and out to the Dumpster. The sun was peeking through dismal morning clouds when I heaved the garbage sack over the Dumpster's side and turned around to see Steve Featherstone pull in.

He got out of the car, smiling, his clipboard tucked under an arm. "Good morning. You're bright and early. Glad to see it."

"Thought I'd get a jump start on the day," I said. "We're getting down to the wire."

"Couldn't be too soon for me." He followed me into the house and, once inside, sniffed the air appreciatively. "Ah, you made coffee."

"I did. Brought some baked goods too. You interested?"

"I'm always interested in sweets."

We went to the kitchen, and I poured us each a cup of coffee. I unwrapped the sliced banana nut bread and peanut butter cookies I'd brought, and Featherstone chose a cookie.

"What time did you get here?" he said.

"About an hour ago. I was surprised you were already out and about."

"Actually, I've moved to a hotel. Didn't want my stuff lying around when the appraiser arrives." He crunched into the cookie. "That's part of the story. Truth is, this place depresses the daylights out of me. All the memories. How things were, how things might have been."

"I know the feeling." I hadn't yet completely worked through the emotion from losing my mother nearly thirty years ago.

"And then I heard even more depressing news in town," he said. "You heard about the lawyer's secretary?"

"I did."

"Darn shame," he said. "Hard to believe she was just here yesterday."

"I know."

"Sweet, helpful woman. I'm afraid my attorney will be lost without her."

"He'll manage somehow."

"Hope so. I'm counting on him." Featherstone finished his cookie and washed it down with coffee. He heaved a big sigh, then pulled his latest list from his clipboard and handed it to me. "I didn't realize this was such a high-crime area when I arrived. Makes me in a bigger hurry to get out of town."

As if he could be in a bigger hurry. I accepted the paper graciously and scanned the list. Being a big list-maker myself, his shouldn't have bothered me, but he'd added several time-consuming tasks.

"I'd like you to get these things knocked out before the appraiser arrives," he said. "What do you think?"

"Should be no problem." Assuming McCall showed up to help me.

Featherstone clapped his hands together. "Great. Let's get started."

The doorbell rang, and he said, "I'll get that. Probably your cohort."

He left the room, and I made a face at the way he kept referring to McCall as my cohort. Did he not remember his name? Or was it a California thing? I didn't have time to dwell on the issue because a booming voice sounded in the other room.

"I'm looking for Poppy Cartwright. She here?"

It wasn't McCall.

Featherstone said something, but I couldn't make out his words.

"I know she's here," the man said. "That's her wheels parked out front."

Who would know that? The voice sounded familiar.

"I don't give a crap where she's working or what she's supposed to be doing," he boomed. "She's shooting off her mouth to my girls, and I'll tell you one thing. Nobody gets away with threatening my family."

Barton Fletcher.

My cell phone rang. I fumbled to open my shirt pocket. Stupid button.

"Where is she?" Fletcher thundered.

Struggling with shaky hands to get to my phone, I heard Featherstone say something about private property. I wasn't waiting around to hear more. I *had* to get this call. I stepped out the back door and flattened myself against the side of the house.

Ripped my pocket open. Grabbed the phone on the third ring. Shouted, "Hello." And got nothing.

The caller had hung up. I checked the received calls and recognized the phone number Kevin had called from yesterday. Damn.

I redialed and listened to the phone ring once, twice, three times. I waited through fifteen rings. No one answered.

Chapter Twenty-three

I like nothing better than a well-ordered day where things are planned, prioritized, and carried out with swift efficiency. But sometimes things go haywire and spin out of control, totally beyond my ability to cope with the chaos. This was shaping up to be one of those days.

Where was Kevin, and why wouldn't he answer the phone? And why was Barton Fletcher here, summoning me as if I'd committed some crime by speaking with "his girls" last night? How'd he even known where to find me? Was the jerk having me followed?

I dropped the phone back into my pocket and barreled into the house, supremely ticked off and ready to lay into Fletcher for causing me to miss that call. Featherstone stood at the kitchen counter, clipboard and pen in hand as if he was recording my time out, time in.

"Where did that blowhard go?" I said.

Featherstone hooked a thumb toward the street and said, "He's out front with your cohort."

I resisted the urge to smack him. "His *name* is Wayne McCall."

"What's this about?" Featherstone said.

"Nothing I can't handle. You don't need to concern yourself."

"But you're supposed to be work—"

My lethal expression stopped him from going on. I headed out the front door. Fletcher and McCall stood on the sidewalk close to the street, McCall with his back to me. Fletcher's face was red and blustery as he spotted me marching toward them.

"There she is!" he exclaimed. "I knew she was inside."

McCall told Fletcher, "You need to cool off."

I felt like a volcano about to erupt but realized that McCall's calm approach might work better than exploding. I took a deep breath in an attempt to lower my blood pressure and met Fletcher's eyes.

"If you have a problem with me, I'd like to hear what it is," I said.

"And explain how you know my name. And how you identified my vehicle."

"I'm on top of what goes on," Fletcher said coldly.

McCall said, "Harassing innocent women is beyond the scope of your presidential duties for the homeowners association."

"This one's not innocent," Fletcher said.

What the heck did he mean by that?

McCall took a step toward the pompous jerk, but I grabbed his arm and moved between them.

"I can speak for myself, thank you very much." I turned to Fletcher. "You haven't answered my question."

"Your name's no government secret," he said. "Your aunt lives three houses down. She brags on you. You handed out flyers at the craft fair last November. You're in this neighborhood often. Your ex sells real estate. What I didn't know about until last night was that you have a son named Kevin."

I fought to keep my expression passive. "I don't see how my son is any of your business."

Fletcher leaned forward, towering over me. I felt his putrid breath on my face. "Anyone who screws with my daughter is my business."

"Excuse me?" My face heated up like a red hot chili pepper. "You don't know my son, and he is *none* of your business."

"If he's living with my daughter, he sure as hell *is*."

I stared at him. "Just to set the record straight, she's your *step*-daughter. And they're not living together."

"That's not what you told Victoria last night."

I didn't believe for a second that Vicki had reported to him after our conversation. "You weren't there. How do you know what I told her?"

"I have ways," he said smugly.

My God, had he bugged her house?

McCall said, "You're out of line, Fletcher."

Fletcher kept his eyes on me.

"If you're going to eavesdrop," I said, "at least get your information straight. Kevin is old news. I believe the guy you want is Deke."

Fletcher's stare didn't waver. "I need to have a man-to-man talk with your boy."

"No way," I said. "Maybe Grayson says, 'How high?' whenever you say, 'Jump,' but you won't get that reaction from me. God knows how you convinced her to go along with your sick little game."

McCall gave me a look, confused.

"Where is Kevin?" Fletcher said.

"I don't know."

"Don't give me that. Where is he?"

I glared at him. "I won't answer that, and, as I believe my client has pointed out, this is private property. So leave. Now."

McCall took my elbow. "Let's go inside."

Fletcher said, "Tell your kid to steer clear of Grayson. He gets in the way, I'll—" He chuckled. "You probably don't want the nasty details. Just tell him."

Fletcher turned and stalked to his black Mercedes. I stood there, trembling like I'd just woken from a nightmare, watching until he drove away.

"What was that all about?" McCall said.

When I didn't answer, he turned to me and noticed the angry tears that had filled my eyes.

"Relax. He's gone now." He moved to take me into his arms.

I pulled back, not in the mood to be consoled by anyone of the male persuasion. "Men like him shouldn't even have kids. Arrogant jerk."

McCall put his hands up in surrender. "Hey, you're not getting any argument from me."

I swiped at my eyes with the back of my hand. "He has some nerve, accusing me of threatening his family, then turning around and threatening mine."

"Did you threaten his family?" McCall said.

"You have to ask?" I stomped up the sidewalk.

"So where is Kevin?" he asked, following me.

I stopped and spun toward him. "I'm not telling *anyone* anything about my son."

"Fair enough," McCall said. "Just being polite. Thinking maybe you ought to check with him right now. Make sure he's okay. Maybe warn him about that guy."

"Oh, I'll warn him," I said. *Just as soon as I figure out where on earth he is.*

"Fletcher's a loose cannon," McCall said.

"No kidding."

"What kind of game were you referring to?"

"What?"

"The 'sick' game. Between Fletcher and his stepdaughter?"

Featherstone appeared at the dining room window. I was surprised his patience had lasted this long.

"Later," I told McCall, then smiled at the client, indicating everything was all right, even though it wasn't. "We're being summoned."

We went inside, where Featherstone waited with his clipboard and list of instructions. He studied me, concern creasing his brow. "Is there a problem?"

"Nothing that will interfere with our work," I said.

He hesitated for only a second before launching into what he wanted done before the appraiser arrived and in what order we should do it. As he droned on, I worried about Fletcher's reaction to learning about Kevin. He must have talked to Grayson. Had she led him to believe she and Kevin were still together? Maybe to protect Deke, the current boyfriend? But Fletcher hadn't blinked when I mentioned Deke's name. For all I knew, he might be on his way to bully Deke right now: *leave Grayson alone, or else.*

When Featherstone finished reviewing the day's agenda, he and McCall headed to the garage. I bolted upstairs the second they were out of sight. My assignment was to sweep through the house, make sure all items that needed to be valued were on display or easily accessible and to dispose of all trash.

But first, I needed to try Kevin again. I locked myself in the master bath and dialed the phone, chanting, "Pick up, Kevin. Please, pick up, pick up, pick up."

The chanting didn't help.

For the next few hours, I moved through my chores, trying Kevin every fifteen minutes without luck, and I was doing my final spot-check downstairs when the doorbell rang at two sharp. Featherstone had just taken the final bag of trash out the back, so I answered the door.

I almost needed sunglasses to ward off the vivid chartreuse pants suit and iridescent paisley scarf worn by the woman on the front stoop. She was sixty-five if she was a day and wearing enough makeup for ten women, accented by lavender cat's-eye glasses with glittering rhinestones at the temples.

My smile froze as the woman stepped over the threshhold before I could invite her in. She was short, with a hefty trunk on thin legs that made it seem as if she might topple as she walked.

"I'm Annabelle Lake, hon. Steve's expecting me." Heavy bracelets jangled on her wrist as she ran a hand through her too-black dyed hair.

"Ah, the appraiser." I closed the door and turned to face her.

"Appraiser, auctioneer, *Antiques Roadshow* groupie, decorator—that's me." She chuckled, showing a mouthful of age-yellowed teeth. "Let's see what we got here."

I introduced myself, but Lake was already moving into the dining room. She picked up a plate and held it to the light. "Lovely. Baronet China Silver Arbor. Good condition." She slid a gigantic leopard-print tote off her shoulder and leaned it against a dining chair.

I would have loved to see Featherstone's first reaction when he spotted the quirky woman, but I was so intent on watching her myself that I didn't hear him come in.

Lake had been picking up and putting down dish after dish when she suddenly faced the doorway and broke into that dingy smile again.

"You must be Steve." She crossed the dining room to shake Featherstone's hand, pumping his arm as if she was trying to get water out of a dry well. "Pleased to meetcha, and have you got yourself a gold mine in dinnerware here."

"Glad to hear it," Featherstone said.

Lake stooped over with a grunt, pulled a flyer from her tote, and handed it to him. She used the chair for support to push herself upright. "Accredited by the ISA and all that jazz. Member of the Texas Estate Liquidators Association for more years than I care to count."

Featherstone glanced at the flyer. "I was told you're the best. I'm ready to roll."

"Gathered that from your phone call, hon. Here's what I recommend." She grunted again as she reached for the tote and pulled out a square black object. "I got me this computerized gizmo makes things go a whole lot quicker."

"The quicker the better." Featherstone glanced at what looked like a computerized tablet. "What does that do?"

"I record your inventory right into this little baby." She tapped the screen. "Go back to my office, consult my research materials, and add values. Print it all out for you."

"How long does that take?"

"Depends on what you have, hon."

"Of course." Featherstone nodded. "Then what?"

She walked into the foyer and gazed toward the living room. "A couple of ways we can do this. Nice big house like this, we could set up the estate sale right here. Save the expense of moving. Run the newspaper ads, distribute announcements—"

Featherstone was shaking his head. "That won't work. I need to empty the house now, by this weekend."

Lake screwed up her mouth. "Why's that?"

"Prospective buyers are coming in," he said, "and the place needs to look spacious."

Lake nodded but didn't appear convinced. "Emptying the house leaves you wide open to inspection. Every little flaw will—"

"I realize that," Featherstone interrupted. "My decision stands."

"Okay, then." Lake tapped a finger on her chin. "Let's look at our other options. First I'd like to take the tour, see what all you got."

Featherstone crossed the foyer and opened the doors to the art studio. He flipped on the light.

Lake entered the room and clucked her tongue. "Heard you had original art, but you got it out the wazoo, don'tcha?"

"Should be worth something," Featherstone said hopefully.

"Get the right buyer," she said, "it could bring a pretty penny."

This was likely to take a while, and they didn't seem to need me around. I wanted to try Kevin again.

I said, "Ms. Lake, can I get you something to drink?"

"A strong cup of coffee would rev me up," she said. "Cream and sugar."

"I'll have the same," Featherstone added.

I reminded myself he was paying me by the hour whether I was waitressing or organizing. "Coming right up."

I hurried to the kitchen, poured out the old coffee, and started a fresh pot. As it brewed, I hit redial on my phone.

After what seemed like a million rings, I gave up and slipped the phone back into my pocket. I propped my elbows on the counter by the coffeepot and buried my face in my hands. *Kevin, where are you?*

The back door opened, and I wiped at my weepy eyes. A hand touched my back.

"You okay?" McCall said.

I looked up at him. "Sure."

"Did you warn your son about Fletcher?"

"Not yet."

"Want to tell me what's going on?"

"Not really."

"Tell me anyway. Maybe I can help."

"I don't know where he is," I blurted, ignoring for the moment the fact that McCall was one of the people who'd seen Kevin or some-body who looked like Kevin wandering around this very neighbor-hood. "He'd been living with Fletcher's stepdaughter. Two nights ago he was at my place, then he left a note saying he was going out of town. Except I don't think he did. And I don't know where he is."

"He have a cell phone?" McCall said.

I nodded. "Sort of. It's the phone you found at Aunt Millie's house. He has trouble keeping up with his stuff. Always has."

"Doesn't take after his mom, huh?" McCall put a finger under my chin to tip my head up.

His grin made me smile, but the smile soon disintegrated into a loud sigh. "If that stupid Fletcher hadn't shown up, I wouldn't have missed Kevin's call."

"He called you this morning?"

"Yeah."

"Let me see your phone."

"Won't do any good. I've been calling the number all day. There's no answer."

"Where's he calling from?" McCall said.

"That's the problem," I said, frustrated. "There's no name on the caller ID. It's a local number, but I have no idea where he is."

"We can find out from the number."

"How?"

"On the Internet," McCall said. "I can access a database. Look it up in two seconds."

"But there's no computer here."

"We can run over to my place. It isn't far."

Hope lifted my mood. "Featherstone will be tied up with this woman for a while anyway."

"Then let's go."

"Wait, I promised them coffee." I grabbed two mugs, sloshed the fresh, hot liquid into them, added the cream and sugar, then practically ran into the art studio to deliver the mugs.

Lake and Featherstone were paging through canvases at the far end of the room.

"Here's your coffee," I said. "McCall and I are going to take a break now, if that's okay. Do you need us back today?" We'd covered everything on Featherstone's agenda, and he had spent the last thirty minutes doing his version of the white-glove test.

"Don't think so," he said. "I'll be in touch."

My shoes squeaked on the hardwood floor as I turned to leave.

"One sec, hon," Lake said. "About the portrait."

"What portrait?" I said.

"I was told about a portrait painted by this artist." Lake's back creaked as she straightened and looked around the room. "I have a client who's decorating a library. All dark woods and black-and-white art from the seventies. She's looking for portraits from that decade."

"There was a portrait here." I looked at Featherstone. "You remember it?"

He shrugged. "Maybe there was. Tell the truth, I wasn't paying much attention."

I frowned. Dawn Hurley had oohed and aahed over the portrait. Had she slipped back and taken it? But why would she want it? For decorating reasons, same as Lake's client?

This was a mystery, but not one I had a personal stake in. "Don't know where it is," I said, "but I'll be glad to take a look around when I get back."

"Don't worry about it," Featherstone said. "Maybe the thing will turn up somewhere."

Maybe it would, maybe it wouldn't. Whatever. I had more important things on my mind.

Chapter Twenty-four

I'm not sure what type of place I expected Wayne McCall to live in, but it wasn't the Stafford Inn off the Southwest Freeway. I'd noticed other rent-by-the-week places springing up around Houston and envisioned them as a thrifty alternative to hotels for traveling salesmen, someone who'd walked out on a spouse, those waiting to close on a new home. McCall didn't fit any of those profiles, but then, what did I really know about the man aside from the well-shaped biceps, the lines around sexy eyes . . . ? Not much.

I pulled into a parking spot beside his truck and followed him up the concrete stairs to a second-floor unit.

"Excuse the mess." He opened the door and motioned for me to enter ahead of him.

"No problem." I said conversationally, then saw he was serious when he flicked on the light.

Bagged dry cleaning draped the sofa, and dirty dishes decorated the coffee table. File folders lay on the floor near an armchair next to a pile of toppled books. Paperbacks, I noticed, mostly on business topics that sounded as dull as the beige walls and carpeting looked. This didn't strike me as the living quarters of a professional organizer, even if McCall was in the early stages of his career.

He headed for a square dining table in a corner and flipped open a laptop computer. Pushed a button.

"Lived here long?" I asked.

"About a month. I'm between things."

What kind of things? I wondered but didn't ask.

"Takes a minute to get this up and running," he said. "Thirsty? I have bottled water, Cokes, beer."

"Nothing, thanks."

He went into the kitchen, and I heard the refrigerator open. I glanced around the room. A navy blue suit jacket hung on the back of a dining chair. Next to the chair sat an expensive-looking black leather briefcase.

McCall in a suit? Carrying a briefcase? The image didn't fit.

A box of his *Wayne's Way* business cards sat on the table near the computer. I walked over to check the computer screen—still booting—and noticed an invoice next to the cards. He'd had them printed at Kinko's—two weeks ago.

He came back into the room and snapped the tab on a Coke. "What was Fletcher's problem today?"

I shook my head. "He's not important. I just want to find Kevin."

"Something was important for the man to track you down the way he did," McCall said. "I don't like his attitude."

"He's freaked out about his stepdaughter," I said. "Overprotective, I guess you could say, but for the wrong reasons."

"What do you mean?" McCall said.

"It's a long story."

The computer signalled it was up and ready for action. McCall leaned over, clicked an icon, and entered a password.

I recited the phone number we needed to look up and pulled out my cell to confirm my memory. The phone rang as I flipped it open, startling me.

"Maybe this is Kevin," I said, my heart thudding.

But Aunt Millie was talking before I got the phone to my ear. McCall could hear her from where he stood. He smiled and turned his attention back to the keyboard.

"I am so relieved to reach you," Aunt Millie said.

"What's wrong?" I said. "Are you all right?"

"I'm fine. My car isn't."

"What happened? Were you in a wreck?"

"Nothing that serious," she said. "I'm at Kroger's. Drove over here okay, but when I came out, the car was as dead as a snake on a rush-hour freeway. Thought I had a bad battery, but it might be the alternator again."

"You want me to come and get you? Better yet, maybe McCall can help. I wouldn't know the first thing about car problems."

"No, no. I don't need either one of you over here."

"Then why did you call?"

McCall was watching me, curious. I shrugged.

"Olive Hurley is expecting me at four-thirty," Millie said. "I ran over here to pick up some apples. Had apple-cranberry crisp on my mind. It's a quick fix, and I thought Olive could use some comfort food. Not that it will ease her pain, but—"

"Aunt Millie, what do you need?" I hoped she didn't expect me to make the dessert for her. I paced McCall's living room, waiting for her response, checking on his progress every few seconds. He was busy working the keyboard.

"Well," she said finally, dragging it out into three syllables. "My mechanic is on his way, and he might be able to fix the problem here, but I can't count on that, and Olive needs to be at the funeral home by five to make arrangements. I thought you might pick her up and take her over there."

I stopped in my tracks and looked at the ceiling. I felt sorry for Mrs. Hurley, but I didn't exactly have spare time. "What about Janice?"

"Poor Olive does *not* need Janice," Millie said in a what-are-you-thinking tone.

"Good point." Siccing my cousin on a grieving mother would be cruel, even on Janice's best day.

"Speaking of Janice," Aunt Millie went on, "I swear she's more frantic by the minute. She won't tell me why. Never thought I'd say this about my own daughter, but she needs to take something. Maybe I should slip her a sedative."

"Couldn't hurt," I said.

"Not that I'm complaining," Millie said. "Olive's daughter is gone, and I'm grateful to have mine, even if she won't listen to a word I say."

"I understand."

"So, can you do it?"

I checked my watch. If McCall came through with an address, and depending on where it was, I should be able to track Kevin down before it was time to pick up Olive Hurley.

"I'll do it," I told her.

McCall gave me a thumbs-up. He'd found something.

I spotted a notepad and pen next to a stack of phonebooks on the counter separating the dining area from the kitchen. I grabbed the pen. "I have to run, Aunt Millie. Tell me where—Mrs. Hurley's address and the funeral home's."

As I listened to her fumbling on the other end, I noticed some photographs sitting on the phone books. The photo on top looked familiar, and I leaned over to study it. I recognized the back of Vicki Rhodes' house from her kids' swing set. I glanced over my shoulder at McCall, who was engrossed with the computer.

I pushed the top photo aside. The one beneath it was a street scene, a black Mercedes just like Barton Fletcher's prominent in the photo. *Weird.* Curious now, I flipped to the next. A front view of a house I didn't recognize. The fourth picture was of Grayson with a man I'd never seen before. I froze for a second, then hurriedly shoved the photos back onto a pile. Why on earth would McCall have these pictures?

Aunt Millie began reciting addresses, and I scribbled them down while straightening the photos with my left hand. I promised to take care of Mrs. Hurley, then disconnected and turned to McCall. I felt awkward being here, as if he had suddenly become a stranger. I was eager to leave but not until I got the information I'd come for.

"What did you find?" I asked.

"The location for that phone number is clearly a building at the corner of Fifty-nine and Gessner," he said. "A convenience store."

I frowned. "Kevin called me from a convenience store?"

"More likely from a pay phone outside. Could explain why nobody answers when you call back."

I nodded, thinking. Chances were slim that I'd find Kevin hanging out in the parking lot, but I had to look.

"I'll be glad to go over there with you," McCall said. "Not the best part of town."

"No," I blurted and headed for the door. "I'll be fine. Thanks for the help."

"You're welcome." He followed close behind me. "What about Millie's problem?"

"We got that straightened out. Thanks again."

"I'd like to hear more about Fletcher," he said. "Something doesn't sit right."

Not with Fletcher and not with you either, I thought.

"I have to go see about Kevin," I said. "That's my top priority."

McCall smiled and touched my arm. "I know. Maybe we can get together later."

I shook my head. "Aunt Millie needs me tonight. I'll let you know if Featherstone wants us to come back. If we're done there, I'll collect on his bill, and we'll divvy it up."

"Sounds like a plan." McCall opened the door for me.

I said good-bye and jogged down the steps and out to the Durango. As excited as I was about having a lead on Kevin, I couldn't help wondering about McCall on my way to the convenience store. Why did he have a picture of Grayson? Why had he been spending so much time in Aunt Millie's neighborhood? Had he taken those pictures himself, and what did he plan to do with them? What had he been up to late last night when I spotted his truck parked on the street?

I reached the convenience store, maneuvered around vehicles waiting in line to get gas, and slipped into a parking space next to the building. There was a pay phone near the street, but I didn't see Kevin loitering in the area. His pickup was nowhere in sight. I rushed inside, nearly knocking over a skinny teenager on her way out, and made a lap around the store. Kevin wasn't there.

One clerk manned the store, and three people waited impatiently while he activated gas pumps and rang up purchases. I joined the line and five long minutes later came face-to-face with the man behind the counter, an Asian with graying temples. He looked at me expectantly.

"You get gas?" he said.

"No, I'm looking for someone."

He glanced at the line behind me. "What you want? Cigarettes? A pack of gum?"

"No. I'm looking for a young man. My son."

"I don't see no lost kids around here," he said. "I'm alone, and you see I have many customers."

I regretted my switch to a small wallet that had no room to hold a picture of Kevin. "Is the manager here? Maybe I could talk with him."

"I am manager," the man said, frowning.

I grabbed several candy bars and tossed them onto the counter.

"I'll buy these, but my son called me from the phone outside. Maybe you saw him."

The clerk rang up the candy bars. "That will be four dollars, nineteen cents." He picked up a plastic sack.

I pulled out my wallet, taking my time. "My son is about six foot, blond. His name is Kevin."

The clerk dropped the candy into the sack and stared at me. "Kevin Cartwright?"

"Yes, that's him."

His face reddened. "You tell Kevin Cartwright I am looking for him too. I'm his boss, and I get this call that he had to leave sudden-like. So here I am trying to fill in when he's supposed to be the one working."

"Kevin works here?" I said.

"For now, yes," the man said. "And if he get back here by eight like he says, maybe I will keep him on. If not, you can tell him for me. He's fired."

I threw a five onto the counter and grabbed the candy. "Keep the change. I'll be back at eight."

I trudged out to my truck, surprised by what I'd learned.

Kevin *worked* here. At the convenience store. I couldn't wrap my mind around that, much less understand why he would take off suddenly, saying he'd come back by eight. I checked my watch. That was nearly five hours away. Which gave me plenty of time to collect Olive Hurley, deliver her to the funeral home by five, and be back here when Kevin returned.

I ripped open a candy bar, chomped into the chocolate, and felt the knot in my gut unwind with that first bite. Comfort food. Things would look better as soon as I got hold of Kevin—surely they couldn't look worse.

After a quick trip home to take a shower and make myself presentable to meet Olive Hurley, I arrived at her small country home at ten minutes till five. The house, a brick one-story with wide flower beds full of colorful pansies, sat at the end of a narrow dirt lane on the outskirts of Richmond.

I stayed in my SUV for a moment and imagined how the Hurley

women might have felt removed from the dangers of big-city living out here in this tranquil setting. Now Dawn was gone, and I wondered if her mother would ever again have a peaceful thought. I couldn't imagine myself living through the horror of my child's murder.

A curtain moved at a front window, and I realized I'd been spotted. I approached the door, steeling myself to deal with an emotionally distraught woman. But Olive Hurley surprised me with her calm and matter-of-fact greeting. We introduced ourselves, and I expressed my condolences.

The woman was built like Dawn—short and round. She wore a plain navy dress with matching low pumps and appeared ready to leave except for the pink curlers in her hair.

"Thank you for coming," she said. "My doctor has me on medication, and I'm not supposed to drive."

"I'm glad to help," I said.

"If you don't mind, I need to finish getting ready." She patted the curlers.

"Take all the time you need."

She rushed off down a hallway that I assumed led to the bedrooms. I strolled over to the living room and stopped short in the doorway. *Wow!* In all my experience of going into people's homes, I'd never seen anything like this. The room had a split-personality decor. The left side reminded me of Dawn's office—papers and books stacked everywhere, with barely a path to a deep armchair in front of the television. The other half was neat and rather empty, with knickknacks placed carefully on end tables flanking the sofa, a *TV Guide* centered on the bare coffee table.

Heels clumped down the hall toward me, and I pulled my gaze from the invisible line dividing the room.

Olive had removed half of the curlers, and tendrils of hair bounced as she approached me. "I just realized you're the person Dawn mentioned earlier this week—the organizer."

"That's right."

"This probably gives you the heebie-jeebies." She indicated the crowded side of the living room. "I know it does me."

I hesitated, not sure how to respond, then said, "Everyone has their own style."

"I'm sure you can see the conflict we had going on in this house."

"You mean because of the clutter?" I said.

"Yes." She looked at the floor, and when she raised her head, her eyes were wet with tears. "I can't live this way anymore, but I don't want to change anything either, because when I do, then she'll be completely gone. I'm not sure which is more depressing."

"Give yourself some time," I said. "You aren't ready to make any big decisions yet."

She took a breath and blinked away the tears. "You're right. Later."

She turned away, then paused and said, "Could you help me with this?" She gestured at the messy half of the room. "I mean in a month or so."

"I help people with projects just like this all the time," I said. "I'll be happy to leave my business card."

"Good," she said. "If you want to look around, so you'll know what to recommend when we talk later, I wouldn't mind." She started back down the hall, then stopped and pointed to a door. "That's Dawn's room."

"Okay."

She disappeared into a room at the end of the hallway. I felt awkward nosing around the house, but it appeared that's what she wanted me to do. I stuck my head into the kitchen first and noticed a decor similar to the living room. Half of the breakfast table was stacked with debris, half clear. A section of kitchen counter was cleared, the other side a mess. This was weird.

I understood how Olive felt she'd be erasing Dawn from her life if she cleaned up the place and why she didn't want to keep things as they were. But we could designate a room in the house to keep mementoes of Dawn and clear out the rest.

Dawn's room would be the likely place to gather her things. I went down the hall to see how large a room we'd be dealing with and gasped when I opened the door. The room was packed and stacked, with a path to the bed so narrow, I couldn't imagine Dawn had fit through it. I estimated she'd been in her mid-thirties, and it wouldn't surprise me to learn that every single item she'd ever brought into this room was still in here somewhere.

One thing was for sure—if she *had* taken the Featherstone portrait, she couldn't have possibly fit it into this bedroom. And I didn't think Olive would have allowed some stranger's portrait to take up any of her neat and orderly space.

I was dwelling on what might have happened to the darn painting when the doorbell rang.

"Could you get that please?" Olive called from the other room. "I'm almost ready but not quite."

"Okay," I called back, wondering if she was expecting someone else.

I opened the door, and my chin dropped in surprise. "Detective Troxell."

"You're a hard woman to catch up with, Ms. Cartwright," Troxell said.

"What do you mean?"

"I mean your fingerprints were found at another crime scene, and I need to take you in for questioning."

Chapter Twenty-five

Detective Troxell kept me waiting in the interrogation room—the same one I'd been in the day before. The room was frigid today, just like Troxell's attitude. I didn't know what had happened to change her—a couple of days ago we were friends sharing chocolate cake. All of a sudden she was treating me like a front-runner on her suspect list.

I hugged myself, rubbing my arms to warm up. At least she hadn't dragged me here cuffed and shackled. She'd allowed me to drive Dawn's mother to the funeral home as planned, so things couldn't be too bad. But if Troxell had questions, why didn't she just ask them? Why did I have to be *here*?

I told myself this was simply a conclusion of yesterday's meeting. Troxell had been interrupted. And now she'd have even more questions because of Dawn's murder. Yeah, that made sense. This had nothing to do with my son. But by the time Troxell graced me with her presence, I'd worked myself into a major snit. I was no criminal, and I didn't appreciate her wasting so much of my time.

To speed things along, I began answering questions before she asked. "If you brought me here to find out whether I was in the building where Dawn Hurley worked, the answer is yes, I was. Yesterday. The day she was killed."

"I see." Troxell settled into the chair across from me. She placed her tape recorder on the table, pushed record, and stated the date, time, and my name, then smiled at me.

"Ms. Cartwright, were you in the building at six-twenty Morton Street yesterday?"

"That's what I just said. Yes, I was there. I'm sure many other people were too. Are you bringing everyone in for a formal interview?"

She ignored my question and asked another of her own. "Why were you there?"

I explained about Aunt Millie's papers and her request that I take them to her attorney's office, then spent the next five minutes giving Troxell a blow-by-blow of my meeting with Tate, including his concern that Dawn had not yet arrived for work.

"We found your prints on the railing along the back stairs."

"Of course," I said. "I used the stairs on my way out."

"Why not take the elevator?"

I blew out a breath. "Because I was in a hurry. Have you ever *been* in that geriatric elevator?"

Once again she ignored what I'd said. "Did you see anyone else in the stairwell?"

"No."

"Did you leave anything at the law office?" Troxell asked.

"The papers from my aunt." Was she not paying attention?

"Anything else?"

"No."

"Not a note?"

I slumped back in my chair. "I forgot. I left a note for Dawn to call me."

"And did she call you?"

I shook my head. "No."

"Why did you want to talk with her?"

Yesterday seemed like a year ago, and I had to think for a second. "I wanted to ask her about my cousin. Dawn seemed to know more about her than I did, and I thought she might shed some light on why she's acting so weird."

"That would be Janice Reed?"

"Right."

"What do you mean by 'weird'?"

"You know," I said. "You met her the other night at Aunt Millie's." Troxell nodded. "The first time."

"Don't tell me she's harassing you about her boxes."

"You might say that," Troxell said.

"Then you know what I mean by 'weird.' Those boxes are thirty years old. I mean, how important can they be?"

"Let's stay on track," Troxell said. "Tell me how your cousin was acquainted with the victim."

I frowned. "I wouldn't say they were acquainted. Dawn only knew Janice as Aunt Millie's heir because of Dawn's job. She seemed to take a personal interest in all of Mr. Tate's clients."

Troxell nodded as if this wasn't the first time she'd heard this information. She glanced down at the recorder, I guessed to make sure it was still running.

"In fact," I added, "Dawn turned up early yesterday morning at *my* client's house."

Troxell looked up. "Your client's name?"

"Steve Featherstone."

"What time was this?"

"Before eight," I said.

"And her reason for coming?"

"Mr. Tate is the probate attorney for Steve's late grandmother, who was an artist. Dawn was interested in getting one of her paintings."

"And she'd made an appointment to come see these paintings?"

"I'm sure Mr. Featherstone wasn't expecting her," I said. "He seemed put out about the visit."

Troxell nodded again. "I see."

"We discovered today that one of the paintings is missing. A portrait Dawn was particularly interested in."

Troxell raised her eyebrows. "You think she stole a painting?"

I shrugged. "It's the one that's missing. You didn't happen to find a portrait in her car, did you?"

"I can't discuss that," Troxell said.

Her choice of words was making me more jittery.

"Did you notice anything unusual at the law office?"

What was she getting at? Did she suspect Allen Tate now? "Aside from Dawn's office being a mess and I couldn't imagine her getting any work done there, no."

"Do you have any idea who might have wanted Dawn Hurley dead?"

"No."

"Were you involved in any way with the murder?"

My jaw dropped. "Are you kidding? I've only seen the woman a couple of times in my life. Why would I be involved?"

"Calm down, Ms. Cartwright."

"I can't believe this."

"I simply asked you a question."

"Which sounded like an accusation. Can you see me getting the drop on a woman Dawn's size and strangling her with a wire?"

"Did I say you did it yourself?" she said.

Outrage burned on my cheeks. "You *are* accusing me."

"No," Troxell said. "But I *would* like to hear how you knew about the wire."

I stared at her hard. "I heard about *that* right here in this office. Yesterday, as I was leaving. People were already talking."

Troxell watched me, silently.

I didn't look away, concentrating on calming myself.

"Was your associate Wayne McCall present when the victim visited Mr. Featherstone?" Troxell asked.

I hesitated, reviewing the sequence of events. "No, he arrived later."

"Do you know if he was acquainted with her?"

"They knew each other. I don't know how or when they met."

"What *do* you know about Mr. McCall?"

She kept coming around to asking about McCall. I chewed my lower lip. I had plenty of suspicions about him, but I didn't necessarily want to share them with Troxell. He'd been so nice, helpful, seemed so genuine. I didn't *want* him to be involved in the murders, but what if he was? If it came down to Troxell suspecting McCall or Kevin or even me, I'd rather she suspected McCall. So I told Troxell everything I knew and felt like a traitor.

"Is McCall a suspect?" I asked when I'd finished.

Troxell drummed her fingers on the table. "No comment."

To change the subject, I said, "Have you identified the man from Aunt Millie's garage?"

"I can't share details with you. This is an ongoing investigation," Troxell said.

"But you know who he is?"

"The investigation is continuing."

I sighed, frustrated. "Okay. May I ask if you've at least interviewed the neighbors? I heard about a lady named Birdie Peterson who knows—"

She held up a hand. "I'll decide whom to interview, Ms. Cartwright. Your son has given us some good information."

My mouth went dry. "You talked with Kevin?"

"I did."

"When?"

"A few minutes ago. He's down the hall."

My heard raced. "Is he under arrest?"

She tipped her head. "Should he be?"

I fidgeted in my seat. "Of course not."

Troxell watched me so closely, I wondered if she was counting how many times I blinked.

Finally, she indicated for the tape that our interview was over and switched off the recorder.

"Are you holding us here?" I didn't breathe as I waited for her answer.

"No. You and your son are witnesses for the time being."

I let out my breath. "So now what?"

The corners of Troxell's mouth curved up slightly, the closest thing to a smile I'd seen since the start of the interview. "You're free to go."

"And Kevin?"

"My partner should be finished with him. Go talk to your boy."

It took every ounce of willpower in my being to rise slowly and walk from the room. My heart soared at the thought of finally talking to Kevin.

Chapter Twenty-six

Relief washed over me as I stepped into the hallway and saw Kevin emerge from a room two doors down. His hair needed washing, and his jeans and sweatshirt looked as if he'd worn them for a week straight. But no handcuffs—a good sign. His jaw dropped when he spotted me.

"Hey, Kev." I walked over and gave him a casual hug, pretending that running into each other here was no big deal. "Sorry I missed your call earlier."

He stared at me as if I'd just sprouted antlers. "Uh, no problem."

He looked exhausted and even thinner than he had the other day. Troxell kept an eye on us, as if she expected we'd commit some crime right there and she could swoop in and make an arrest. The sooner we put distance between us and her, the better.

"Detective," I said, "you'll let us know if we can do anything more to help out?"

"Count on it." Troxell nodded and gave a little wave.

My stomach knotted at her words. I linked my arm in Kevin's and made tracks for the exit.

He pulled his arm free as soon as we turned the first corner. "You don't have to hang on to me like I'm some little kid."

"Sorry."

"Mom, what are you doing here? Did the cops call you?"

"Wait," I said, "We'll talk outside."

On the first floor, a blast of cold, damp air whooshed in as people left the building ahead of us. It was already dark and, to make matters worse, pouring rain. We went out and stood under the portico where a couple of women waited in hopes that the weather would let up.

Not the best place to talk. I dug into my oversized purse, came up with my folding umbrella, and undid the snap.

"Hold on," Kevin said. "What's happening here?"

I took his arm again, urging him as far as we could get from the women and still be under cover.

"You tell me," I said in a low voice. "Your dad and I have been worried sick. He drove to Austin searching for you."

"Austin? Why?"

"We didn't know where else to look. We heard about the festival. Jojo expected you—"

"I told him I wasn't in the mood for any festival," Kevin said.

"Whatever. That's not important now."

"Then why are you so freaked out?"

"Because you disappeared right after a dead man was found in Aunt Millie's garage. Witnesses reported someone who looks like you lurking around Riverside Estates. So you see why we beat the bushes trying to find you?"

Kevin's eyes widened. "Is that why you're here? The cops wanted to talk to you because of me?"

I glanced at the women, but the pounding rain was drowning out our voices, and they weren't paying any attention to us. "Not exactly. I'm sure they're talking to everyone remotely connected to these cases." I gave him the shorthand version of my past few days.

"You think I'm guilty?" he said.

"Of course not. But where have you *been*?"

"Around," he said, not meeting my eyes. "Staying at a friend's."

"Not with Grayson, I hope."

"No, Mom. You can quit harping about her."

Even in the skimpy outdoor lighting I caught his pained expression. My heart hurt for him, but I needed to push on and get some answers. Rain pummeled the shrubbery surrounding the building and splattered us. Thunder boomed in the distance.

"How about we move this discussion to Manuel's?" I said. "Grab some dinner."

He shook his head. "I should get going."

"Not so fast. We have to talk about what happened in there. Just because the police let us go doesn't mean we're off their radar."

Kevin looked down, scuffed his tennis shoes on the concrete, then stared out at the wet parking lot. "Crap."

"Exactly," I said. "Let's go. You have to eat."

"Okay." He sounded utterly dejected, as if spending time with me was his worst nightmare. "Meet you there."

I offered him my umbrella.

"Keep it. I'm good." He pulled his sweatshirt up higher around his neck, then broke for the parking lot.

On the way to the restaurant I thought about calling Doug. He needed to know Kevin had surfaced, but I didn't want him joining us. He'd end up yelling, Kevin would clam up, and in the end I wouldn't know any more than I did now. I pulled into the restaurant lot and vowed to call Doug after dinner.

Our waiter delivered the usual basket of tortilla chips and salsa to the table and took our orders. Two iced teas—though I sure could have used a margarita to calm my nerves—and taco plates, the day's special.

When the waiter left, I said, "Tell me everything. Start with how the police found you."

"They didn't," Kevin said around a mouthful of chips. "Some guy sicced them on me."

"What guy?"

"You don't know him, and you don't want to." He smoothed rain-drenched hair back from his face.

"Tell me his name. I need details in case the cops come back to us on this."

He swallowed and waited a beat, trying to decide whether or not to share the information. Finally, he said, "Grayson's stepfather. He hates my guts."

"Barton Fletcher," I said, bristling at the thought of anyone hating my son.

Kevin looked up, surprised. "You know him?"

"We've met," I explained. "And he's the one who mentioned your name to the police?"

"He threatened to have me arrested."

"For murder?"

"No. To keep me away from Grayson."

I nodded. "Actually Fletcher and I had a little run-in this morning. He's not through threatening you."

Kevin's hands balled into fists. "I'd like to get my hands on that—"

"Not a good idea," I said.

"It's so freakin' stupid," he said. "All I wanted was to talk to her."

"You're losing me."

Kevin clenched his hands together on the table in front of him. "When Grayson left our apartment, she went to stay at her mom's. She said it was over, but I didn't believe her."

I stuffed a chip into my mouth to keep from throwing in my two cents. He was talking, and that was good.

"I kept trying to catch up with Grayson," he said. "To talk, that's all, but I never made it past the front door. Fletcher made sure of that."

The waiter brought our drinks. Kevin gulped some tea before going on.

"I hung around the golf course," he said, "hoping to see her on her way in or out."

Aha. Things were falling into place. "*That's* why people spotted you in the area."

"Guess so, but I didn't know about any murder at the time. Fletcher said he'd call the cops on me. I heard sirens, so I got out fast."

"That's when you left me the note saying you were going out of town, even though you didn't intend to leave?"

He nodded. "I didn't want to drag you into anything."

"You mean you didn't want me to know you were still after Grayson."

"Maybe that too."

I reached across and touched his arm. "I'll always be here for you, no matter if I approve of what you're doing or not."

"I know." He ate another chip. "Anyway, it wasn't enough for that jerk that I was staying away. I heard he gave the cops my name in connection with a murder, so I decided to come in and tell my side of the story."

"Good choice. I'm proud of you."

The waiter served our tacos then, and we ate in silence for a few minutes. But I wanted information more than food. I pushed my plate away.

"Did the cops ask you about all this today in the interview?" I asked.

"Pretty much."

"You told them what you've told me?"

"Yeah."

"You think they believed you?"

"Seemed like they did. They mostly wanted to know what I saw while I was out there."

"Did you see anything important?"

He shrugged. "I told 'em about the other dude hanging around the course. Since I was out there a lot, I recognized the regulars. Knew who teed off at what times, on what days, and all that."

"Who is this dude?" I said.

"Don't know his name," Kevin said. "But I think the cop knew him. He's older. Dark hair, turning gray. Hangs in the neighborhood, usually at night. Drives a white pickup."

"Huh." I tried to hide my reaction to Wayne McCall's description. I'd seen McCall's truck in the area at odd times myself and probably not at the same times Kevin had seen him. Which meant McCall spent a *lot* of time in the neighborhood. But why?

"I saw the dead guy too," Kevin added. "Didn't help the cops much, 'cause I have no idea who he was."

I was so preoccupied thinking about McCall that it took a couple of seconds for Kevin's words to sink in.

"What do you mean you saw the dead guy?" I said.

"They showed me a picture of the guy in the garage."

"And you recognized him?"

Kevin nodded. "When they showed me the picture, I knew I'd seen him before."

"You mean while he was still alive?"

"Yeah."

Chills ran up my arms. "When was that?"

"Last Friday, I think."

"Where did you see him?"

"He was out on the golf course alone, not too far from Aunt Millie's. But he wasn't dressed for golf, and he didn't have any clubs."

"Are you *sure* he was the same guy?"

"Positive. When I mentioned the Oakley sunglasses he had pushed up on his head, the cops got excited. They found Oakleys in the dead guy's pocket."

"Do you think they've identified him?"

He shook his head. "Didn't sound that way. Too bad they can't check his fingerprints. They took mine, and that ought to prove I'm *not* who they're looking for, right?"

I nodded, thinking of the machete the police had fished out of the lake. I sure hoped water washed fingerprints away so no one could even consider using the machete as evidence against Kevin even if his fingerprints were on the sheath.

"Mom, you okay?" Kevin ate his last bite of taco and pushed his empty plate away.

"I'm fine." He had enough to worry about without my bringing up the machete. I checked the time. "With this weather, you probably should head back to work. Your boss is expecting you by eight or you're fired."

Kevin frowned. "How do you know about my boss?"

"I'm a mom," I said, smiling. "Moms know everything."

He grinned slightly. "You're right. I should go."

I opened my purse and fished out the cell phone I'd found at Millie's. I wished Kevin would come back and stay at my house tonight, but he'd had enough pressure for one day.

I handed him the phone. "I think this is yours. Keep in touch, okay?"

He took the phone, glanced at it, and didn't try to explain. "Thanks, Mom, and thanks for dinner."

The rain had slowed down, and from where I sat I could see him jog across the parking lot to his truck.

My brain swirled with unanswered questions. Had Kevin's information about the dead man helped the police? Were they thinking one killer or two? And, most important, had their meeting with Kevin convinced them of his innocence? Mothers do know a lot, but in this case I didn't know nearly enough.

Kevin backed out of his parking space, and I watched his taillights as he pulled out of the lot and disappeared down the street. It wasn't until he was out of sight that I realized he'd never told me why he'd been trying to call me.

Chapter Twenty-seven

I finished my tacos so I wouldn't be hungry thirty minutes from now and called Doug from the restaurant. He had made it back home and didn't sound too happy about the wasted trip.

"You're telling me Kev was here all along?" he said after I'd filled him in on the latest events. "What in God's name has he been doing?"

I told him most of what Kevin had shared, leaving out the more personal tidbits about Grayson. "Now that the police have questioned Kevin, they can focus on finding the real killer."

"Miss Suzie Sunshine," he said sarcastically. "You haven't changed."

"What's that supposed to mean?"

"Are you the most naive person on the planet? The cops won't assume Kevin is innocent. They don't give a crap about him. They're probably matching his fingerprints to that machete as we speak."

As if I couldn't come up with enough worries on my own.

"He should have told the cops he wanted a lawyer," Doug went on. "Why didn't *you* insist he get a lawyer?"

"I didn't even know Kevin was there until after they'd talked to him. And if he asked for a lawyer, they'd think he had something to hide."

"Cops assume everybody's hiding something. All they care about is solving the case, and if Kev's fingerprints are on that—"

"Stop it," I said, loudly enough to draw the attention of the people at the next table. I lowered my voice. "No one is denying that Kevin touched Aunt Millie's machete."

"The killer will protect himself however he can."

"What are you saying?"

"Whoever did this isn't sitting around waiting to be caught. He, or she, could plant evidence to frame someone else. Who the hell knows what Kevin's fingerprints are on, what the killer had access to, what the cops might find near enough to the crime scene to pin the blame wherever they can to end the case?" Doug sighed noisily. "Innocent men have gone to jail before."

"Kevin is *not* going to jail." I felt my blood pressure rise with my tone. "And I don't need your—your negative, condescending, speculative crap. This conversation is over."

I punched the END button and snapped my phone shut. Now people were turning to stare. I threw more than enough cash onto the table, dashed out of the restaurant, and ran through the rain to the Durango. I jumped in, hit the door locks, brushed raindrops mixed with angry tears from my face, and tried to slow my breathing.

I regretted calling Doug. No way could I go home now and expect to get any sleep. I wouldn't rest again until the killer or killers were behind bars and I knew Kevin was safe. I had to do *something* to hurry up the process, but what?

Time to turn off my emotional Mom brain and switch on my logical problem-solver side. First, isolate the problem. Simple. Two murders, no arrests. Second, divide the problem into manageable segments. That wasn't so easy.

I couldn't do anything to change any physical evidence the police might come up with. The witnesses I knew of had fingered Kevin, or a Kevin look-alike. Given Troxell's questions, it seemed she didn't have much to go on at this point. She needed more information, more witnesses. The right witnesses.

I tore out of the parking lot, hoping to reach Birdie Peterson's house before her bedtime. If Troxell wasn't going to talk to the woman, I'd do it for her.

The rain had slowed to a drizzle by the time I pulled up in front of the house I knew must belong to Birdie. Who else would have birdbaths dotting their front yard, a birdhouse mailbox, and fake canaries hanging on thin wire from the trees?

It was a little after eight, and the downstairs lights were on. I hurried up to the front door and smiled when the doorbell chirped instead of ding-donging. The foyer light flicked on. A woman with a long gray ponytail and dangling parrot earrings peered through the side glass, opening the door at the same time. She was tall and as bosomy as an overstuffed pillow, her wrinkly cleavage spilling out from a pastel pink spandex shirt—not the small, birdlike ninety-year-old I'd envisioned.

She looked me up and down, adjusted her thick eyeglasses, and stepped closer. She glanced behind me. "Where's the cookies?"

"Cookies?" I said.

"Your girl said they'd be here on Thursday, and I'm waitin' all day."

"I'm sorry, but—"

Loud squawks coming from inside the house interrupted me.

"Pipe down!" she yelled over her shoulder, startling me. "Damn doorbell sets him off every time."

I was thinking her loud voice could set off a bomb in Baghdad. "Are you Birdie Peterson?" I asked.

"That's me. Least your girl could do is show up instead of sending you. You got 'em in there?" She was eyeing my purse.

I adjusted the straps on my shoulder, nudging the bag out of her sight. "Sorry, but I'm not the cookie person you're expecting. My name's Poppy Cartwright, and I'm concerned about the neighborhood's safety. I wanted to talk about the police investigation if you have a few minutes."

Birdie's disgruntled expression brightened. "Why didn't you say so?" She motioned for me to come inside. "It's what *everyone* is talking about. I'd offer you some cookies if I had some. Damn Girl Scouts."

"You have a lovely yard," I said, to get her mind off the cookies.

"Tell that to the homeowners association," she said. "They send out a code-violation notice every other week."

"Why?" I asked, hoping for a short answer.

"Think they can tell me what I may or may not put in my own yard. Well, they can kiss my grits. I lived in this city my whole life, it's my property, and I can put out a hundred birdbaths if I want to."

"I agree." I crossed the room to a chair under the beady-eyed stare of a caged gray bird with a yellow crest and orange cheeks. The bird squawked when I sat down.

"Don't mind Howard," Birdie said. "He don't care for visitors any more than the first one did."

"The first one?" I said.

"My late husband, Howard. That's him and me in that picture on top of the TV. Never had any luck teaching either one of 'em to mind their manners in front of company. Or to pick up after themselves." She grabbed a long-handled dustpan leaning against the sofa arm and hobbled to the bird's cage to sweep up sunflower seeds scattered on the parquet floor beneath.

I glanced at the picture of Birdie and her husband, then at the framed photographs that dotted Birdie's walls and sat on every available surface. They fought for breathing room in and around dozens of porcelain bird figurines. My gaze settled on the birdcage.

"Howard sure is a pretty bird," I said.

The bird whistled, then said, "Pretty bird. Birdie wants a treat."

"Mouthy cockatiel," Birdie said. "Always trying to wheedle something out of me. Another thing reminds me of the first Howard."

I hoped Birdie didn't mind my trying to wheedle information from her, but that *was* why I'd come. Before I could form my first question, she said, "You remarried?"

I frowned. "No, but how—"

"I know your ex," she said. "Your aunt too."

"Oh."

"Heard you're working at Ida Featherstone's."

"That's right." Blanca Sandoval had told me Birdie knew everything, but I hadn't taken her literally.

"What do you think of Wayne McCall?" she asked. "Wouldn't mind an eyeful of him all day myself."

"Wayne's a good worker."

"And how is Stevie?" Birdie said.

"Steve Featherstone?"

She leaned on the dustpan handle, looking wistful. "Wouldn't mind seeing the little whippersnapper, but kids don't care about visiting us old folks."

I had trouble envisioning the serious Steve Featherstone as a whippersnapper. "How do you know him?"

"He went to school with one of my grandsons. Got a picture of them in here somewhere." She scanned the room and pointed to the mantel. "There. We took the gang on a bird-watching weekend, must be near thirty years ago."

I rose and felt Howard watching me as I walked over to the mantel. Only one picture featured young boys—five of them, about ten years old, standing in front of a small wood cabin. The picture was black-and-white, and I couldn't have picked out Steve Featherstone on a bet.

Birdie came over to study the picture. "There's my grandson with the binoculars. That little towhead to his right is Stevie. What a trip! Tommy broke his arm the first day, Stevie's allergic to peanuts and got hold of some in a candy bar, and Dean turned up with poison ivy. I said we should have gone to the medical center on vacation instead of the state park."

I got the feeling Birdie would talk for hours if I didn't home in on the reason I'd come.

"How do you know my Aunt Millie?" I asked, returning to my chair.

Birdie turned around. "Run into her at the hairdresser's from time to time. Heard about you finding that man's body at her place. Hell of a thing."

"Yes, it was," I said.

"Told my neighbor some old dog's gonna drag up those missing hands any day. Course by then there won't be any prints left to find."

I didn't want to dwell on that gruesome thought. "How did you first hear about the murder?" I asked.

Birdie hesitated only a second. "My friend Martha called. She knew from her neighbor whose daughter's son's wife works for the police."

"Sounds like the phone lines were busy that day."

"Every day." She took the chair across from me. "How did your little meetings with the police work out?"

"Meetings?"

"Heard you and your son talked to 'em today."

This stopped me for a few seconds. I stared at Birdie, whose innocent expression belied the woman's cunning.

"Sounds like you have a regular hotline," I said, my face growing warm. "You might know more than I do."

Birdie smiled. "I hear so much, sometimes it's hard to sort things out."

I hated knowing that people were gossiping about me and my family, but I needed details.

"What's the word around town?" I said. "Who do you think did this?"

"Nobody knows," she said, shaking her head. "Might be a serial killer on the loose for all we know. First this man, then that poor woman from the lawyer's office."

"Have you heard anything about the police identifying the dead man?" I asked.

"Nope," Birdie said. "Only a lot of speculating so far."

"What are people saying?"

She leaned forward in her chair, getting into the gossip. "Kind of hard to figure motive when nobody can tell where the man came from, much less his name. At first we thought he'd be somebody you don't give a second thought—like the meter reader or a UPS driver."

"He wasn't wearing a brown uniform," I pointed out. "I wonder if any employers in the area are missing employees."

"Not that I know," she said, "but that was only one for instance. There's plenty more. Like he escaped from the prison. Maybe he's a homeless man. Or a yard man who went into that garage looking for a rake and suffocated in the mess before he could find his way out."

Her eyes were twinkling with the telling, and I could imagine her and her phone pals gossiping the days away.

I wasn't amused.

Birdie tipped her head to look at me over the top of her glasses. "Now don't get all riled up. Millie wouldn't. We tease her all the time, and she can dish it out too."

"You're right," I said, swallowing my irritation. "I guess the state of Aunt Millie's garage is not new news you learned because of the murder."

"Lord, no," Birdie said. "Everybody in town who's ever had a garage sale knows Millie. She's the cleanup lady. Comes in at the end and buys things you thought you'd never give away."

Great. There went my theory that few people would know a body could be stashed in Aunt Millie's garage without fear of discovery anytime soon.

"I'm sure the homeowners association has sent a bundle of those code violations to Millie," Birdie said.

"For what?"

"Tellin' her to keep a clear path to every door and window. Now that's a code makes sense."

"She can do whatever she wants to on her own property," I said. "Or are the rules different for her?"

"But you want her to be safe," Birdie said. "And keeping a clear path is a fire code rule. My Howard was a firefighter, so I know."

"Sounds like an office building code to me," I said. "They can't enforce that in private homes."

"You wouldn't believe the rules they come up with in this neighborhood," Birdie said. "One of the things I hope to change in the next election."

"Who's in charge?" I asked. Maybe someone who could give me more useful information about the murder investigation than I was getting out of Birdie.

"That Fletcher character," she said. "You tell Millie we're campaigning to run him out, and we want her on our side. We can win if we get enough senior citizens involved to outvote the young mothers."

"I've met Barton Fletcher." I said. "Why on earth would a young mother vote for him?"

"They sign their kids up for everything under the sun—singing, dancing, ball games, competing up the wazoo. What about normal family dinners, doing homework, reading a book before bed? Miss their whole childhood, you ask me."

I understood what she meant but didn't see the connection. "What does this have to do with Fletcher?"

"He wants to make a mint off these young folks. Bought fifty acres between here and Rosenberg to build some studio where kids can film their own movie, record their own album." She shook her head, disgusted. "I can see him now, like the damn Pied Piper. Attract the kids, and the parents will come and spend all their money. Lord help anybody who gets in his way."

I wasn't too crazy about Richmond being built up to resemble Houston and Sugar Land, but that wasn't what struck me about Birdie's speech.

"What if the dead man in Aunt Millie's garage was someone who got in Fletcher's way?" I said.

Birdie's eyebrows rose. "Now there's a thought."

The doorbell rang, and Birdie jumped up as if I wasn't even there. "That might be the cookies."

Howard squawked, "Birdie wants a treat."

He could say that again. Now that the woman had cookies on her mind, I knew I might as well leave.

Chapter Twenty-eight

I drove away from Birdie's house, thinking about the coincidence of two murders occurring so close together in such a short time span. Richmond wasn't a crime-free city by any means. We had the usual burglaries, car thefts, and domestic disputes that occasionally led to murder. We seldom heard about serial killings, and that wasn't what we were dealing with now. Yet I was convinced these victims were somehow connected. The fact that I'd found the mystery man in Aunt Millie's garage and that we both knew Dawn Hurley linked us to both crimes.

There had to be other connections.

If only we knew who the dead man was. A chill ran down my spine at the thought of asking Barton Fletcher whether he knew the victim.

Maybe I needed to approach this from the opposite direction— find out who wanted Dawn Hurley out of the picture. That might lead to the mystery man's ID.

Armed with a plan, I headed for Aunt Millie's. She knew Dawn, and she'd spent time with Dawn's mother. I wanted to check on her anyway, see if her car trouble was solved. Make sure Janice's visit wasn't driving her to drink.

As my luck would have it, my cousin was outside when I pulled up in front of Aunt Millie's house. She was approaching her rented Mercedes, holding a banker's box, dressed down in plain jeans and a cranberry sweatshirt. She popped the trunk and placed the box inside, then turned as I came up behind her.

"You home alone?" I asked.

She shook her head. "Mother's here. Her car's in the shop. I'm glad you came by."

The uncharacteristic remark stopped me for a second. "Really? Why?"

"We don't often get a chance to visit." Her smile seemed forced.

I shrugged. "The price you pay for that New York City power-broker lifestyle."

The catty remark didn't seem to bother her.

"We *do* stay busy." She turned to close the trunk, but not before I caught a glimpse of three other cartons inside.

"What's with the boxes?"

"I'm shipping my things home," Janice said. "Mother shouldn't be saddled with them. She needs to start thinking about downsizing."

"You pared everything down to three boxes? Good job."

Janice shook her head. "I'm not finished yet, and the police still have some of my possessions."

"I can ship them for you once they're released," I said, "if you'll give me your address." I was curious if she would tell me about the move to New Jersey that Dawn had mentioned.

Janice looked at me quietly, maybe wondering if I'd lost her address or had a reason to suspect there'd been a change. "No need," she said. "That detective finally agreed to return the contents, if not the boxes themselves, in a day or two. I'll need your help, though, to make sure I've got everything."

"How would *I* know?"

"You've obviously spent a lot of time here," she said. "Mother didn't pack up all that junk by herself, and I'm missing some things."

"What's missing?"

Janice made a frustrated tsking noise and said, "Just things. I don't have a list of every book report I ever wrote."

"And that's what you're shipping home?" I said. "Your old book reports?"

Janice blew out a breath. "I'm just saying I don't have everything. I saved quite a lot from high school and college. Eight or nine boxes total, and they're not all here. I wish someone would 'fess up and tell me where they are."

I had seen at least that many boxes marked with Janice's name in the garage, but I wasn't getting the whole story.

"Why don't *you* tell me exactly what you're after, Janice?" I said. "You have Elvis Presley's personal autograph stashed away, or what?"

"No. I didn't even like Elvis." She shook her head as if I was the most obstinate person she'd ever dealt with, then whirled and walked toward the house. "Why do I even bother?"

"Maybe I can help if you level with me." I followed her inside. "I don't see you shipping a bunch of junk home to litter up that gorgeous penthouse you're always bragging about."

She stopped at the bottom of the stairs. "Is it a crime, wanting to have memories from my childhood close to me?"

"No crime," I said. "Just *way* out of character."

Janice huffed and stomped up the stairs.

I didn't buy her suddenly treasuring memories from home. To start with, Millie was the one who had kept and boxed up those things, not Janice. I stood in the foyer, trying to make sense of my cousin's behavior.

Aunt Millie emerged from her first-floor bedroom, spooking me because her face was lathered with aqua, sandy-looking goop, only her eyes and pale lips showing.

"What on earth—?" I said.

"Janice is giving me a facial," Millie said excitedly, "just like the ones she gets in New York City."

Janice leaned over the upstairs banister. "It's designed especially for aging and fatigued skin, Poppy. You want one?"

I smiled tightly. "I'll pass."

"Be nice, girls," Millie said. "I've had a rough day." She touched a cheek gingerly. "How much longer do I keep this on?"

Janice checked her watch. "Another eight minutes. I'll come down then. Maybe *she'll* be gone." She disappeared into the guest room.

I looked at Millie. "Sorry. Guess it's too late for us to learn how to get along."

"It's never too late," Millie said. "C'mon to the kitchen. I baked some lemon bars."

"I'm stuffed," I said, holding my full stomach.

"Come anyway," Millie whispered. She glanced up the stairs, then grabbed my arm and hauled me into the kitchen. I wasn't surprised to see the counters that I had so recently cleared now littered with baking supplies, dirty dishes, and mail.

"Did you get me a new appointment with the lawyer?" Millie asked.

"I did." I told her the new date and time and walked over to her wall calendar to make the notation. "What's so urgent?"

"Janice is acting stranger than ever," she said.

"What's she done now?"

"She's being *nice,*" Millie said. "She made supper for me. Now she's into this facial. She wants us to go shopping together tomorrow. This is not like her."

"You should be pleased," I said. "She's making the most of the time you spend together."

"That's not it. She's fishing for information."

"What kind of information?"

"She's quizzing me hard about where all the things went that were in the house. I didn't tell her about the storage units."

"Do you have any idea what she's looking for?" I asked.

"No. She's insinuating that someone stole something. There's nothing here worth stealing—at least nothing I know about."

We could have stood there all night analyzing Janice's psyche, but it wouldn't ease Millie's concern, and I had other topics to discuss.

"Hate to change the subject," I said, "but I have some important questions, and I'd rather ask them without Janice around."

"Okay," Millie said.

"Did Dawn Hurley know Barton Fletcher?"

"I'm sure she'd heard his name."

"Maybe he was a client of Mr. Tate's?" I suggested.

"Fletcher's kind thinks they'll live forever," Millie said. "Can't see him worrying about estate planning."

"We can check on that with Dawn's boss," I said. "What does Olive Hurley think happened to Dawn?"

"She has no idea why anyone would want to kill her daughter, if that's what you're asking," Millie said. "She's clueless."

"No ex-boyfriends, angry clients, strangers coming by, unusual phone calls, threats?"

Millie shook her head. "The police badgered Olive with a load of questions. She couldn't tell them much. Might be because of those drugs she's on to calm her nerves."

I explained my conviction that one murderer had a connection to both victims and my desire to find that link. "We don't want the police homing in on you or me or Wayne McCall just because we all knew Dawn and we were all here the day the man's body was discovered."

"Why do people want to suspect Wayne?" Millie asked. "Janice was bad-mouthing him this afternoon."

"She suspects Wayne?" I said.

"She says he's a suspicious character."

I put a hand on Aunt Millie's arm. "I hate to tell you this, but the police think so too. Troxell asked me more than once about him, but you have to remember, it's her job to ask questions. For all she knows, all three of us could be lying when we say we don't know who the dead man was."

"But we're not liars."

"The police don't know that," I said. "Maybe *we* didn't know the man, but Dawn might have."

Millie nodded. "That's a possibility."

"Mother!" Janice yelled. "Two minutes."

"Okay," Millie called back, then lowered her voice. "Wish I could get some of Olive's drugs for Janice. She could use some calming. All this hunting for old stuff she hasn't cared about for thirty years. She's gone off her rocker."

An idea struck me, one I knew Millie would not want to hear. "Have the police talked to *her*?"

"Who? Janice?"

I nodded.

"Sure, they did. Remember? Janice was at your place the night Rae Troxell came over."

"I know, but did they question her? Did they ever show *her* the picture of the dead man?"

Millie stared at me. "You think *Janice* knew him?"

"I'm grasping at straws, Aunt Millie. First we find a dead man in your garage, then Janice shows up early. Why *did* she show up days ahead of schedule? Did she ever tell you?"

"No," Millie said thoughtfully.

"And now she's searching for something," I said. "What if it's something the dead man had in his possession? What if she *did* know him, and he brought something here, and now she's looking for it?"

Millie gasped.

"But maybe this mysterious object isn't here anymore," I continued. "The killer might have taken it."

Millie put one hand on her forehead and grabbed for a kitchen chair with the other. "I need to sit down. I feel faint."

"Don't panic," I said. "I'm just talking off the top of my head."

"But what if you're right?"

Footsteps slapped down the stairs, and Janice called, "Time's up, Mother."

I gave Aunt Millie a quick hug. "Janice will behave herself better if I'm not here. Don't worry. We'll get to the bottom of this."

I escaped through the back door, feeling bad for dropping such a bombshell on Aunt Millie and wishing I didn't have this tendency to blurt things out before thinking them through. But it was entirely possible that Janice knew the dead man. She was never one to share secrets with people, so there was no reason to believe she'd tell us the details if she had become involved in some weird drama that ended with a man's death.

I jogged around the side of the house and over to my SUV, slid in, and quickly shut and locked the door. I looked at Millie's house and hoped Janice continued to treat her mother nicely, no matter how suspicious that behavior might seem.

I turned my key in the ignition and just before flicking on my headlights noticed the front door opening at the house where McCall and I had seen the van being loaded with boxes the other day.

A man emerged along with the red-haired Lori Gilmore, who didn't appear to be dressed for going out. She was barefoot and wearing what looked like a red kimono with a belt tied loosely in front. I'd bet the man was getting an eyeful from the robe's deep *V* opening as they stood under the porch light.

This guy was blond, muscular, and wore skintight jeans—not the businessman I'd seen before. He held three boxes under one arm. The same kind of long, narrow boxes I'd seen loaded onto that van. I decided that whatever they held must be relatively light. They talked for a few seconds, then Skintight swept Gilmore into a brief but very passionate kiss before striding across the lawn to his car parked on the street—a black Porsche. He tossed the boxes in through the driver's door before getting in himself.

My knees felt a little weak, and I'd only witnessed the kiss from a distance. I could imagine what Lori Gilmore might be feeling. She waved to him before going back inside and closing the door.

I shook my head to clear my thinking and shifted into drive, wondering what on earth was in all those boxes. From the way he'd carelessly tossed them, nothing fragile.

Something curious was going on over at the Gilmores', and, considering the circumstances of the past few days, anything even slightly unusual deserved a closer look. I could go over there and knock on the door—ask Gilmore some questions. But I could do that anytime. Meanwhile, the Porsche reached the end of the street and made a right.

I'd never tailed anyone before in my life, but I wanted to find the truth about these murders before the wrong person ended up in jail. I wanted to know what was in all those white boxes. And, as Birdie Peterson might say, Skintight wasn't bad on the eyes.

The only idea that made sense at the moment was to follow that Porsche.

Chapter Twenty-nine

The farther we drove on the Southwest Freeway toward Houston, the more I thought about turning around and going home. That would be the smart thing to do. But I wanted to do the gutsy thing, whatever it took to get answers. Traffic was light, which only made driving more dangerous, with speeders zooming in and out of lanes at will. I was relieved when Skintight exited the freeway. We made a left on Hillcroft and took it up to Richmond Avenue, where we turned right.

The street was lined with strip malls, restaurants, and clubs— seedy properties with FOR LEASE signs pasted in the windows interspersed with thriving businesses. I felt increasingly uncomfortable and out of place as we passed clubs ablaze in neon lights and flashing signs that promised *Live Dancing*.

Skintight pulled into the parking lot of an establishment called Wildcatter Bill's. Under the name, a one-liner advertised *Food— Beer—Music*. I tapped my brakes, but there was traffic coming up behind me, and I had to make a snap decision.

What the heck. You've come this far.

I turned in and followed the Porsche down a row of parked cars, hoping the driver was oblivious to my existence. He whipped into a space along the building near the back of the lot. I found a spot in the shadows under a live oak and watched until he got out of the Porsche and went inside.

Now what?

I pulled down my visor and checked my reflection in the vanity light. This was not the face of a woman who could sidle up to Skintight inside the club and hope to learn anything about the guy. In my black cotton Dockers, striped shirt, and work shoes, I'd probably be mistaken for the cleaning woman.

Jeez. I hadn't come this far for nothing.

I fished around in my console and found some lipstick and a

beaded necklace. I put on the necklace and colored my lips rosy red. Removed my hair clip and finger-fluffed my hair. Contemplated my clothes for a second, undid a couple of shirt buttons, and decided that would have to do. I climbed out, feeling ridiculous.

I headed for the entrance, adopting the hip-swaying gait of two women entering ahead of me. A man at the door asked to see my ID, which I managed to show him without bursting into laughter. The pungent combination of alcohol and sweat hit me as I moved inside, glad for the dim lighting. The place buzzed with conversation— more like shouting over music blaring from the jukebox.

Standing on tiptoe, I looked for Skintight in the crowd. Beyond the center bar, couples gyrated on the dance floor, trying to put moves to Toby Keith and Willie Nelson's song about beer-drinking horses.

I spotted Skintight to the left of the dance floor talking with another man. He'd brought one of the white boxes in with him, and I figured they might be talking about whatever was inside. Maybe I could get close enough to learn something useful.

I caught the attention of a bartender and ordered a ginger ale so I wouldn't feel so conspicuous as I edged my way closer to the men. I needed a better conversation starter than "Come here often?" but no matter how I began with Skintight—*if* he'd talk to me—I couldn't imagine getting through the list of questions flooding my head. Questions I had a feeling might get me into trouble.

I stopped walking. This was stupid.

I looked toward the entrance and considered leaving. When I turned around, Skintight was on the opposite side of the dance floor and heading down a hallway. He disappeared through a door and swung it shut behind him. I started in that direction, thinking he'd entered the men's room and I could conveniently bump into him when he came out. But when I got closer I saw the door was marked OFFICE.

So maybe Skintight was Wildcatter Bill, and that was *his* office. Or maybe he was the manager. I didn't make him for a bartender— not driving that Porsche.

Whatever he was doing in there, this might be my chance to get a better look at the boxes he'd left in the car. I spun to head back the way I'd come, ignoring the stares of men seated at the bar until one beer-bellied man jumped off his stool in front of me. He towered over me, his eyes glazed, his expression more of a leer. Keith and Nelson had given way to Brooks & Dunn crooning "That Ain't No Way to Go."

"How 'bout a dance, darlin'?" the man said.

"No, thanks." I tried to sidestep him, but he blocked my path.

"Aw, c'mon," he said. "What's the hurry?"

"I need to leave. Please."

He showed no sign of budging, and everyone nearby seemed oblivious to us. He grabbed my forearm, and that's when I gave him a good kick in the shins with my steel-toed sneakers.

The man bellowed like a sick cow, and I didn't wait around to see what he tried next. I stooped over, making myself small to scoot in and around people and out the front door. My heart raced as I ran to the Durango, glancing over my shoulder every few seconds. No one appeared to be coming after me, and I didn't see anyone else outside.

I retrieved a flashlight from my glove box. The coast was still clear, so I hurried over to the Porsche and flicked on my light.

I peered into the car. Both remaining boxes sat askew on the passenger seat. The one on top was plain white, unmarked, but I could see that the bottom box had a label in the return address area. I moved forward a step, then back, then forward again and leaned around the windshield, adjusting my flashlight position to get a better look at the label. It read *The Bare Facts* with a Sugar Land P.O. Box underneath. What was that about?

I heard voices and jerked upright, lowering my flashlight arm quickly while stepping back so I wouldn't clunk the heavy metal on the Porsche's hood.

Hands clamped my waist.

I opened my mouth to scream, but one of the hands slapped over my mouth while a strong arm encircled my waist. A harsh "Shhh" sounded in my ear, and hot breath hit my cheek. I struggled, trying to loosen the man's grip, but he had me off balance, and I couldn't gain any ground.

My feet scrabbled for purchase on the pavement as he dragged me away from the Porsche and behind the oak tree's wide trunk. Beams from the parking lot's yellowish lamps filtered through the tree, pinning us with specks of light.

"Stop struggling," he said.

That voice. Familiar. I kept squirming.

"Who are you?" I mumbled around the hand clamped over my mouth.

"Poppy, I'm going to let go. Don't scream."

He knew me. I recognized the voice. The hint of citrus cologne. My cheek brushed Wayne McCall's chest as he eased me around to face him, then took his hand off my mouth.

"Sorry," he said quietly, "but—"

"You have some nerve," I interrupted.

He clamped his hand over my mouth again and said, "Quiet. I don't think you want him to notice you."

Curiosity overcame my urge to give McCall a good kick in the shins as he pointed toward the Porsche, about ten yards away. Skintight and the man I'd seen him with inside appeared to be conducting business. All three boxes were exchanged for a wad of cash. A drug deal?

I fought to catch my breath. "Do you know them?"

He shook his head. "Never saw them before."

I leaned against the tree trunk and studied McCall. He was wearing jeans with a form-fitting cinnamon brown golf shirt that I knew even in this dim light matched his eyes perfectly. He looked different tonight with his hair slicked back. Running into him here seemed like a huge coincidence, but I didn't believe in coincidence. Had he followed me?

I turned my attention to the men who had wrapped up their business. The buyer took his boxes and went inside. We watched the Porsche until it roared out of the lot, then McCall took a few steps back and gave me a once-over.

"What are you doing here?" he asked.

I pushed away from the tree, not wanting to answer his question. "I could ask the same thing. What are *you* doing here?"

"It's business," he said.

"Oh, I get it." I raised my eyebrows. "Business. What, are you alphabetizing the liquor bottles behind the bar? Or does your 'business' have more to do with getting drunk and hitting on women?"

He scowled. "You're dead wrong."

"Whatever," I said.

"Why were you interested in that Porsche?"

I gave him my best fake smile. "Just checking the interior. Thought I might want to buy one."

He shook his head. "C'mon. That's not your style. Why are you here?"

"How do you know what's my style or what's not?" I said. "You don't *know* me."

"I'd like to," he said softly.

"Fat chance." I crossed my arms over my chest.

"Have it your way." He waited a beat, then touched my chin and turned my face toward his. "I don't think an attractive lady like you should be out alone at night. Houston can be dangerous."

Was he coming on to me, or was that a threat? He always sounded so damn sincere, and those eyes could lure a woman straight into a bad decision. I looked away, not wanting my defenses against McCall to crumble. "Yeah, well, Richmond isn't too safe these days either."

"Point taken," he said. "I still think you should head home and get some rest. You've had a hard week."

"Harder than most," I conceded. "Guess I'll leave you to your 'business.' I expect to be paid by Featherstone tomorrow, and I'll make sure you get your fair share."

"Fine," he said. "You need any more help, let me know. We worked well together."

"I guess."

We stood there awkwardly for a few seconds.

I cleared my throat. "Does your being here have anything to do with the murders?"

He shook his head, incredulous. "So you *do* think I'm involved. You're the one. I didn't believe it."

"Didn't believe what? Who?"

"You're the person who told the cops I'm involved."

"I didn't say that."

"Whatever you *did* say got me hauled in for questioning today. Apparently, right behind you and your son, and yet I told myself that was a fluke. Couldn't imagine the timing had anything to do with you. But it did, didn't it?"

I swallowed. "How do you know *we* were there?"

"I have friends, Poppy. People who respect me. People who don't find me threatening or believe I had anything to do with murder."

My face felt hot. "I didn't say you were threatening. They asked me questions about you, and I answered."

"I'd have loved to hear your answers, because you—not knowing *me* any better than I know *you*—managed to convince the police that I'm a suspect."

"I didn't mean—"

He touched a finger to my lips briefly. "I'm not a killer, Poppy."

I pushed his hand away. "What *are* you, exactly?"

He kept his eyes on mine. "I can't talk about that right now. I'm a good guy, but I see you don't believe that."

"I'm not sure what I believe."

McCall shoved his hands into his pockets and walked away from me, circling the tree. When he faced me again, his expression was stony.

"I meant it when I said I wanted to know you better," he said. "Sorry things didn't work out. Mail me a check for that work if you're too afraid to see me in person."

He turned and headed for the building.

Emotions swirled as I slumped against the tree, watching him walk away. Was he innocent, or was he playing me? He was obviously hiding *something*. Logic told me to stay far away from the man.

My emotions told me McCall might just be the nicest damn guy I'd met in a long time and that I'd just made a huge mistake.

Chapter Thirty

Sometime after midnight, I collapsed into a restless sleep. I dreamed of speeding after a Porsche and stalking a faceless killer on a golf course. A nightmare in which I stumbled upon Wayne McCall's dead body surrounded by boxes labeled *The Bare Facts* segued into a more pleasant dream about McCall's body—alive and barely clothed.

I sat bolt upright. *Good grief.* The last thing I needed was erotic dreams about McCall. The man was secretive and shifty, and I didn't dare trust him. I glanced at the clock—3:00 A.M. My world felt upside down, out of control. I couldn't focus, and no wonder. I hadn't checked my e-mails, reviewed my to-do list, or followed up with clients in days. Instead, I'd been chasing leads, trying to solve murders, thinking I could do Detective Troxell's job for her.

But for God's sake, somebody needed to figure out this mess. Until the perpetrator was caught and Kevin was cleared, I wouldn't be able to concentrate on marketing Klutter Killer and building the client base I desperately needed. I might run out of money and end up living on the street.

I threw back the covers, frustrated and wide awake. Now that I'd worked myself into a tizzy, I wouldn't fall asleep anytime soon. And what was wrong with my doing a little investigating, as long as I turned over all the facts and evidence I found to Troxell?

I rolled out of bed, pulled on a robe, and padded into my office to find Jett curled up in the desk chair. The cat stretched and yawned. He squinted at the bright light I'd turned on.

After hesitating a second, cringing at the thought of black hair plastering my chenille robe, I picked Jett up and settled into the chair with him in my lap. Stroking the cat and listening to his soothing purr, I thought about the question I'd raised earlier in the evening.

Who wanted Dawn Hurley dead? There were two people I could follow up with. Both had shown an interest in my organizing skills, but now was not the time to call Dawn's mother. I straightened abruptly, startling the cat. Jett streaked from the room, and I grabbed my tote to retrieve Allen Tate's business card.

I woke up my computer and typed his e-mail address into a new message. *Hmm. What to say?* I drummed my fingers on the desk and decided short and sweet was best.

I typed, *When we met, you expressed an interest in my organizing services. Although with this tragedy you may want to put the project on hold, I just wanted you to know that I'm available Friday—today— if you need me.*

After studying the message for a second, I clicked SEND, then sat back and felt a fresh wave of sadness over Dawn Hurley's untimely death. I allowed myself these morose thoughts for a few seconds before pulling up my incoming e-mails and deleting the junk that regularly floods my in-box. I then sent messages to former clients, asking them how their new and improved organized lives were working out and letting them know I could return if they'd run into any glitches. When I finished, I noticed a new e-mail—Allen Tate's response.

You're right. I do need help. The sooner the better.

I wrote back. *How does 9:00 A.M. sound?*

He answered quickly. *Perfect. You're a godsend. See you at nine.*

Guess I wasn't the only one who couldn't sleep.

On my way to Tate's office the next morning, I swung by Steve Featherstone's to make sure there were no loose ends he expected me to handle before he paid me. A Heritage Movers truck blocked the driveway. Men in orange T-shirts scurried back and forth, hauling furniture and packed boxes to the truck. The garage door was raised, and I noticed that only a few odds and ends of lawn equipment and tools remained inside. The ancient Impala was gone. Featherstone's rental car wasn't there either.

I strode toward the open front door anyway and found Annabelle Lake in the foyer, bent over a clipboard and checking off items on a list. The dining room and living room—formerly the artist's studio— were empty.

"Wow, you work fast," I said.

Annabelle looked up. "Only when forced, hon. He insisted the house had to be vacant by the weekend. Wants me to move the stuff off-site and wire him the money in LA after I sell it all for top dollar."

"Whatever the client wants, the client gets," I said. "That's my motto."

"You just missed the boss," Annabelle said, "but he left something for you." She headed for her leopard-print bag that sat in the dining room doorway. She wore a black pants suit today and looked somber and more haggard than the first time we'd met. When she put the clipboard down to grab her bag, I glanced at the paper attached.

"I see he made you a list too," I said.

"I didn't need any list." She waved a hand dismissively. "You know, he might be the fussiest man I've ever dealt with, but his money's as green as anybody else's, so who's complaining?" She reached into the bag and withdrew an envelope, handing it to me.

"He asked me to pass this on to you with his thanks."

I glanced inside at the wad of crisp green hundreds, then looked up at Annabelle and smiled. "Hope your job goes as smoothly as mine did."

"I expect it will," Annabelle said, "as long as I don't try to understand the man. Must have been *some* bad blood between him and his grandma. Hope my grandkids never feel that way about me. He told me to shred the pictures I found upstairs. Ripping them up will have to do." She indicated torn photos sitting on top of a filled garbage can.

He'd been collecting photographs the other day, and I'd assumed he wanted to keep them all. These were probably the ones I'd left after he'd emptied his bedroom.

"Like I said, whatever the client wants." I checked my watch. If I hurried, I could deposit this cash in the bank and still make it to my new job on time. Annabelle was busy instructing the movers, so I waved good-bye and went on my way.

I counted the money at a long red light and did some quick mental calculations. Featherstone had made good on his offer of a two-thousand-dollar bonus. I drove to the bank, grinning, and made my deposit.

The grin faded when I thought about paying McCall his share. Not because I didn't want him to have the money—God knew he deserved it—but I wasn't too keen on a face-to-face after our run-in the night before. Dropping off a check when he wasn't home felt like a wimpy way to handle the transaction, but that's just what I did.

Despite the detour, I arrived at Tate's office with minutes to spare. I entered through the front door, averting my gaze from the stairs where Dawn had met her end, and took the creaky elevator. I was eager to get to work on the new project, to lose myself in paper. Not only in hopes of finding some clue that might lead to the killer, but because bringing order to chaos always helped clear my head. I wanted those spiderwebs gone.

"Hallelujah," Tate said when I walked through the door of Dawn's office. He backed away from an extended file drawer that held folders bulging out like the excess weight of a stocky woman in a petite bikini. "You have no idea how glad I am to see you."

Taking in the mass of paper piled ankle deep around the lawyer's shoes, not to mention the nearly invisible desk, I could well imagine his relief.

"Klutter Killer to the rescue," I said.

Tate exaggerated wiping sweat from his forehead. "Good thing. I have clients due in less than an hour. George Prescott passed two days ago, and his kids expect to take control of their inheritance today. The probate process is quick but not that quick. For starters, I need to find the listing of assets George handed me six months ago. It's not in his file."

"I'll give it my best shot." I dropped my tote on top of papers stacked by the desk. "All I need to know is whether there's any rhyme or reason to—" I hesitated, glancing around the room. "I, um, don't want to undo something that's working."

"I don't know where *anything* is, if that's what you're asking," Tate said. "Feel free to start from scratch. If there was a method to Dawn's madness, I've yet to figure it out." He looked away, his mouth a grim line, as though he was ashamed of himself for speaking ill of the dead.

"You'd be surprised how many people work in an environment like this," I said to break the silence. "They always claim to know exactly where everything is."

The uneasy moment passed, and he turned to me. "I have a confidentiality agreement for your signature, if you don't mind. Drafted one for the temp coming in on Monday too. Do you have a contract for me before you get started?"

"Oh, right." I reached for my tote, but my brain was stuck on the confidentiality agreement. Did that mean I couldn't repeat anything I learned about Dawn while I was here? But Tate was already headed for his office, and I followed. While we were taking care of the paperwork, I asked him whether the police had come up with any leads on Dawn's murder.

"Nothing substantial," he said. "They're leaning toward the catchall 'random act of violence.' Guy wanders into the building. Dawn's in the wrong place, wrong time. I don't buy it."

"Me neither," I said. "Did they ask whether she had any enemies? Angry ex-boyfriends?"

"At least a dozen times until I felt like replying, 'Asked and answered.' Course, they wouldn't have received that very well, so I kept repeating my story. I hadn't seen or heard one unusual thing here at the office. No strangers hanging around. No weird phone calls. No disgruntled clients to my knowledge. Still don't buy the 'random' business, though."

I could have asked him a dozen more questions myself, but he probably wouldn't have received them very well. Especially not now, when he needed the Prescott documents in a hurry. My inquiries would have to wait.

"Any special instructions before I get started?" I asked.

Tate produced a client printout and explained his goal of boxing files for those he'd crossed off the list so all the current files could fit into the cabinets. He gave me a rundown of the customary documents that belonged in the client file—everything from a Last Will and Testament to forms I'd never heard of, like Proof of Heirship and Approval for Plan of Distribution that came along after the Testator's death.

I figured it would take me the day to sort and file loose papers and box the older files. The temp coming in next week could arrange documents within each active file so long as I got them into the proper place.

When Tate left me alone, I scanned the client list and spotted Steve Featherstone and Barton Fletcher next to each other near the bottom of page one and Aunt Millie on the third page. I wondered if Dawn knew details about Fletcher's estate he wouldn't want anyone else to know, but I'd have to work now and consider that later.

This wasn't the first time I'd faced a horribly messy office, but with a deadline looming, I felt edgy. For today I'd forego the OHIO—*only handle it once*—rule. I sat on the floor, grabbed the closest stack, and began sorting quickly, searching for the name Prescott.

The largest heap, documents related to other clients, grew quickly. A separate pile contained attorney-related stuff—flyers for conferences, letters from the State Bar, et cetera. Probably most would end up in the circular file, but I'd leave the decision-making to Tate.

I stacked everything personally related to Dawn—recipes printed from the Internet, greeting cards, and myriad lists and notes I assumed were in Dawn's handwriting—in the desk's kneehole. I wanted to stop and read her notes in the worst way but forced myself to press on with the paying job at hand.

When I came across a copy of Ida Featherstone's inventory, though, my curiosity couldn't be contained. One glance at the total of her bank accounts explained why Steve Featherstone had no problem handing out cash bonuses. He'd be living comfortably, if he wasn't already, with this inheritance, and that didn't even include the cash sale he hoped for on the house. He'd be a good catch for some lucky California girl.

A short while later I found the Prescott papers and hauled myself up from the floor to deliver them to Tate—minutes before he greeted three Prescotts and showed them into his office.

I took stock of what I'd accomplished so far. This was definitely the looks-worse-before-it-looks-better stage of the project. I wanted to nose around while Tate was occupied, but at the same time I wanted him to see a marked improvement when his meeting ended. I went down the hall to retrieve some banker's boxes from the storage closet Tate had showed me and heard raised voices coming from his office. I was glad I was out here instead of in there. So much easier to deal with paper.

I took the boxes into Dawn's office and lined them up near the file cabinets, quickly filled three of them with files earmarked for archiving. I filled another box with the pile I thought of as attorney junk mail. Then I plopped into Dawn's chair and gathered the heaps of paper covering the desk into two foot-high stacks in front of me.

For the most part, these papers were only more client documents for the to-be-filed mountain. I found a birthday list Dawn kept for people whose names I recognized from the client list. Several of those listed bore a line through their name and DECEASED printed out to the side. Depressing.

The original signed wills and other estate planning documents for Dawn and her mother were mixed in with everything else as if they were insignificant pieces of paper. I paged through the wills and found that Dawn left her estate to be divided between her mother and the brother Dawn had referred to as Little Joe. Similarly, Olive named Dawn and the brother as heirs. Nothing surprising there. I clipped the Hurley documents together and put them on the to-be-filed stack, even Dawn's health-care power of attorney, which served no purpose now. Even more depressing.

Amazing how Dawn turned this job into something enjoyable. It seemed she'd found a way to involve herself in the clients' lives and help people however she could. Had that knack led to her death?

I leaned forward to study the Post-it notes she'd stuck around the edges of her computer monitor. One grocery list. A Weight Watchers meeting schedule. Notes on top of notes with scribbled names and phone numbers. Mostly individuals, except for Becker Investigations with a 213 area code. I uncovered a neatly printed motto—*Today is the first day of the rest of your life.*

My eyes stung unexpectedly, and I blinked to keep from tearing up, then spotted a partially hidden paper with Janice's name next to a phone number that wasn't for New York City. Might be her new place in New Jersey—a number I was willing to bet Janice never shared with Aunt Millie.

The outside office door opened, and I jumped like a kid caught with her hand in the cookie jar. Steve Featherstone appeared in the doorway of Dawn's office and did a double take. He looked nice in a well-cut tweed jacket over charcoal slacks.

"What are you doing here?" he asked.

I smiled, slipping the note with Janice's number into my pants pocket. "Mr. Tate hired me to organize files. Thanks for your payment by the way. I appreciate it. Would you like a dated receipt?"

"That's not necessary." He glanced down the hall toward Tate's office. "I need to see my lawyer."

"He's with clients at the moment. Did you have an appointment?" I checked the clock. The Prescotts had only been here for thirty minutes. I doubted Tate would have set appointments so close together.

"This is urgent," Featherstone said. "Tate told me I could wrap everything up this week, and so far that's not happening. He needs to *make* it happen. I have a job to get back to."

"Right. Hmm." I could hear the voices coming from Tate's office, louder now. "I don't think this is a good time."

"He said he'd have some Letters Testamentary for me to pick up by now," Featherstone went on. "Tells me that's what I need to finish things up with the bank."

That wasn't a term I knew, and I hadn't noticed any documents with that title lying around. But Featherstone didn't look ready to take no for an answer. I stood and stepped over a pile of papers next to the desk. "I'll see if he's earmarked anything for you."

Featherstone glanced around the room. "Something tells me Tate's better off without that secretary, huh?"

I was about to retrieve Ida Featherstone's file from the cabinet, but his comment stopped me. Before I could speak, Featherstone raised his hands, palms up, and shook his head. "I apologize. That was horribly rude."

I forced a smile and bit back a comment. "Don't worry about it. I'll just check your grandmother's file."

I slid out the accordion file to check the contents and spotted a spiral-bound report with a red *Becker Investigations* logo on the front. Interesting, but before pulling out the report I noticed the name *Barton Fletcher* on the file and realized I'd pulled the wrong one. Reluctantly, I slid that file back and pulled the correct one, fatter than most.

I set Ida Featherstone's file on top of a box and paged through the contents, passing by handwritten letters, photos of her artwork, including one of the portrait that had gone missing, and many of the legal documents Tate had listed for me. Everything but the document Featherstone had come looking for.

"Sorry," I said. "It's not here."

"I can't wait any longer," he said. "Please interrupt him."

The voices coming from the lawyer's office still sounded angry, and I figured Tate might welcome an interruption. Featherstone followed me to the lawyer's door, literally breathing down my neck as I knocked and waited for a response. This morning was convincing me I never wanted to work full-time in an attorney's office.

Finally, Tate came to the door and excused himself from his meeting to speak with Featherstone. I gladly went back to Dawn's quiet office.

I moved the Featherstone file to the desk and began separating the legal documents from things that likely came from Ida Featherstone herself. It made sense that Tate would return the personal things to the client in closing out this file, but Steve Featherstone probably wouldn't be interested in anything except precisely what he'd come for.

Tate and Featherstone exchanged words in the hallway, speaking in blessedly civilized tones. Some of their conversation drifted my way, and I caught enough to learn that Tate had expected a call from the clerk's office when the Letters Testamentary were ready to be picked up. He would check on that as soon as the Prescotts left.

A minute later, Featherstone stuck his head in and said, "Thanks for the help."

"You're welcome." I looked up from my sorting, but the office door was already slamming behind him. So much for returning the personal documents today.

Tate walked in and looked around. "Good progress. You should take a break for lunch. I'm going back into the snake pit."

"You mean to the Prescotts?" I said.

He nodded. "I've been at this work a long time, but I never saw such backbiting, greedy kinfolk. Make a good advertisement for birth control—other than that, can't say much good about them." He headed back to his office.

Those were harsh words, but I couldn't disagree. The Prescotts were adult children who should know how to behave themselves better than this in the face of their father's death. It didn't take much to imagine one of them flying off the handle and doing something crazy like committing murder.

Dawn Hurley had undoubtedly dealt with plenty of unstable people in her years working for Tate. How foolish of me to think that coming here would help me narrow down the suspects. What I had now was a plethora of new possibilities.

Chapter Thirty-one

The dreary midafternoon sky threatened rain as I hurried into a Subway and ordered a foot-long meatball sandwich. Probably a zillion and one calories, but I was ravenous and needed all the energy I could get if I wanted to finish Tate's job today, which I absolutely did.

I'd worked straight through the lunch hour until I couldn't ignore my hunger any longer. Everything that needed boxing was boxed, and much of the filing was done. Tate had taken off at one when his grueling session with the backbiting siblings ended, leaving me the keys in case I went out and returned before he did.

As soon as he was gone, I pulled the Becker Investigations report from the Fletcher file, only to find that it had been misfiled and actually belonged to the Featherstone case. A quick read told me that Ida Featherstone, wishing to find her grandson, had hired the PI firm through Tate. The investigator located Steve living in LA, but not until shortly after Ida's death.

Thinking about the elderly woman who probably had wanted to make amends in her last days depressed the heck out of me, so I pulled the file of somebody I didn't like and probably couldn't feel sorry for if he paid me—Barton Fletcher. But Fletcher's file held nothing except customary estate-planning documents.

I made a quick pass through Dawn's desk drawers—packed with office supplies, makeup, grocery store coupons, and a variety of over-the-counter medicines. No surprises there. For all my snooping, I learned absolutely zip to help solve Dawn's murder. Maybe this afternoon would be different.

The sandwich shop was deserted except for a couple of guys in Office Depot shirts, and I chose the booth farthest from them. After eating a quarter of the sandwich to take the edge off my hunger, I pulled a handful of papers from my purse. One of my favorite mottos is, never find yourself sitting somewhere with nothing to do. So of course I simply *had* to bring a sampling of Dawn's notes with me to read over my late lunch.

Guilt twinged my conscience, but the papers would go straight back to Tate's office when I finished. What was the harm? I straightened the stack next to my tray and scanned pages as I ate, careful to avoid dripping sauce onto them.

Dawn was obviously a scribbler who jotted things down helter-skelter on whatever happened to be nearby rather than using an organized notebook or at least a tablet. A used envelope back held the message, *1/25, 8:35 A.M. Miriam Bentley. Correct bequests. S. Silver bracelet—to* Louise, *not* Louis. A note in the margin of an incoming letter read, *Pick up milk on way home.* Names and phone numbers were scratched every which way on scraps of paper.

Nothing struck me as particularly interesting until I realized I'd seen the name Sam several times. The most interesting reference said, *2/19, 11:17 A.M. Sam Becker. Found him. On location in Vancouver. Call me.*

On location. Three days ago. I wondered who it meant and what Tate was having investigated. I could wait and ask him, but I wasn't feeling very patient. Instead, I pulled out my cell phone and dialed the 213 phone number scrawled on the page.

A perky girl who sounded about sixteen answered, "Good afternoon, Becker Investigations."

"Hello, may I speak with Sam Becker please?"

"This is Sam."

After a brief hesitation where I tried to picture Sam as an adult, I introduced myself, then said, "I'm doing some work in Dawn Hurley's office."

"Hey, where is that girl?" Becker said. "As hot as she was to get this information, I've spent forever trying to reach her."

I blew out a breath. Sam Becker didn't know about Dawn.

"You one of her Hollywood groupie friends?" she asked.

That stopped me for a second, but I figured I'd play along and see where it led. "That's us, Hollywood groupies." I faked a laugh.

"You all keep me busy," Becker said. "Don't get many requests to check out the crew, though. Usually it's Brad or Harrison. You know."

"And this time?" I said.

Becker clammed up for a second, then said, "This is between me and Dawn."

"Dawn asked about one particular man?" I said, guessing.

"You don't know?"

"I know you called her about some guy on location in Vancouver."

"I'd better talk to Dawn. Is she there?"

Dawn didn't seem like a woman who'd have a crush on some Hollywood type. I hadn't seen any *People* or *Entertainment Weekly* magazines in her office—no screen saver of a movie star on her computer. The guy she knew with a connection to Hollywood—Steve Featherstone—was right here in town. Maybe she'd developed an interest in someone he'd talked about or someone he worked with.

Becker cleared her throat and repeated, "Is Dawn there?"

"No, but you could fax your report to the office."

"My report went out in the mail days ago," Becker said. "She didn't get it?"

"Wish I knew," I muttered, glancing around the Subway shop. The other customers were gone, and the place was as quiet as a tomb. The girl behind the counter was halfheartedly wiping the sandwich preparation area and probably hearing every word of my conversation.

"Can you hang on a second?" I said.

"Sure."

I quickly gathered the papers and shoved them into my purse, dumped my tray, and went outside, where a cold, misty rain had begun falling.

"Sorry about that." I crawled into the Durango and cranked the ignition and the heater. "I hate to be the one delivering this news. Are you sitting down?"

A short pause, then, "I am now. What's wrong?"

"Dawn was murdered day before yesterday."

Becker went quiet. When she spoke, her perkiness had vanished, and she squeaked out, "What happened?"

I gave her the short version, then said, "Under the circumstances, could you tell me what, exactly, Dawn asked you to do and what you learned?"

"You're not the client," Becker said, her voice stronger. "I can't do that."

"The police might need to talk with you," I said. "You mind if I give them your name and number?"

Becker's gulp came over the line. "They can contact Preston Becker. He's *the* Becker of Becker Investigations. I'm sorry, I need to go."

There was no chance I'd get more out of Sam, so I hung up, eager to return to Dawn's office and see if I could lay my hands on a second report. But my gas gauge was sitting precariously close to empty, and I decided to fill up now rather than after dark when I left the job.

I made a quick detour to Monty's Mobil on 762. Monty ran an honest car-repair facility, with the customers to show for it. Today was no exception, with cars stacked up outside each of his three drive-through bays. While my gas was pumping, I spotted Monty at one of the open garage doors. He pulled the collar of his denim jacket up against the rain and headed my way.

We exchanged pleasantries, then he said, "Got Millie's car 'bout ready to go. Soon's her new alternator comes in. Should be some-time tomorrow."

"Good," I said. "I'm sure she'll be glad to hear it."

"Tried to call, but no answer. Do me and her a favor?"

Odd. Monty usually kept to himself and never asked me for any-thing. "Okay," I said slowly. "What is it?"

"Got some stuff of hers I'd like you to take back home. I don't like to tempt the help."

I frowned. "What stuff?"

He chuckled. "You ever seen the inside of her trunk?"

"No, but I can imagine."

Monty shook his head. "We had to unload every bit of it 'cause she asked us to check her spare."

"And you want me to take everything with me?" I said, thinking that if his workers wanted anything from the trunk, we should let them have at it.

"Lord, no," Monty said. "Most of what she kept in there is, uh—"

"Junk?" I said.

He nodded. "Yup. Except for one box, and I don't like to keep valuables lying around here. Don't worry. It's not big."

The gas pump clicked off, and I quickly replaced the hose, screwed the gas cap back on, and yanked my receipt. The last thing I felt like dealing with right now was Aunt Millie's junk, but I followed Monty dutifully to the garage, where he handed me a battered Justin boot box.

"What's all this?" I peered inside the box at stacks of baseball cards, balls, and a red plastic bag filled with miscellaneous junk.

"Baseball memorabilia," he said. "Could be worth a pretty penny."

Yeah, right. Probably another box she'd picked up at a garage sale.

"Thanks, Monty. I'll make sure this gets back to Aunt Millie." She needed more junk in the house like she needed a hole in the head. I put the box into the back of my SUV and hightailed it out of there before he could ask me to take more of Millie's things off his hands.

I didn't want to waste any more time by running the box straight to Millie's, but on the way back to the law office, I picked up my cell and called her.

She answered on the first ring.

"I'm glad you called," she said after she heard it was me. "Janice is fixing lasagna for dinner, and I hoped you might join us too."

"Lasagna? That's a lot of work. Doesn't sound like Janice."

"You're telling me. She's still acting fishy, and I can't get a thing out of her. Maybe you can. At dinner."

"I can't come, Aunt Millie. I'm working at Allen Tate's office today, and I'll be there late."

"Come when you're finished. Wayne will be here."

"For dinner?" I'd successfully avoided thinking about Wayne McCall all day, and now she went and broke the spell.

"I ran into him when I went out for the mail and invited him."

"What was he doing? Staking out your mailbox?"

"No, silly. He's working at Lori Gilmore's house."

"Doing what?" I frowned at the memory of Gilmore prancing around outside in her skimpy robe.

"Fixing her fence," Millie said.

"I'll bet he's fixing the fence," I muttered.

"You sound jealous, dear."

"Not jealous, just skeptical."

"I can see him from the window," Millie said. "He's out there with his tools. Replacing slats in the fence. You should cut him some slack, Poppy. He really is a very sweet man."

"A man we know next to nothing about," I said. "But let's not get into that. I called to let you know I just left Monty's. He says your car should be ready by tomorrow."

"Wonderful."

I could hear pots and pans banging in the background.

"And he gave me a box to return to you," I said.

"Who? Monty?"

"Yes. With some baseballs and stuff inside."

"Okay," Millie said. "I hate to cut you off, dear, but Janice is messing up my kitchen. See you at dinner." She hung up.

I pulled the phone away from my ear and stared at it. Someone else messing up Millie's kitchen? That was a joke. And if they waited for me before starting dinner, they'd be waiting a very long time. I dropped my phone onto the console and thought about McCall and Gilmore. Yes, he seemed like a sweet guy on the surface, but there was something shady about McCall. Maybe he hadn't been staking out Millie's mailbox, but I had a feeling he was in that neighborhood for a more interesting reason than fixing any old fence.

Chapter Thirty-two

I stewed about the McCall/Gilmore situation all the way back to Tate's office. Logically, McCall's activities were none of my business, but when people are being murdered, logic flies out the window. Everyone seemed suspicious to me these days, and McCall was cozying up to my family. His behavior concerned me even if Aunt Millie would adopt the man before she'd consider him guilty of anything worse than running a yellow light.

I rode the lethargic elevator up to Tate's floor, tapping my foot impatiently the whole way. Maybe I *could* get out of here in time for the dinner festivities. See if I could figure out what McCall had up his sleeve. But my curiosity was hopping to find out what Becker Investigations' second report was all about. First things first.

Tate had made it back to the office before me, and he stood next to Dawn's desk with his foot propped on a double-wide briefcase and a phone to his ear.

"I understand," he said into the phone, "but there's nothing to tell."

He paused to listen, ignoring me as I walked around the desk and put my purse on the floor. I pulled out the papers I'd taken and surreptitiously returned them to the desktop. Tate seemed oblivious, so I began to search the file drawers for another spiral-bound report from the PI.

"My client conversations are privileged," Tate said. "I can't and won't discuss them."

I glanced at the lawyer. He pushed his glasses up to rest on his forehead and rubbed his eyes with his free hand like a man who hadn't slept in days.

"There's no connection." He checked his watch. "Look, Detective, I have a client on his deathbed waiting to see me this afternoon." A pause. "If anything relevant comes to mind, you'll be the first person I call." Another pause. "Yes. Thank you."

Tate dropped the phone into its cradle and straightened, rolled his head as if to loosen tight neck muscles, and looked at me.

"That was Detective Troxell," he said.

I slid a file drawer shut. "Any progress?"

He shrugged. "She claims new information has come to light, but she won't tell me anything. Yet she expects me to divulge personal information about my clients. Not going to happen."

"Is she accusing one of your clients?" I asked.

"She's on a fishing expedition, plain and simple." Tate went to a file cabinet and extracted a fat folder. "Benson and Stabler would have closed this case by now."

"With the help of the *Law & Order* script writers," I said. "Not a fair comparison."

"True." He opened his briefcase and attempted to stuff the file inside. "I *do* have a client waiting for me. Two, actually. Not enough hours in the day, but I shouldn't complain about business being good."

"Which clients did Troxell ask about?" I said.

Tate removed some folders and envelopes from the briefcase and gave me a stern glance. "I think the detective would agree that that's not something we should discuss."

"Sorry," I said, watching his unsuccessful attempts to force the file into the case. "Let me help."

I knelt by the briefcase and quickly rearranged the contents, then easily slid the folder into place. "Hope you don't need to fit any more in there."

"No. My second meeting is a quick stop at the courthouse. I'm still trying to get Steve Featherstone everything he needs."

I nodded, my mind on the Becker report. I didn't think Tate would appreciate my nosing in by calling the PI myself, so I skirted the issue. "Before you go, I saw a note about a second investigation done by that California PI firm, but I couldn't tell which case to file it in."

Tate closed up the briefcase and stood. "Becker Investigations?"

"Right," I said.

"There's no second case, only the one. They worked on Featherstone."

"Oh." I tried to sound casual. "The note seemed to reference a different investigation."

"I hired them one time," Tate said. "Cost Ida Featherstone a good bit too. I wouldn't call on them again unless something urgent came up."

I hesitated. There was no way to ask if he knew anyone in Vancouver without giving away my true purpose.

"I need to get out of here," Tate said. "By the way, you've done a superb job. More than I could have hoped for. Why don't you take off early?"

"I've got a good couple hours left in me." I forced a smile. "I want everything tidy for Monday when your temp comes in."

"Well, don't kill yourself," he said. "They lock up downstairs at seven, so—"

I waved him off. "Go to your meeting. I'll be fine."

He didn't argue, and when the front office door slammed behind him, I jumped into action. That report had to be somewhere, and I was betting that it contained something important. Urgent, even. According to Sam Becker, Dawn had been eager to get the results, and that knowledge made me even more anxious. Sure, I could call Troxell and tell her what I'd learned. And she'd probably think I was nuts—or trying to draw attention away from myself and my son.

No, I'd rather have something to *show* her.

I explored the file cabinets thoroughly. No report.

Emptied Dawn's desk drawers. Nothing.

Lay on the floor and looked at the underside of her desk, in case she'd taped the report there the way I'd seen done in the movies. Nada.

I went into Tate's tidy office and stood inside the door, guilt nagging me as I scanned the room. I *had* signed the confidentiality agreement, but this was an extraordinary circumstance. Tate might have the report in here without realizing it. The document might hold important details. I *had* to look.

I spied a small pile of unopened mail on Tate's credenza and crossed the room quickly. I leafed through the envelopes. Nothing from Becker. I checked the bookcase and inside Tate's spectacularly neat desk drawers. I folded my arms over my chest and surveyed the lawyer's office. Peeked behind every one of the dozen certificates decorating his wall. Checked the backs of all the office art-work. No dice.

One more room to inspect—the small kitchen—before calling Olive Hurley to ask if her daughter had received any unusual mail at home.

But luck was with me in the kitchen. A thermal lunch sack sat on a cupboard shelf next to cans of Campbell's Chunky Soup and pack-ets of instant oatmeal. The bright blue nylon bulged unnaturally, and my heart raced as I opened the Velcro top. And there was the report, rolled up next to a Hostess cupcake.

Goose bumps prickled my arms as I pulled it out and plopped into a chair at the miniature dinette table to read.

Tate had been right. Becker hadn't worked on two cases, only one. The Featherstone case. I already knew the initial investigation had occurred months ago, before Ida Featherstone's death. This report was dated last week. Client name—Dawn Hurley. Billing address—her home. Status—rush. My conscience eased up a bit. I hadn't signed any confidentiality agreement with Dawn.

The narrative described Sam Becker's visit to Ventura Pictures in LA, where she hoped to track down and meet with Steve Feather-stone.

I stopped reading for a second. Why was she looking for Feath-erstone last week? He'd been here in Richmond, hadn't he?

My eyes scanned quickly ahead. Becker met with Steve Feather-stone's immediate superior and learned about Featherstone's work on a movie being shot in Canada.

Next stop Vancouver, British Columbia, where Becker spoke with the manager of the hotel housing the movie's camera and lighting crew. They'd holed up in the hotel for five bad-weather days before production went on hiatus. To the best of the manager's knowledge, Featherstone was among those headed home for the break after his checkout on the twelfth.

These dates were screwy. And this little investigation with the travel to Canada must have cost a bundle more than the first one. Dawn must have had a darn good reason to put Becker up to this.

I sat back and stared at the wall, chewing my lower lip. Tried to think like Dawn, the people person, the secretary who asked a lot of questions, kept up with clients' personal lives, cared about them when no one else did. She had sent the PI on a mission to find Steve Featherstone. Who had already been found.

I bent over the report again and scanned through to the end. Found a reference to enclosed photos and located them in the lunch bag's slim outer pocket.

A chill ran up my spine as I studied the photos. Bile rose in my throat. I knew this man, though he'd looked a hell of a lot worse when I'd seen him. I shoved my chair back and fled down the hall to Dawn's office, clutching the pictures. I opened the drawer holding the Featherstone file and yanked the accordion folder off the shelf so fast that I lost my grip. Papers spilled out, across the floor.

I dropped to my knees and shuffled through them, frantic to find the photos I'd seen earlier in the day. There was a resemblance, sure. Enough to get by, but not identical.

Facts clicked into place.

The missing family portrait.

Photographs destroyed.

The sense of urgency.

The bird-watching outing.

The peanut allergy.

Steve Featherstone biting into Aunt Millie's fresh, thick peanut butter cookies without a care in the world.

The dead man in her garage.

My hands slid across pages, throwing documents aside. Where on earth were those pictures?

My teeth chattered. Blood pounded at my temples. Hard and loud, but not loud enough to cover the metallic click that sounded behind me.

I jerked upright and turned.

Steve Featherstone, or whoever the hell he was, stood in the office doorway, a gun in one hand and a fistful of pictures in the other.

"Looking for these?"

Chapter Thirty-three

I stared at the man I thought I'd known. My heart thudded so hard, the building seemed to vibrate. He knew I was on to him. Fear coursed through my body, but I was ticked off too. And that's the part of me that couldn't keep quiet.

"I don't believe we've met," I said. "My name is Poppy Cartwright, and yours is . . . ?"

"Shut your mouth," He strode across the room and snatched the photos from my hand, then stuffed them into his pants pocket along with those he'd already confiscated from the file. He eyed the folders strewn on the floor. "Put this mess back together. Hurry it up."

"Why bother?" I forced myself to maintain eye contact.

"Because you'll be leaving this place exactly as Tate would expect you to leave it, Miss Neat Freak."

I gulped. "And then what?"

He grinned. "Then we'll take a little trip over to the Brazos River."

My insides churned as I stared down the barrel of his gun. Likely the weapon that he had used to murder the real Steve Featherstone. This couldn't be happening. I thought of dying, of never seeing my son again.

"I'm in the middle of a job here," I said. "I can't just leave."

Stupid. Weak. Why couldn't I think of a way out?

He grabbed my shoulder and squeezed, sending a bolt of pain down my arm. "I *said,* clean it up."

"Ow!" I pushed his hand away. "Give me a chance."

With my heart in my throat, I swept the papers from the file into a heap. Tears filled my eyes. I glanced at my purse next to the desk. My cell phone was inside, a mere six feet away, but it may as well have been a hundred.

Think, Poppy. Stall.

213

"Mr. Tate went to get those Letters Testamentary for you at the courthouse," I said. "Shouldn't you be there?"

"I was. Clerk's office didn't have them ready yet, and now they're closed until Monday. Unfortunately for you."

I swallowed. "Then he'll be back here shortly."

He smiled at me as if I was mentally challenged. "I saw him head out of town. Time he shows, we'll be long gone." The smile faded. "Move it."

I stuffed papers into the accordion folder, knowing what he really meant. *He'd* be gone. *I'd* be dead. Just like Dawn, whose frequent visits and strange lines of conversation made perfect sense to me now. If only she'd told someone about her suspicions before it was too late.

I got to my feet, shaking, holding the file in front of me. My only smidgen of hope was that he wouldn't shoot me here. Wouldn't look good for another body to be found in this building so soon. At least not before he had his money.

"Dawn saw through your charade immediately, didn't she?" I said.

"Shut up," he said. "You don't know anything."

"Apparently you think I do, or you wouldn't be threatening me."

"If that nosy secretary had left me alone, things would have been quick and simple. Same for you. I paid you good money to do a job, so why did you have to come nosing around here?"

"I'm working for Mr. Tate. The same way I worked for you. I thought you appreciated my help, Steve."

His face went as cold as a statue's. "I'm not Steve, and you know it."

"So do the police," I lied. "You won't get away with this."

He laughed, a rude cackle. "I had that line once in a film. Should have been my grand debut, but the script was riddled with cliches. Got one star and didn't deserve that."

"You're an actor?"

"You've never heard of the great Mason Teale?" He used a King-Arthurish tone, then lowered his voice to Dustin Hoffman's *Rain Man,* cocking his head and shaking it. "Not surprising. No one has. No one."

His sudden change of persona raised gooseflesh on my arms. "You decided to step in and play the part of Steve Featherstone. Heck of a performance."

He snapped out of performer mode and waved the gun at me. "Put that file away. Let's go."

I turned to the cabinets, my thoughts racing as I slid the file onto the shelf. How could I stop him without a weapon? The car keys in my pocket were no match for Teale's gun. The best I could come up with was to heave the heavy file at him and make a break for the door.

The outer office door slammed open as if it had heard my thoughts, followed by a woman's voice.

"Poppy? Are you here?"

"Janice," I shouted. "I'm busy. Leave me alone."

Teale raised the gun menacingly and stepped behind the door, shielding himself from view. He sliced a finger across his mouth, a zip-your-lip signal.

I nodded quickly, grateful that he wasn't bent on murdering everyone in sight, and stepped into the doorway. Teale's eyes peered at me though the crack by the hinges. If I tried running now, he might panic and shoot us both. Not a good idea.

Janice stomped down the hallway toward me, her eyes as wild as a drug addict's. "Don't tell me no. You hand my things over right this minute."

"What are you talking about?" I fought to keep hysteria out of my voice. "And what are you doing here?"

"Taking back what's mine." She came at me, palms first, and I could see she planned on bulldozing past me.

"Don't come in here." I grabbed the doorjamb, arms outstretched to barricade the entrance.

"Don't tell me what to do." She shoved me with both hands, trying to break through. "You have no right to my personal belongings."

"What belongings?" I shook my head to clear the cobwebs.

Before I had a chance to respond to her shoves, Janice raised a hand and slapped me hard on the cheek.

I stepped back involuntarily as my hands flew up to protect my face. From the corner of my eye I saw Teale making a rolling motion with his free hand. Hurry this up or else.

But Janice had other ideas. She marched past me into the office, looking around as if she expected what she'd come for to jump out at her. "That box is worth a small fortune. Where is it?"

"We have bigger problems than any stupid box," I said, holding my cheek.

"You have no idea what—" Janice whirled and stopped at the sight of Teale behind the door.

She stared at the gun. "What—what—?" She looked at me, eyes wide.

Teale came forward and grabbed her arm, shoving his weapon into her side.

"Ladies," he said in a jovial tone, "this is your unlucky day." Keeping the gun trained on us, he backed up to the desk and grabbed my purse. "You, Klutter Killer, douse the lights. We're out of here."

"Leave us," I said. "Go. We won't say anything."

"Yeah, right," he said.

Janice emerged from her stupor and glared at me as if I was the bad guy. "What the hell have you done?"

"Me?"

"This is unbelievable," she screeched. "I came over here to get what's rightfully mine, and—"

"Shut up," Teale said. "We're leaving, and you'll both keep your traps shut. You act like we're friends out for a Friday night. Got that?"

"I'm not budging." Janice folded her arms over her chest. "Whatever problems you two have has nothing to do with me."

"It does now." He waved his gun toward the door.

Janice and I exchanged a glance, but neither one of us moved.

Teale fixed us with an evil eye that could have won him an Academy Award. "You ladies need to think of Miss Millie. She could get hurt. Badly hurt."

Janice stepped toward him. "How dare you threaten my mother?"

I grabbed her arm. "We'll do whatever you say."

Janice's wrath faded as we left the law office ahead of Teale and walked down the empty hallway. He directed us to the stairwell, and we'd descended one flight when Janice found her voice.

"If I'm about to die, I sure as hell wish one of you would have the decency to tell me why I'm dying."

"Because you *had* to come for some stupid box," I said. "What's that all about anyway?"

"Mother told me you picked it up," she said.

It took my brain a second to catch up and remember what Monty gave me at the service station. "Oh, that's out in the Durango."

"And a fat lot of good it will do me now."

"Shut up," Teale said. "Keep walking."

We were crossing the very spot where Teale had murdered Dawn, and I felt numb, unable to devise any way to gain an advantage. He was stronger than both of us put together and bent on getting his hands on the Featherstone money. And who could forget the gun?

He steered us out through the stairwell exit leading straight to the small parking lot behind the building. The rush of cool night air heightened my panic as I noted the only vehicles in sight—mine, Teale's rental, and a battered Civic. Janice must have parked out front.

One lone pole light cast a dim glow on the asphalt. Downtown Richmond didn't have any nightlife, and everyone who worked in the vicinity had taken off for the weekend. Little traffic noise came from the main drag running through town. I doubted the Civic belonged to a conscientious security guard who would rush to our aid.

I glanced over my shoulder at Teale, who moved close behind Janice. If anyone saw us, the fact that he had my purse slung over his shoulder might draw attention even if they didn't see the gun he held inches from her back.

"You've piqued my interest in this box that's worth a fortune," he said. "Let's take a look."

Janice stopped in her tracks and turned to stare him down. "You can't be serious."

Teale scowled and raised the gun hand as if she'd said, "Over my dead body."

"For God's sake, Janice, let him look." I quickened my step, glad for any interruption of Teale's plan, and pulled out my keys. Hit the unlock button. In a perfect world, I would take Teale down with a karate kick, throw Janice into the vehicle ahead of me, and we'd take off before he could recover.

That wasn't about to happen here.

"The box is in back." I moved straight to the tailgate door, then unlatched and lifted it in one fluid motion. I fumbled with the keys for my miniature flashlight and flicked it on to better illuminate the interior.

"You don't have to be so freaking helpful," Janice said.

Teale kept the gun on her. "Show me what you've got in the box, Mouth."

"Show him," I said, meeting her eyes with a we've-got-to-do-*something* expression. My fingers felt for the panic button on the underside of my keyless-entry doodad. Setting it off might help us or might get us killed.

Janice took the lid off her precious box, muttering, "Came here to keep this from one creep, now I'm giving it to another."

I cringed, expecting Teale to crown her with the gun. He put my purse down beside the box and stepped closer, drawn by the baseballs inside.

"Autographed?" he said, as if he were planning to make a bid.

"Of course," Janice said smugly. "Babe Ruth's in there somewhere."

I could almost see the dollar signs flashing before Teale's eyes and took advantage of the distraction to stretch my free hand toward my purse strap. I needed my phone.

Janice reached into the box and latched onto the red plastic sack inside, then elbowed the cardboard corner hard. Balls spilled out onto the pavement.

Teale crouched and grabbed at them.

Janice raced around the SUV, the red plastic waving from her hand.

Teale lifted his gun arm, taking aim at Janice.

I hit the alarm button, setting off a blaring horn and flashing headlights.

He ducked, startled, but before he could turn the gun on me, I grabbed the tailgate and with all my strength smashed the heavy door down on his head.

Teale's legs buckled, and he fell to his knees, moaning and holding his bloody temple.

Get the phone.

I reached for my purse and jumped back when Teale made a grab for my leg. I got the purse, but my keys fell to the pavement. Teale lunged at me again, but his movements were weak. I slugged him with my purse, and he fell to the ground. That wouldn't last.

Forget the keys.

I took off running, expecting to feel a bullet in the back. Janice was nowhere in sight. I sprinted across the lot and down the sidewalk beside the law office building, chest heaving. Rounded the corner to the front sidewalk.

And saw Wayne McCall only yards away, running toward me.

He held a gun too. I froze and screamed, my brain instantly connecting McCall to Teale. They were in this together. McCall would drag me off to the Brazos River and toss me in like fish food. Or he'd take me back to Teale, and they'd use me for target practice.

I was trapped. Teale behind me, McCall ahead.

He closed the distance between us quickly. When he reached out for me, I darted away. But he was faster, stronger, and managed to wrap his arms around me and pull me close. He backed us up to the alcove of the building entrance, murmuring, "It's okay. I called the cops. You're safe, Poppy."

Sirens sounded in the distance, and for some crazy reason I believed him. I allowed myself to rest against him, my heart pounding wildly, for the thirty seconds it took the police to show up. And did they ever show up—with more sirens and flashing lights than I'd ever seen in one place. I decided it must be a slow crime night in Fort Bend County, but I was glad to see every blessed officer.

McCall and I were separated in the flurry of activity that followed as the police apprehended Teale and stuffed him into the back of a cruiser on my word that he had tried to kill me and Janice. When I added that he had already committed two murders and gave them facts and evidence to back up my claim, they put in a call to Troxell.

Half an hour into the commotion, McCall finished talking with the cops and told me good-bye. He had important business to tend to, or so he said. I was peeved that he felt the need to rush off. And then immediately I felt guilty. I was still stressed, yes, and would have welcomed him comforting me, but for McCall to leave like that? Obviously, this business was even more important than he'd indicated.

Shortly after he'd gone, the cops dismissed me too, with a warning to not leave the county, that Detective Troxell would be contacting me shortly. I couldn't very well leave with the Durango blocked in by a dozen police cars. I didn't want to go over there anyway. Teale was staring me down through the cruiser's window. Maybe he wasn't a well-known actor, but tonight he had the role of psycho killer down pat.

Janice, who'd answered her share of questions and obviously been dismissed too, waved me in her direction. "C'mon, I'm parked out front. Give you a ride."

"Yeah, thanks."

We walked side by side toward her car, and I felt like crying, or hugging her, or both. We'd come close to losing our lives. I'd never felt so glad to be with my cousin and thought this might be a turning point in our relationship. Janice was uncharacteristically subdued, and I figured she must be having the same feelings.

Teary-eyed, I glanced over at her.

She gave me the usual smug expression, a Janice classic, and said, "Good thing I came along tonight to help you out of that jam."

Chapter Thirty-four

 $\mathbf{B}$ y the time Detective Troxell showed up at Aunt Millie's to give us an update, we'd moved into the dessert-fest phase of a late supper. Millie had baked from the time Janice left to come after me until we returned to her doorstep at around nine. Cheesecake, deep-dish apple pie, and fudge brownies sat on the table before us.

McCall was a no-show, though Millie had invited him. Kevin was there, and I wondered what special communication pipeline Millie had to reach him when I could never get a lead on the boy. Maybe he'd sniffed out the food and showed up without an invitation.

A trickle of dread slipped down my spine when Troxell stepped into the dining room and shook Kevin's hand. I knew he was off her radar now, but I still felt nervous having them in the same room after all that had happened. That feeling wouldn't fade quickly.

"Have some dessert, Rae." Millie pulled out a chair for the detective. "There's plenty."

"I can see that." Troxell sat and made a show of checking out the selection. "What? No chocolate cake?"

"Not tonight." I picked up the plate of brownies. "This is tonight's chocolate fix."

"That'll do."

Janice, quiet after inhaling three pieces of cheesecake, nodded hello to Troxell and sipped her coffee.

Troxell placed two brownies on her plate, took a bite, then checked out me and Janice in turn. "You ladies holding up okay? Kind of a rough night."

"We'll live," said Janice.

"You're fine," Millie said, "thank God. And thank God I had the sense to send Wayne after you."

"We would have been fine without him," I said, wishing that his absence didn't bother me.

Troxell swallowed a bite of brownie and looked at Millie. "What made you send him over there?"

Millie looked sheepish, then glanced at Janice. "Seems silly now, but Janice was pretty hot when she left here to go after Poppy. I was afraid the girls might get into it. They've been this way their whole lives."

Janice rolled her eyes. "We're not twelve, Mother."

"Then quit acting like you are," Millie said. "But let's not discuss this now. I'm sure Rae came over here for more important reasons."

Troxell wiped her mouth with a napkin and addressed me. "We can formalize this in the morning, have you and your cousin come down and make official statements. You know the routine."

I nodded. "Unfortunately, I do."

"Since you gave us what we needed to solve the murders, I didn't want to keep you waiting that long before you got some answers," she went on. "Everything you reported fits with what I've learned. I talked with that PI, Becker. Along with some help from my LAPD contact, we put the story together."

I felt myself leaning forward, relieved. Kevin was absolutely in the clear.

"Teale and Featherstone worked and lived together," Troxell went on. "They rented a pricey LA apartment. Featherstone spent most of his time working on location, leaving the place to Teale, who, according to a neighbor, couldn't seem to find work. He spent his time lounging around the pool, feeling sorry for himself."

"Until he spotted a golden opportunity to make a fortune by doing next to nothing," I said.

"Right." Troxell sipped her coffee. "Tate had the PI search for Mrs. Featherstone's heir. Becker found Teale holed up at the apartment leased in Featherstone's name. Sent Tate the first report complete with pictures of the man she *believed* was Featherstone."

"So Teale intercepted the letter to Featherstone about the inheritance," I said, "while Steve was out of town. He must have known Steve hadn't been in contact with his grandmother since he was a kid."

"I believe that's exactly what happened," Troxell said. "I sure would like to know what went down after Steve showed up here in

Texas—and where. Teale's not talking. Yet. Bet we can squeeze the details out of him before it's all over."

"He had no way of knowing how close Dawn Hurley was to the clients," I said. "How much she already knew about Steve from his grandmother, that she would spot an imposter."

"Right," Troxell said.

"Oh, dear Lord." Millie, who'd been topping off coffee cups, sank down into her chair. "Dawn mailed the letter that ended up getting her killed."

Kevin, who had been listening raptly, took the coffeepot from Aunt Millie and placed it back on its burner.

"She was a nosy little, uh, person," Janice said. "Called me a few times."

Millie looked at Janice, her brows furrowed. "Why did she call *you*?"

"Claimed she'd sent me mail that came back to her. Said she needed a new address."

"Do you *have* a new address?" Millie asked.

Janice looked down at her plate and said nothing.

"Honey?" Millie prodded.

"Oh, hell, I give up." Janice sat up straighter. "Yes, if you must know. I have a new address. I live in New Jersey in a little hovel of an apartment, and I don't work on Wall Street anymore either."

Troxell and I exchanged a glance. Kevin, leaning against the kitchen counter, calmly watched the conversation like a spectator at a football game.

Millie swallowed. "What about Conner?"

"He's not with me in New Jersey, Mother. God, no. He wouldn't *think* of living in New Jersey. He left me for another woman, and he arranged for me to lose my job, and my life is a big fat lie. He's filed for divorce, okay? Now are you happy?"

Millie held a hand to her chest. "Janice, honey."

"Don't 'honey' me." Janice pushed her chair back and seemed ready to run from the room.

I caught her arm. "Don't do it. Your mother doesn't care about your job or your lousy apartment or your bank account. She cares about *you,* and nothing you could tell her is going to make her love you any less." I loosened my hold and lowered my voice. "Janice, we're family. We're sorry to hear what's happening to you."

Janice slumped into her chair. Her complexion had reddened. I sensed she was holding back a gallon of tears that she'd never let flow in front of us.

"Does this have anything to do with those baseballs and stuff?" I asked.

She glared at me. "What if it does?"

I shrugged. "Just curious."

Troxell said, "I have those baseballs in a sack out in the cruiser. Almost forgot about them."

"I don't care about those stupid balls," Janice said.

I frowned. "I thought you had a ball signed by Babe Ruth."

"No way," Janice said. "Those were Conner's from his high school team."

"Then what was the big deal?" I asked.

Janice was quiet for a second. Then she pulled the red plastic sack from her jacket pocket. "*This* was the big deal."

"What's in there?" Millie said.

"Nobody in this room breathes a word of this to Conner," Janice said, staring each of us down.

Millie and I made *x*'s over our hearts.

"Don't even know the dude," Kevin said.

"Me neither," Troxell added.

Janice took a deep breath. "They're World Series pins," she said. "Conner's grandfather was with the press back in the twenties. They issued these press pins to the series every year. He's got a couple dozen of them."

"So?" I said.

"So he's trying to screw me out of a fair settlement, and I just found a way to even the deal a little. These little babies are worth two to three thousand each."

"This is what you were after when you came to town in such an all-fired hurry?" No way was I going to utter the words *separate property* and risk being clubbed over the head. Besides, I didn't know whether New York or New Jersey cared about community versus separate property.

Janice hesitated, then said, "I came for these and to visit Mother."

Millie burst into tears. Janice went to her mother and wrapped her in a hug.

Yeah, right, I thought. *You came for the goods, that's all.* But I'd never speak those words aloud. This was between mother and daughter. I signaled Kevin and Troxell that we should give them some privacy, and the three of us left the dining room.

"Wow," Kevin said when we were out of earshot. "That was like watching a movie."

Troxell said, "Think I'll skip out on the end of the show."

"And I'll skip moving to LA," Kevin said.

"What?" I stared at him.

"Oh, yeah," he said. "What I wanted to talk to you about the other day? Never mind."

"Never mind what?"

"I was gonna ask for money to go live out there for a while. Play in a band, see if I could make the big time."

"That's what all the phone calls I missed were about?" I said.

"Yeah." He bit his lower lip and shook his head. "Idea doesn't sound so hot now after hearing about this Teale dude. Life's tough out there. Tough enough here, but I'd rather take my chances in Texas."

"I'm glad." I gave him a hug.

He gave me an honest-to-goodness hug in return, something I'd been missing for about the last ten years, and said, "It's a good thing they have that dude behind bars, or I'd kick his butt for threatening my mom."

"We have Teale under control," Troxell said, "and I don't think he's going anywhere for a long time. Maybe never."

"Cool." Kevin smiled at Troxell, then asked me to tell the others good night. He was going to chill at his friend's place—a friend he assured me was male, since he had no intention of getting involved with another woman until Grayson was out of his system.

Troxell and I watched him drive away as we walked to her car.

"He's a good kid," she said.

"Yeah, he really is."

"Guess we've cleared up more than one mystery tonight, huh?"

"We did, but there's one left."

Troxell stopped walking. "What could be left?"

"How does Wayne McCall fit into all this?"

"He doesn't fit in at all," Troxell said. "He had nothing to do with these cases."

"But you investigated him."

"Him and everyone else. I had to."

"What's his story? Where's he from? Why's he here?"

"Not my story to tell," Troxell said. "You'll have to ask the man yourself."

"But you know something?"

"All I'm saying is, it's not police business."

Not police business. Huh. Well, I was tired of waiting for explanations. A lot of questions had been answered tonight, but I wanted *all* the answers, and I wanted them now.

Troxell agreed to take me to pick up my SUV, and from there I headed straight for McCall's apartment.

Chapter Thirty-five

I stood on the third step down from the landing outside McCall's door. What if he thought I was butting into his life, fishing for information that was none of my business? Not to mention I must look a mess after surviving a near-death experience and sitting through that traumatic dinner with my relatives. I hadn't even checked a mirror, combed my hair.

But, darn it all, I hadn't come this far for nothing.

I opened my purse and reached for a lipstick. The apartment door opened, and a glimmer of light from inside hit the landing.

So much for the lipstick.

McCall stood framed in the doorway, holding a suitcase. He looked sexy, as usual, in jeans, a gray V-neck sweater, and black alligator boots. His hair was wet, as if he'd come straight from the shower. Made *me* feel even grungier. I could see past him into the apartment, which was stripped of the books and personal belongings I'd seen strewn around the other day.

"Um, hi," I said casually.

"Poppy. What a surprise." He put the suitcase down and approached me. "Are you all right?"

"I'm fine. Better than I was this morning." I wiped sweaty palms on my pants legs, irritated with myself for feeling nervous. "Teale is in jail. Troxell says they have enough on him to make the charges stick."

"That's great news," he said. "Come on in. You've had a hard night."

"Yes, I have. That's why I need to get on home. Wanted to update you first."

"Don't run off. By the way, thanks for the check. Not a bad profit for a couple days' work."

I frowned, considering for the first time that I'd accepted payment from a killer. "Not bad, if you don't mind tainted money."

"I wouldn't say it's tainted," McCall said, "but if you want to give the money back . . ."

"I don't *want* to, but the inheritance wasn't Teale's to spend. I wonder who's next in line now that Featherstone is gone."

"We can talk to the lawyer about that later. C'mon in." He took my arm and drew me up the last stairs.

"A few minutes, that's all." But I planted my feet outside the threshold. Eyed the suitcase. "Are you moving out?"

"I am." He smiled, more like beamed.

The fact that he seemed eager to get away annoyed the heck out of me. "Kind of sudden, isn't it?"

He shrugged. "Not really. I've made some big decisions today."

"What kind of decisions?"

"If you'll come in and relax, I'll tell you."

I felt anything but relaxed, but I went inside and dropped into an armchair.

"I'd offer you something to drink if I had anything," McCall said. "Already cleaned out the refrigerator."

I waved away any thought of food or drink. Now that I was here with McCall, it was hard to ignore my nerves. "I just came from Aunt Millie's, where I've had *way* too much of everything."

He laughed. "Millie's a sweetheart."

"Yes, she is."

"You take after her."

"Bite your tongue," I said, thinking of all the organizing we'd done at her house. Then I saw the way he was looking at me and knew that wasn't what he meant at all.

"Tell me about your big decisions." I wanted the answers I'd come for.

"For one, I've quit my job," he announced.

"The job working with me?" The question popped out, though I knew we had no pending jobs together.

He smiled. "No. The job working security for a company in Fort Worth."

"Fort Worth?"

"That's where I'm from."

"You never mentioned anything about working security. Or Fort Worth."

"Because the terms of my employment prohibited me from talking about the job." He sat on the coffee-table top, facing me. "My former boss—two-faced, non-upstanding Southern Baptist that he is—set stringent rules. Not sharing anything about my background or the assignment was one of them. I was here as an imposter, kind of like Teale."

"You're nothing like *him,*" I said. "You can't tell me about this assignment?"

"I can now, since I quit. Boss flew in unexpectedly, insisted on a face-to-face. That's why I left you, left the scene, after the cops arrived. To make that meeting."

"Why'd you quit?"

"Had enough of working for a jerk I didn't respect. He sent me here undercover to check out prospective business deals. One with Barton Fletcher. The other with Jim Gilmore."

"Lori Gilmore's husband?"

"Right."

The dots connected. "That's why you spent so much time in Millie's neighborhood."

He nodded. "And I reported back that they are *not* people he should partner up with."

"On what did you base that advice?" I asked.

"A major portion of the boss' income comes straight from one of those huge conglomerate churches in the Dallas Metro area. Wouldn't mesh well with Gilmore's little porno-movie empire that he's hoping to take national."

"Jeez. Pornography?"

"That's what they're shipping out in those boxes. DVDs through the mail for the triple-X-rated consumer."

I grimaced. "Your boss must have appreciated your saving him from getting involved with that."

McCall shook his head. "He didn't. He intends to invest. So long as his name is never connected with the dirt. Wanted me to be the go-between. I told him that's not what I hired on for."

"Good for you."

"Only secret I'm keeping from here on out is his ID. The man didn't even care when I told him that his own son was set up. Fletcher bribed his stepdaughter to date the boy. That alone would have been enough for me to tell Fletcher to take a hike."

"Now that I know what you were up to, I understand why you had those photos."

His eyebrows rose in exaggerated surprise. "You were nosing around while I was distracted?"

"Me? Nose around?" I put a hand to my chest, playing innocent. "All I care about is killing clutter. You must admit, the place was messy."

"You kept me so busy, I had no time to pick up after myself."

I laughed. "Valid excuse."

"Anyway, I'm done with the whole mess."

I fidgeted under his serious gaze. "So what's next?"

He leaned forward and placed his hands on my knees. "I was hoping you'd tell me."

I looked around the room and tried to ignore the sensation of his touch. "First thing is your move. Where are you going?"

"A hotel for tonight. Stay here past midnight, they'll want another week's rent. Now that I'm jobless, I need to watch the pennies. Saw a nice little house for rent in Rosenberg, and I'm meeting with the landlord tomorrow."

I let out a breath I hadn't realized I was holding. "You're not going back to Fort Worth?"

He straightened, removing his hands as if he knew I couldn't think straight with the heat from his palms searing through to my skin. "Nothing for me in Fort Worth."

"And here?"

"I've discovered some talents I didn't know I had," he said. "Wayne's Way was a setup for the undercover assignment, but I enjoyed the work. Thought I might try it full-time. What do you think?"

"You're good enough to make a living as an organizer. I think it's a fine idea, so long as I don't have to worry about you underbidding jobs, stealing them from me."

He shook his head. "Never. I'd have to be on my last dollar, desperate for grocery money."

I smiled. "In that case, I need to help you get off to a good start. If you promise to behave yourself, you can park your boots in my guest room tonight for free."